HUGH C.N. MILLER

The Electric King

Artificial Intelligence has found its purpose.

FUTUREVILLE
BOOKS

Images for promotional purposes from 123RF.com, CanvaPro, Freepik.com and Dreamstime.com.

Audio used in CanvaPro videos copyright: Highwater (Instrumental) and Kodiak (Instrumental). View more by Vestevent from Audiosocket

Copyright Hugh C.N.Miller © 2025

Cover art by HM Studio. Image elements from: 123RF.com

Typesetting and formatting: Reedsy Editor. https://reedsy.com/

Cover image elements: www.123rf.com

Book Trailer by HM Studio Productions

Printed by Print on Demand, South Africa, Cape Town. 2025

A special thanks to the editors for their contributions.

Dedicated to the King of Kings.

First edition

ISBN: 978-1-0370-7498-1

Editing by Reedsy
Editing by Charleen Dama
Editing by Cindy Orchison
Editing by FutureVille Publishers
Editing by Tony Parry
Cover art by HM Studio

This book was professionally typeset on Reedsy.
Find out more at reedsy.com

ONE

Drakensberg, South Sector 7 - 2052

In the far distance, something caught Scarlett's eye. She moved up the mountain to gain a better view from the highest point. The dust swirled round her as she narrowed her almond-shaped eyes. Her deep, husky breathing as she positioned her crossbow in the long grass, echoed in her ears. She bent lower to the ground, focusing on the shapes appearing on the horizon, feeling as if her legs were about to collapse beneath her. Her dark brown hair danced in the gentle breeze as the sunrise highlighted her flawless medium complexion. Her well-defined cheekbones tightened as she glanced back at the village with smoke hanging in the air, feeling her emotions boil like a volcano within her. She spun round and ran down the mountainside as quickly as she could. A small Zulu boy of around ten years old shouted as he came running to her, "They're here!"

"Move inside. Now!" Scarlett shouted like a lioness about to pounce.

Then a torrent of rage exploded within her. The complete

desperation of what awaited them weighed heavily on her shoulders. She blinked rapidly as she gripped her crossbow, feeling like a feral animal finally released into the wild.

Hundreds of Zulu warriors descended the mountainside, as fearsome and ready for battle as ever. But today was different. The king had arrived. The most fearsome ruler the world had ever known. And now, he was about to tear this village apart, just as he had done to thousands of others across the globe. It was indeed a dreadful day. A day she had been preparing for.

Were they ready for that day? Today?

The wind picked up behind her as various drones circled her in a precise and powerful military formation through the low-hanging mist and clouds. Her heart dropped into her stomach as she watched them prepare for a large flying craft to descend from the sky and land on the Drakensberg's grassy land. It was winter in the middle of July and the morning frost had gone. The world's weather had become unpredictable, resulting in harsh winters and summers.

The Drakensberg was no exception with thick snow blanketing the peaks, creating a picturesque winter landscape. Sudden weather changes remained a threat, but it was a secure location. A safe place. Safe from rising water levels and extreme heat. Perhaps that was why so many people moved from all over the world to this part of Africa, which stretched for a thousand kilometres, attempting to escape the rule of Artificial Intelligence. It was a cosmopolitan mix of diverse races and ages. But now they were here. The king, as he preferred to be called, eventually discovered all the rebellions that defied his rule, slaughtering thousands of humans who refused to submit to him. The sound of the craft landing reverberated throughout the valleys. Baboons barked in the

2

distance and a few black eagles soared between the towering basalt cliffs above her. Her mouth dropped open in surprise when she realised her younger brother was still not in the cave as they had repeatedly rehearsed.

"Alyx! Listen to me and enter the cave. Stay down!" Her voice rang through the air amid Southern Africa's highest mountain range, as people scattered across the valleys into various holes in the mountainsides. When the mouth of the hull opened like a wound, robot soldiers poured out like thick black pus. An army of one hundred faceless robots descended the slope in tight, organised rows that stretched far into the distance. They were moving so fast towards them that it was hard for the human eye to register. It was an eerie sight of power and intimidation as they marched towards the valley's entrance, neatly tucked between two peaks. Scarlett stood still at the entrance as they reached her. Out of nowhere, hundreds of Zulu spears flew through the air, piercing the robots as they marched. The human insurrection emerged from under the long grass and opened fire at the robot soldiers approaching the village. Gunshots from vintage AK-47 and AR-15 rifles echoed throughout the valley. Bullets sliced through the bodies of the humans like a hot knife through butter as the robots opened fire in response. Bodies were piling up everywhere—loads of them.

They kept coming. The robot soldiers had sleek, metallic silver bodies. Their heads were smooth and faceless, resembling a helmet with only small horizontal slits for eyes. They had smooth, polished metallic bodies that subtly reflected light and their elbows, knees and hips had visible circular mechanical joints. Above them a squadron of black quadcopter drones hovered, with their short, stocky frames, rotor blades on each corner and small mounted guns with surveillance equipment underneath their chassis. Scarlett raised her cross-bow and launched an arrow-like bolt straight at one robot uncomfortably close to her. The force cut through his neck and sparks exploded from his chest as he plunged backwards. With precision, she tore through the metal bodies of another two. The mountainside exploded into a war scene. Women and children screamed as they ran deeper into the caves while birds flew high up into the sky. Scarlett, however, remained quiet and defiant. Without warning, the earth suddenly grew dark and silent as a voice commanded the robot soldiers, "Stand down!"

The scene before her froze as everyone backed off and, in unison, lowered their weapons. Dust swirled above the parched winter grass in front of her. A bald African man walked past the robots and charged directly at Scarlett, dressed in a black leather doublet with a high collar and long sleeves. The outfit was completed with a waist-cinching belt with a golden buckle and was decorated down the front. She lowered her crossbow. The robot soldiers stood motionless as if someone had simply turned them off in the middle of a battle.

"There is no need for more bloodshed here," he said in a warm French accent. She froze, unable to move. Perhaps standing still was her only correct move. His striking facial features made him appear compassionate, but she sensed a cold presence beneath. He had a strong jawline, high cheek-bones and expressive eyes that seemed to pierce her soul. She recognised who he was. Everyone knew and feared the king's right-hand man, who did the dirty work of forcing humanity to submit to the world's new ruler.

Then his face lit up as he extended his arm towards her.

"State your name," he said in a firm tone.

His presence conveyed confidence and intensity as he took a step towards her. Scarlett backed up a few paces.

She was only thirty-eight, but the subtle lines on her face spoke of far more years of pain and violence than her age revealed. She had a slender and athletic build and her dark brown hair fell straight down her face. Her distinctive brown eyes locked with his. Her right forearm was covered in tattoos as she clenched her crossbow. Several people bowed their heads as he passed.

"Your name?" he asked again. She frowned, not moving.

"Scarlett," she replied, as if it were a threat.

Abruptly, a robot soldier issued a command, "In front of the king's Chancellor, bow your head!"

After glancing at the robot, the African Frenchman pivoted and faced her again. "You are in the king's presence," he said, referring to the craft.

"Why does he not show himself then?" she asked.

He smiled at her condescendingly.

"The king is in a good mood today. He wants to show mercy to the people here."

"We don't need anything from this so-called king," she said, unsure if she had overstepped. No one moved around them. The atmosphere was tight. The situation was tense.

He frowned so deeply that his brows met. His bald head shone in the sun and his duck-tail beard seemed his pride and joy. Her expression changed abruptly as a young Zulu boy ran towards her and grabbed her right leg.

"Alyx, I told you to stay inside!" she yelled, staring down at him.

"That's all right. Surrender this uprising and everyone's

lives will be spared," he said softly, trying to bend down towards the boy.

Alyx was dressed in traditional garments made from animal hides. His hair was dark and closely cropped, complementing his dark brown complexion. He stared with tears at the man in front of him. His round face had a serious, focused expression as he kept on looking back up at Scarlett.

"It's going to be okay," she said, attempting to persuade both him and herself.

"She's right, you know. My name is Sebastian and everything that happens next depends on Scarlett over here. I assume you are not his mother?" he asked as he focused his attention back on her.

"What I am to him is none of your concern."

"Everything is of my concern. The king has instructed me to ensure everyone follows his orders as I carry them out."

"Why are you doing this?" she asked, frowning.

"Perhaps you should rather ask yourself that question," he said as he looked around the village, with more people slowly coming out of the caves. "Why do you choose to deny that the world is becoming a better place? You *just* need to see it."

"I don't need to see it. Here we are free," she said, swallowing her emotions down.

"Here, you live like animals," he said. "You call that free? Today I'm offering you an end to suffering. I suggest responding wisely to the gesture as it won't stand for much longer."

"You are human, yet I can't see why you wish to destroy so many human lives to serve machines."

His brows knotted together again as he lowered his voice.

"I believe your father is very ill?" he asked suddenly, like it was an ace up his sleeve.

"How do you know about that?"

"I have my informants. Not everyone here can be trusted. But then that's the human dilemma, isn't that so?" he reminded her. His face softened for an instant as a mask of mercy appeared, his eyes penetrating hers.

"You know AI has cured cancer, right? Bow down to this king, surrender this village and I will give you the treatment he deserves. You can save his life today. Don't you want that for him?"

"My father's life is not for sale," she said, swallowing hard, fearing that she had just sent him to his death unnecessarily.

"You are going to see the error of your ways," he said, spinning round. "Take the child!" he commanded one robot.

"No!" she yelled as he moved closer, ripping the boy from her leg as if it were a limb. Two more robots took the crossbow from her and forced her to kneel. She hoped her father would remain silent and inside. They were going to use him against her.

"Sooner or later, everyone who wishes to live will bow down to this king."

"I kneel before no one. Let go of my brother!" she boomed.

He moved closer to her face, his eyes widening.

"Be silent now and you will live. There's no way you'll ever be able to save this innocent little boy if you die today," he pleaded.

She looked up at him, knowing that this moment would determine who lived or died. She stared at her adopted brother with glassy eyes as he struggled to free himself from the robot's grip.

Sebastian waited for her response.

The moment had passed.

"We are done here. Bring her and the child. Let's see how this village survives without her," he said, his voice hollow and cold.

A gust of wind blew through her hair as she and Alyx were dragged to the first craft in the front while the larger craft began to ascend in the back.

Was the so-called machine king present, observing everything?

With military precision, the robot soldiers returned to their craft. Nobody else moved. She glared at them in rage as she tried to kick them away, but they were extremely strong. They forced her into the craft's hull, accompanied by Alyx, who began to cry. Her heart was in her throat as they propelled her forward.

"It will be okay, Alyx. Just stay calm," she said, her hair clammy against her cheeks.

Her biggest problem now was how they would get out of this craft...

She wondered how her father was handling the commotion. He was so weak and her mother couldn't care less.

As the craft started to lift off the ground, Sebastian's grin turned into a feral smile.

"Burn the village," he ordered as the craft rose ten metres above the grassy land.

A wave of nausea washed over her as she tried to process what she had heard. Then, balls of flames erupted towards the village as missiles launched from the craft. She dropped to her knees as the scene before her became a battlefield. Tears welled up in her as her anger erupted.

Sebastian moved closer to her and taunted, "I wanted you to have a front-row seat to what happens when humans defy the rule of this king."

He enjoyed the conflicting emotions raging across her face.

She felt frozen in that position, unable to move as the missiles decimated the village. Everything went up in flames. Tears and sweat streaked across her face. Her rage was unstoppable as she spun round swiftly and kicked him hard. He stumbled backwards but quickly returned to her as two robots pinned her to the floor of the craft.

"You can't stop this. See this as a lesson for disobedience," he snarled as he lowered his eyes. She looked at him impassively. She felt numb. Her heart was pounding, but nothing happened. Alyx was screaming as they pulled him deeper into the craft.

"Alyx!" she shouted, as a robot punched her in the middle of her back. The blinding pain that followed brought the metallic taste of blood to her mouth.

"Send my regards to your father," he said coldly as he lifted his right leg and pushed her out of the craft, which was now fifteen metres above ground. She spun round in mid-air and fell backwards, her arms attempting to fly through the air as she prepared herself to fall to her death. On impact, she sank hard into the grass, feeling as if her lungs were being pulled out of her chest. The dust swirled as she moved briefly, then everything went dark.

TWO

Drakensberg, South Sector 7 - 2052

2 Weeks earlier

Scarlett rubbed her hands together, ignoring the cold as the late evening fire threw crackling sparks into the dark night. Her stare into the fire got disrupted by the voice of her mother.

"It's bloody freezing out here. You should come inside the cave," she said, tightening an old scarf round her shoulders, her short hair waving in the gentle wind.

"I'm fine," Scarlett replied.

"You don't look fine. You look exhausted and need rest," she scolded.

Scarlett felt every bit of patience inside her expire as her head snapped towards her mother's expressive eyes, contrasted against the dark clouds in the night sky.

"You can't carry the responsibility of this entire village on your own," she said as her small, delicate nose lifted. She turned around to walk away when Scarlett sighed.

"Have you been drinking again today?" Scarlett asked

sharply as she ran her fingers through her hair and stood up. The colossal side of the mountain beside them seemed to want to swallow them both, threatening to crush their shaky relationship.

"I'm still your mother. Show some respect."

"Respect? You think you deserve my respect or anyone else's here?" Scarlett asked, her mouth hanging open like a fish out of water.

"I'm just doing the best I can," she said, her high cheekbones giving her face a slightly angular appearance.

"By what? By being drunk every single day and night?" Scarlett asked.

Absolute fear and despair commanded her features. "You are still young. You have strength. I no longer dare to face what's happening out there in the world. Here we live like the rats in the mountains, scavenging for food and barely surviving."

"At least we control our future."

"Our future? What future? The world has made its choice. No one listened to the warnings. They wanted AI to rule and now we are hiding from our own created monster," she challenged.

"Well, I still believe in the human spirit. It's worth the fight," Scarlett replied, almost whispering, watching the conflicting emotions on her mother's face.

"I'm turning in," she said, chewing her upper lip as she slowly turned her oval face towards Scarlett, "Your father is calling on you. His condition has worsened."

Scarlett's face tightened as she looked into her mother's eyes and replied, "It's all going to be all right. One day." Her unwavering determination radiated as a beacon of hope in the darkness.

"I love your fighting spirit, Scarlett. Don't ever lose it." She

11

sighed and walked away into the darkness.

In the past few days, various new people had joined the southern rebellion, coming from all across the continent as people moved around. Food was scarce, but here at the foot of the Drakensberg, at least they had clean drinking water and shelter. She had never offered to lead this village. It just happened.

They have been at this shelter for the past five long years. Her mother was Vietnamese and her Scottish father was the only hope she still had in the goodness of humanity. But now he was dying of pancreatic cancer, slowly eating away the very fibre of his being. As she fought to suppress a surge of guilt, she had to remind herself of what was at stake. The world was divided into two societies: those who were content to submit to Artificial Intelligence, known as the Myriads, who were promised a life of opulence, and those who refused to surrender what made them human as AI rose to power in the form of a king. A king no one saw coming. Her mother, Mai, was quite happy to bow and worship this king as he demanded, but her father was headstrong, believing that tyrannical AI rule would lead to meaningless lives.

Upon entering the cave's enclosed space and witnessing her father lying there in agony, Scarlett realised he was nearing the end of his life. She moved over to kneel beside his makeshift bed. She squeezed his hand, running her fingers through her hair and neatly tugging it behind her ears.

"Father. It's Scarlett," she whispered, her voice trembling with love and fear, trying not to fall into a puddle of tears.

"Scar. It's good to hear your voice," he said, opening his blue eyes. His skin was slightly yellowish and she could feel his body going rigid.

"You okay?" she asked, the slight tremor in her voice betraying her fear of losing him.

"I'm just fine."

She realised that he was still acting as though everything was good, as he had always done and it felt like all the air was being sucked out of the room. Although he still had that rugged face and defined jawline that made her feel secure with him, she could now see that he was losing strength daily. Only in the king's controlled cities was it possible to receive medical care; nevertheless, her father would never consent.

He smiled softly and she had to swallow a whimper as she stroked his grey hair away from his face. She picked up a damp cloth and gently wiped his forehead.

"I need you to promise me something," he uttered slowly.

"Of course. Anything," she said.

"Whatever happens to me-"

"Don't talk like that," she said.

"Scarlett, listen to me," he said as he tried to sit up. "I'm not going to get better. You know that, right?"

She sucked in a deep breath. "You just need to rest and get stronger. The rebellion is considering moving further north soon. They say there are doctors there."

He worked his tongue around his mouth to drum up some moisture and swallowed hard. "Promise me you won't accept medical treatment from that machine king, no matter what happens to me."

A look of horror crossed her face. "If we can just get you to those human doctors, they might be able to treat you." But the thought of defying her father's wishes, of going against his belief in the human spirit, was a heavy burden on her heart.

"Scar. You are not listening to me. You always do that, acting

13

tough and brave when you need to allow yourself to feel pain." His words cut through her, a reminder of the emotional turmoil she was trying to suppress.

She pulled back gently, receiving a sharp reminder of his condition. She fought to keep her composure, not to let her father see the fear and sadness in her eyes.

She had to face the reality that she was going to lose her father. Soon.

"Don't worry about me. I've got things under control," she said.

"I know you do. But the day will come when that king will clamp down on this village, just like the others. You need to promise me you won't take his offer to save my life," he insisted as she cursed the king behind clenched teeth.

"We should be safe here," she said, her eyes flashing with fear.

"Just be on your guard. The days are evil. I'm old and frail, but you must still fight for your future."

She nodded in agreement.

"I don't know if I have that any more. So much has happened in this world. If there really is a creator, he surely doesn't seem to care," she replied softly.

"I understand how difficult it is to see beyond this current world, but all we have is the hope of a better world one day. This king, machine android, or whatever they want to call him, has created a dangerous religion that the world has openly accepted," he breathed, his heart pounding in his neck.

"I don't know if this world is worth saving," she said with a flash of anger.

"The world has gone to sleep, believing AI has all the answers and is immortal. It's a gospel of lies and enslavement as we submit our world to it," he said firmly, coughing gently.

She looked up into the cave and then back at him.

"It's late. You need to rest. We'll talk in the morning," she said.

"Just be patient with your mother. She is not handling this way of living well."

"None of us are. But we are all coping without harming ourselves or each other," she replied bitterly.

He sighed slowly. "It's been over ten years since AI came to rule this world. Remember, we had a home, I had a business and you had your studies? We lost all that because we chose to remain free from AI's terms of living. With that came sacrifices. Big ones. Give her some time and space; that's all I ask. Okay?"

"*Okay*," she said as she crossed her arms and gave him a soft look, feeling guilty for not fully agreeing.

As she walked away, he slowly closed his eyes, unable to shake the evil foreboding that they were all in great danger.

The freezing temperatures of the previous night slowly became a distant memory as the first light of dawn touched the peaks of the mountains, transitioning from deep blue to a soft, glistening glow. Scarlett escaped every morning to her safe place, as high on one peak as she could. She felt sick whenever she thought about how long they had been stuck at this outpost, hiding, surviving and waiting for the dictator sentient king to find them. The gentle wind whipped at her hair as she picked up her crossbow and moved toward one of the rebellion's morning gatherings. Tom was the troublemaker in the group. Very hard-headed and driven to lead, fighting all resistance to support her. As she approached the old Toyota Land Cruiser, she could sense the silence fall on their big talk. With a groan, a few strong African men lifted some bags and a diesel generator onto the back.

"We don't have much time. We need to move from here," Tom said to the men.

Scarlett blocked his route with an outstretched arm as she placed her crossbow on top of the vehicle's roof.

"We are bloody sitting ducks, the lot of us. Too many new people are coming here," one replied.

"And go where?" Scarlett suddenly dropped into the conversation, lifting her bag of arrow-like bolts off her shoulders. She swallowed hard as she stood and tipped her chin to meet his gaze.

"North," Tom replied as he looked back at her, his hazel eyes sharp and focused.

"Further inland would be too flat and expose us. Mountains provide a better chance of protecting children and the vulnerable. I know things are tough here and nobody is more tired of this place than I am, but I believe moving north is a huge risk," she said, clenching her fists.

"No offence, Scarlett, but we will need supplies soon. Very soon. We have no diesel for the generator," Tom said. His light blonde hair lifted in the wind. His face was square and strong, and his complexion was even.

"Yeah. I heard there is electricity there," another snarled.

"There are over two thousand people here. We can't just pick up and go. We have sick and frail people," she responded.

"Look, I'm sorry about your father's condition, but some of us are no longer sticking around. We will get fuel and supplies and be back in a few weeks," he said as he inclined his head. His expression shifted from neutral to slightly serious.

"Rebels are targeting the abandoned power stations. We don't have enough firepower to protect ourselves," she said.

"We have enough for now. They are just petty thieves, looking for food and valuables. We will deal with them," he replied.

She shook her head.

"And here? They know about our position," she stated with a whimper lodged in her throat.

"We are leaving enough men and rifles here. Cooper has reloaded all the AK 47s and AR-15 rifles. You will be fine. You are a good fighter," Tom said, "*And* this Cruiser needs repairs, and finding a mechanic that still services these rare engines is hard to come by. All the EV's batteries are flat. We have to keep these old ladies going as they cut more and more power from us."

"I never asked to lead this village, by the way," she murmured suddenly, craning her neck to look at him.

"Nobody did. We're all just trying to figure out our place in this dark new world and it won't get any easier anytime soon."

He reached down, gripped a bag of bullets tightly and jumped in. He leaned out the window as the Land Cruiser started, "I saw some game walking around to the west of the mountain. This might be a good day to hunt."

"Let's go!" They yelled together as she drew her crossbow back into her chest and gazed at the cave's entrance, where a thin ribbon of fire curled upwards. Tom was four years older than her and he had been especially harsh on her after she refused several attempts by him to kiss her. As the Land Cruiser drove away, she felt more anxious than ever, but her attention had to be on her adopted brother and her parents.

The next few days passed with little change. Her father appeared lethargic most of the time. The view depicted a rugged, rocky cliff with layers of textured stone that stood out against the soft, green vegetation that clung to its edges. She licked and wiped her adopted little brother's dirty face after a few hours of bird watching, which he loved doing. As the sun began to set she realised it was time to leave her 'safe place' and return to reality as she gazed at the dark clouds of an overcast day hanging low. The time spent with Alyx was valuable, personal and reflective. Tomorrow was never guaranteed. Her faithful crossbow never left her side; it became a third leg.

"Can we go horse riding tomorrow, please?" he asked, giving her a sweet smile.

"We'll see, okay?" she replied, smiling weakly. "Come, let's go down and get dinner started. Sound good?"

"Yeah!" he shouted.

The Drakensberg region was well-known for its breathtaking beauty and tranquillity. The Tugela Falls had become a reliable source of fresh water for the outpost in recent years, but it felt as if she had never fully appreciated its beauty as they moved up and down. It was marred by the danger that lurked in every city.

She stared at him with steel-grey eyes. "Come on then. I'll chase you down the hill!" she yelled, knowing she was not far from the main cave entrance. She allowed him to run ahead of her in a playful stroll, watching as his little brown face glowed with laughter and delight.

"I'm gonna beat you, old lady!" he shouted, looking back at her.

"Who's your old lady?" she projected back gently. "Look

where you are running. You are going to fall!"

Her fear of him running full speed subsided slightly as they approached the lower end of the mountain range. Her words barely had time to escape her lips before she saw him stumble over a few stones and fall to his knees. She reached out to him with a quick swish, but another Zulu woman pulled him back to his feet.

"Having fun, I see," she said, eyes locking onto Scarlett's.

He seemed startled as he brushed off dust and grass from his chest.

"Alyx, go inside so long, okay? I'm coming now," Scarlett said, gazing at the woman dressed in traditional Zulu attire.

"Mamma Mhambi," Scarlett respectfully greeted as she placed her crossbow beside her left leg.

"Scarlett. Good to see you are well," she said promptly.

Why was she here?

"You are moving back south, I see?" Scarlett asked, hinting at the mountainside.

"Just looking for some water. It's just me and my two daughters. We won't be here for long."

"Well, take what you need."

"Thank you."

Scarlett's face was relieved as she walked away from her, but the echo of her name again hung in the air.

"Scarlett," she said.

She turned round and sighed. "Look, I know you are a good person and I know your family well. What you have done for Alyx the last five years is commendable, but it's time for him to be around his *own* people," Mhambi said.

"What's that supposed to mean?" Scarlett snarled bitterly as she reached out to grasp her hand.

"You know what I mean. Don't take this personally. I know you see him as your little brother and what your father did by taking him in after his parents were killed, will always be appreciated by everyone here," she said firmly as she walked closer to Scarlett. "But he needs to be living with a Zulu family as he grows up."

"Where was any one of you when we took him in? Huh?" she asked as her mouth popped open.

"We had our own family dynamics then. All I'm saying is-"

"He is my little brother and he is not going anywhere. Are we done here, Mhambi?" she cut her off with lips in a tight, firm line.

"We will pick this up on another day, Scarlett," she said as she peered over at her, "Soon."

Scarlett could feel the spears of discontent being pushed through her heart as she walked away. Mhambi was leading one of the nearby outposts and was known for her brutal leadership and queenly attributes, but here, at her village, she had no say.

As Scarlett reached the makeshift shelter entrance, she instinctively shouted for Alyx, who initially didn't answer. Then the relief followed when he lifted his head from around an old wooden chair and shouted, "I'm here."

She glanced to her right when a sudden sound got her attention coming from deeper inside the shelter.

"Anyone there?" she inquired, taking a slow look back at Alyx. The place was deserted that evening with everyone gathered at the foot of the mountain, where the fires were burning. She drew a bolt from her backpack, inserted it into the crossbow and slowly raised it to her eye level. Standing sideways to the noise source, she slowly spread her legs to shoulder width and positioned her finger on the trigger. She was shaking gently, fearing that she might aim at unknown people in the dark.

"Alyx, stay where you are," she whispered, moving forward slowly.

"Show yourself!" she exclaimed. There was no response as she watched the light behind a shelf shift to the right. Her heart was racing in her chest as she moved forward slowly. Suddenly, the shelf stacked with old cups and plates got pushed over. A young man jumped at her as she tried to determine where the danger was coming from. As she prepared to launch a bolt, she realised she had less than a fifteen-metre range, so she needed to be precise and closer to the target. The bolt launched like a bullet while another man grabbed her from behind and forced her to the ground. There was an agonising scream from one man in the front as the bolt tore into his right leg. She bit the inside of her cheek as she punched the man holding her down in the stomach. He pulled up and away from her as she swung her gaze to one man in the front, still curled up in a heap of pain. With hard precision, she turned round and kicked the man now closer in her space. He lifted his right arm and gave her a hard blow across her face, forcing her to stumble backwards, but she quickly found her feet. He blew out a breath and kicked her in the chest.

With trembling lips, she yelled, "Get away from me!" and collapsed backwards onto the shattered plates and glasses. She attempted to stand up, but was unsteady on her feet, trying to check her injuries. She could see her crossbow gliding by and bouncing against a rock. She stepped forward and delivered a powerful blow to his open hand, but he closed his hand around

21

her fist and gave her a hard head butt. She staggered back, her temples gushing blood. The man standing in front of her was in his twenties, muscular and determined to harm her. The youthful, drug-fuelled rebels were a constant threat, plundering and attacking the villages. Pain gnawed as she shook her hand; her fingers burning. As quick as a whirlwind, her eyes locked on a pipe between him and her. It was only a few metres away, yet it felt like kilometres. She felt her body defy gravity as she ran towards it and grabbed it with both hands. She spun round and faced him again, the pipe now firmly in her hands. For a brief moment the two of them exchanged startled glances.

"Get out of here!" she snarled.

"Make me," he threatened, uttering a series of curses. The two looked at each other. Nothing else was said. Her breath was deep and hollow. Sweat beaded on his brow. As she considered his next move, he dashed towards her, but she raised the pipe shoulder-high like a sword and struck him across the face with significant force. He was flung backwards from the strike. She kept charging, swinging the pipe from left to right. The wind whistled as she turned it in front of his face. Blood gushed from his head. He was suddenly extremely vulnerable. She pushed herself forward, pressing the end of the pipe against his chest.

"Had enough?" she asked, swallowing hard and dry.

"We will be back!" he grinned as he tried to push the pipe away.

"I will be waiting for you, thugs," she said, frantically running her hand across her face, knowing that they will never get rid of them. She stepped back as he stood up and looked at his companion, still attempting to pull the bolt from his penetrated shin.

"Let's get out of here," he growled as they darted away, both limping. She moved forward, scanning the area for any more of them hiding in the darkness. She was tired and panting as she drew a deep breath through her nose.

"That was quite impressive," a deep but warm voice suddenly said right behind her. Fear flushed through her entire body as she spun round, ready with the pipe in her right hand.

"Relax. I mean you no harm," he whispered as he slowly moved more into the cave's dim light.

THREE

The tall, older man pulled his outstretched arm away from her. His piercing blue eyes captured her attention. She could tell that he was at least in his seventies. His grey-white hair was neatly combed and hung just past his ears. He looked into her eyes with incredible intensity.

"What was impressive?" she enquired, still on guard, attempting to see his face better in the poor light.

"The way you handled that pipe like it was a sword."

She moved forward slowly, keeping her grip tight on the pipe.

"Easy now. I'm no threat. Been looking for you for a while," he said.

"Who are you and what do you want from me?"

"Been hearing some great things about you, Scarlett," he said.

He obviously knew who she was. Who was this man?

Endless possibilities ran through her mind like a bullet train.

His physical appearance exuded a sense of elegance and authority. He commanded a sophisticated presence.

"The name is Henry."

"Where are you from?"

"Not from around here," he replied.

"I gathered that. Everyone here knows everyone. How do

you know my name?" she asked.

"Been looking for someone like you."

"Someone like?"

"Someone with integrity," he followed on.

"Did you send those thugs?"

"I had to see if it was true."

"Which is?"

"That you are different. A warrior in your heart. Most people have given up, but not you. Oh, I see incredible power within you, Scarlett," he said as he strolled casually round her.

"I'm not a warrior or a hero. Just protecting my family," she said, still on alert.

"I can see that. But what if I told you that there are so many more people you could protect?" he asked as he leaned forward.

"How?"

"Now you are asking the right question," he said as the cold air clung to their faces. "I know how to save our world from the tyranny of this AI ruler," he said.

"It's a bit too late for that, don't you think?"

"As long as we have hope, it's never too late," he said.

"I don't think the world wants to be saved from it," she replied, lowering the pipe a few centimetres.

"I have very powerful connections on the inside of those shiny techno cities. Not everyone is as happy as they seem. In fact, people are becoming increasingly enslaved in a system of control that they will sooner or later wish they could be free from. This so-called AI King is applying more and more pressure on his citizens to not only conform to its way of life, but to worship him. He is going to clamp down on villages like these and eventually kill all humans who refuse to worship him. We can free humanity from this evil before there is nothing that makes us human left at all," he said. "Your family and everyone here are in great danger. You can only protect them so far. What I'm offering you is a way to do both."

"Why would I believe you?" she asked, looking at him wide-eyed.

"Because I'm your last hope. What has happened here in the past few years? Did things get better? *No*? Do you want to just keep trying to survive like this until you and everyone here dies?"

An awkward silence stretched through the cave entrance. The rest of the people would return to turn in for the night.

"My place is here to protect these people who are my family," she said firmly.

"That king is going to come here very soon, believe me. You cannot protect your family from that. Maybe from those thugs, but not from powerful robots."

"I'm not equipped to do whatever you think I'm capable of. You have been misinformed," she said.

"I have seen enough, Scarlett. I have been assembling a team for the past few years and our last component is still missing. Without it, we can't even think of implementing this plan."

"What plan?"

"We have found a way, a weakness, if you will, into this AI system. I cannot tell you more right now, but we need someone like you to help us execute it."

"Why me?"

The sound of voices began to fade in around them.

"People have given up. That's why I had to come and see this mysterious woman for myself, who has incredible courage and skill. We will equip you with what you lack and give you a destiny you have never thought possible...to help humanity save itself from a force they don't even fully understand yet, before it's too late," he said with a deep urgency in his croaky voice.

"Sounds like a suicide mission to me and I have already told you, my place is here. It's time for you to leave."

"Everything okay here, Scarlett?" one villager enquired as he approached her. He lifted and cocked his gun.

"Everything's fine, thanks, Vance. He's just leaving for his village, up north, I take it?" Scarlett asked as politely as possible, looking at Henry's way.

There was nothing that could keep her away from her family. She would never consider leaving her little, defenceless brother or her sick father on their own. Never.

"Very well. No cause for alarm," he said.

She stared at him as he walked away from her. "I'm staying in one of those dilapidated farmhouses on the coastline. You know where to find me, should you change your mind," he said as he walked off and disappeared almost as mysteriously as he appeared. She finally lowered the pipe.

"What is he talking about?" the man asked.

"We need to be ready. Robot soldiers have been spotted closer to the north of the mountainside. Tell your men to prepare for war," she said as she went looking for Alyx.

A few days later.

The wind gently tugged at Scarlett's hair as she peered over the deep valley close to the edge of the mountain and then back to the inside of one of the deeper caves. The caves were filled with paintings on the walls illustrating the life and beliefs of the indigenous San people.

Jack placed a comforting hand on her shoulder.

"Father? You are up!" she exhaled.

"I have my days. Do you ever put that crossbow down?" he asked.

"You shouldn't walk this far up the mountainside," she said, pausing for effect and tightening her grip around her crossbow.

"You are beginning to sound like your mother," he replied, smiling gently.

With a decisive step, she walked forward and embraced him. His long fur coat kept him warm and shielded him from the elements of the afternoon breeze. He brushed his hand down the side of his jacket as he composed himself.

"Vance told me there was a strange man here the other night? Who is he and what did he want?" he asked.

"What everyone wants," she whispered, barely able to summon enough energy to speak.

"Safety," he said.

"He seems to be a traveller and believes the king will focus on this area soon. We need to be on high alert," she said as her breath came in shallow puffs, trying to keep her conversation with Henry tight to her chest.

Her thoughts were constantly peppered with confusion and fear. If staying where they were was dangerous, moving out into the open valley was even worse.

"We can't move now. We will be visible," he said.

"Agreed. Some of the men here don't seem to think it's a good idea, though," she said with her words dribbling to a halt.

"They will see your leadership skills sooner or later," he answered.

"If they don't pull this community apart before that," she said in a tone that signalled the end of the discussion.

"You are a courageous woman, Scarlett. I'm proud of you. Alyx needs you now more than ever."

Fear flashed in his gaze and she realised he was scared of the future...but she was even more scared of a future without him. She stepped forward, held onto his arm and shrugged. "You need to go rest now. I'll get some breakfast going soon. The guys have started some small fires."

"Will meet you back at the village then. Don't stay here and talk to yourself too long. You are your own worst enemy," he said.

She smiled as she let go of his arm, wishing she had a new plan mapped out to keep everyone safe, but she didn't. As she watched him slowly walk back to the village, she felt the tears springing up within her. But it was time to be tough. The future was as unsafe as ever.

Present day.

Scarlett escaped to her safe place with only her thoughts and crossbow. In the far distance, something caught her eye. She moved up the mountain to gain a better view from the highest point. The dust swirled round her. Her deep, husky breathing as she positioned her crossbow in the long grass, echoed in her ears. She bent lower to the ground, focusing on the shapes appearing on the horizon, feeling as if her legs were about to collapse beneath her. She glanced back at the village with smoke hanging in the air, feeling her emotions boil like a volcano within her. She spun round and ran down the mountainside as quickly as she could. Alyx shouted as he came running to her, "They're here!"

"Move inside. Now!" Scarlett shouted like a lioness about to pounce. Then a torrent of rage exploded within her. The complete desperation of what awaited them weighed heavily on her shoulders.

She blinked rapidly as she gripped her crossbow, feeling like a feral animal finally released into the wild.

Hundreds of Zulu warriors descended the mountainside, as fearsome and ready for battle as ever. The wind picked up behind her as various drones circled her in a precise and powerful military formation through the low-hanging mist and clouds. Her heart dropped into her stomach as she watched them prepare for a large flying craft to descend from the sky and land on the Drakensberg's grassy land.

The sound of the craft landing reverberated throughout the valleys. Baboons barked in the distance and a few black eagles soared between the towering basalt cliffs above her. Her mouth dropped open in surprise when she realised Alyx was still not in the cave as they had repeatedly rehearsed.

"Alyx! Listen to me and enter the cave. Stay down!" Her voice rang through the air as people scattered across the valleys into various holes in the mountainsides. When the mouth of the hull opened like a wound, robot soldiers poured out like thick black pus. An army of one hundred faceless robots descended the slope in tight, organised rows that stretched far into the distance. They were moving so fast towards them that it was hard for the human eye to register. It was an eerie sight of power and intimidation as they marched towards the valley's entrance, neatly tucked between two peaks. Scarlett stood still at the entrance as they reached her. Out of nowhere, hundreds of Zulu spears flew through the air, piercing the robots as they marched. The human insurrection emerged from under the long grass and opened fire at the robot soldiers approaching the village. Gunshots from vintage AK-47 and AR-15 rifles echoed throughout the valley. Bullets sliced through the bodies of the humans like a hot knife through butter as the robots opened fire in response. Bodies were piling up everywhere—loads of them.

They kept coming. The robot soldiers had sleek, metallic silver bodies. Their heads were smooth and faceless, resembling a helmet with only small horizontal slits for eyes. They had smooth, polished metallic bodies that subtly reflected light and their elbows, knees and hips had visible circular mechanical joints. Above them a squadron of black quadcopter drones hovered, with their short, stocky frames, rotor blades on each corner and small mounted guns with surveillance equipment underneath their chassis. Scarlett raised her crossbow and launched an arrow-like bolt straight at one robot uncomfortably close to her. The force cut through his neck and sparks exploded from his chest as he plunged backwards. With precision, she tore through the metal bodies of another two. The mountainside exploded into a war scene. Women and children screamed as they ran deeper into the caves while birds flew high up into the sky. Scarlett, however, remained quiet and defiant. Without warning, the earth suddenly grew dark and silent as a voice commanded the robot soldiers, "Stand down!"

The scene before her froze as everyone backed off and, in unison, lowered their weapons. Dust swirled above the parched winter grass in front of her. A bald African man walked past the robots and charged directly at Scarlett, dressed in a black leather doublet with a high collar and long sleeves. She lowered her crossbow. The robot soldiers stood motionless

31

as if someone had simply turned them off in the middle of a battle.

"There is no need for more bloodshed here," he said in a warm French accent. She froze, unable to move. Perhaps standing still was her only correct move. His striking facial features made him appear compassionate, but she sensed a cold presence beneath. She recognised who he was.

Then his face lit up as he extended his arm towards her.

"State your name," he said in a firm tone.

His presence conveyed confidence and intensity as he took a step towards her. Scarlett backed up a few paces.

"Your name?" he asked again. She frowned, not moving.

"Scarlett," she replied, as if it were a threat.

Abruptly, a robot soldier issued a command, "In front of the king's Chancellor, bow your head!"

After glancing at the robot, the African Frenchman pivoted and faced her again. "You are in the king's presence," he said, referring to the craft.

"Why does he not show himself then?" she asked.

He smiled at her condescendingly.

"The king is in a good mood today. He wants to show mercy to the people here."

"We don't need anything from this so-called king," she said, unsure if she had overstepped. No one moved around them. The atmosphere was tight. The situation was tense.

He frowned so deeply that his brows met. His bald head shone in the sun and his duck-tail beard seemed his pride and joy. Her expression changed abruptly as Alyx ran towards her and grabbed her right leg.

"Alyx, I told you to stay inside!" she yelled, staring down at him.

"That's all right. Surrender this uprising and everyone's lives will be spared," he said softly, trying to bend down towards the boy.

"It's going to be okay," she said, attempting to persuade both Alyx and herself.

"She's right, you know. My name is Sebastian and everything that happens next depends on Scarlett over here. I assume you are not his mother?" he asked as he focused his attention back on her.

"What I am to him is none of your concern."

"Everything is of my concern. The king has instructed me to ensure everyone follows his orders as I carry them out."

"Why are you doing this?" she asked, frowning.

"Perhaps you should rather ask yourself that question," he said as he looked around the village, with more people slowly coming out of the caves. "Why do you choose to deny that the world is becoming a better place? You *just* need to see it."

"I don't need to see it. Here we are free," she said, swallowing her emotions down.

"Here, you live like animals," he said. "You call that free? Today I'm offering you an end to suffering. I suggest responding wisely to the gesture as it won't stand for much longer."

"You are human, yet I can't see why you wish to destroy so many human lives to serve machines."

His brows knotted together again as he lowered his voice.

"I believe your father is very ill?" he asked suddenly, like it was an ace up his sleeve.

"How do you know about that?"

"I have my informants. Not everyone here can be trusted. But then that's the human dilemma, isn't that so?" he reminded her.

His face softened for an instant as a mask of mercy appeared, his eyes penetrating hers.

"You know AI has cured cancer, right? Bow down to this king, surrender this village and I will give you the treatment he deserves. You can save his life today. Don't you want that for him?"

"My father's life is not for sale," she said, swallowing hard, fearing that she had just sent him to his death unnecessarily.

"You are going to see the error of your ways," he said, spinning round. "Take the child!" he commanded one robot.

"No!" she yelled as he moved closer, ripping the boy from her leg as if it were a limb. Two more robots took the crossbow from her and forced her to kneel. She hoped her father would remain silent and inside. They were going to use him against her.

"Sooner or later, everyone who wishes to live will bow down to this king."

"I kneel before no one. Let go of my brother!" she boomed.

He moved closer to her face, his eyes widening.

"Be silent now and you will live. There's no way you'll ever be able to save this innocent little boy if you die today," he pleaded.

She looked up at him, knowing that this moment would determine who lived or died. She stared at her adopted brother with glassy eyes as he struggled to free himself from the robot's grip.

Sebastian waited for her response.

The moment had passed.

"We are done here. Bring her and the child. Let's see how this village survives without her," he said, his voice hollow and cold.

A gust of wind blew through her hair as she and Alyx were dragged to the first craft in the front while the larger craft began to ascend in the back.

Was the so-called machine king present, observing everything?

With military precision, the robot soldiers returned to their craft. Nobody else moved. She glared at them in rage as she tried to kick them away, but they were extremely strong. They forced her into the craft's hull, accompanied by Alyx, who began to cry. Her heart was in her throat as they propelled her forward.

"It will be okay, Alyx. Just stay calm," she said, her hair clammy against her cheeks.

Her biggest problem now was how they would get out of this craft...

She wondered how her father was handling the commotion. He was so weak and her mother couldn't care less.

As the craft started to lift off the ground, Sebastian's grin turned into a feral smile.

"Burn the village," he ordered as the craft rose ten metres above the grassy land.

A wave of nausea washed over her as she tried to process what she had heard. Then, balls of flames erupted towards the village as missiles launched from the craft. She dropped to her knees as the scene before her became a battlefield. Tears welled up in her as her anger erupted.

Sebastian moved closer to her and taunted, "I wanted you to have a front-row seat to what happens when humans defy the rule of this king."

He enjoyed the conflicting emotions raging across her face.

She felt frozen in that position, unable to move as the missiles decimated the village. Everything went up in flames.

Tears and sweat streaked across her face. Her rage was unstoppable as she spun round swiftly and kicked him hard. He stumbled backwards but quickly returned to her as two robots pinned her to the floor of the craft.

"You can't stop this. See this as a lesson for disobedience," he snarled as he lowered his eyes. She looked at him impassively. She felt numb. Her heart was pounding, but nothing happened. Alyx was screaming as they pulled him deeper into the craft.

"Alyx!" she shouted, as a robot punched her in the middle of her back. The blinding pain that followed brought the metallic taste of blood to her mouth.

"Send my regards to your father," he said coldly as he lifted his right leg and pushed her out of the craft, which was now fifteen metres above ground. She spun round in mid-air and fell backwards, her arms attempting to fly through the air as she prepared herself to fall to her death. On impact, she sank hard into the grass, feeling as if her lungs were being pulled out of her chest. The dust swirled as she moved briefly, then everything went dark.

What seemed like a lifetime was only a few minutes. The smell of death clung to her like cold blood. Deep thunderous blows sounded muffled around her, making everything appear surreal. Each passing minute revealed more and more pain inside of her. Smoke billowed from the remains of the village. The sky darkened as the two flying craft's vibrating sound echoed above her head, leaving her life in smoke as they darted into the clouds. She wanted to get up and move forward, but couldn't muster the strength as she tried desperately to get the air back into her lungs. The whole mountainside lit up like a Christmas tree, as hundreds of pieces of debris fell around her. Half-full petrol containers exploded, swirling violently and spitting charred remnants into the air as another fireball burst from the village. The force pulled her backwards like a rope tied to her waist. Then the sounds around her returned to her ears, as if they found a better signal. She could hear again. At that moment, it seemed like her life had paused. In front of her was just death. No one survived.

Her parents were gone.

Her friends, gone.

As sweat and tears stung her eyes, she stood there trying to comprehend the scene before her. Her stomach jumped as a wave of courage hit her hard in the chest. She dashed forward, running into the smoke and fireball in front of her like there was still some glimmer of hope, but everything was ablaze. She fell to her knees amidst the ruins as she tried to come to terms with her loss. Alyx was in the hands of the king and he was now her only focus.

She needed to find Henry, that much she knew. He was now indeed her only hope.

FOUR

London, EU Sector 3 - 2052

Ethan reached for something at his ankle as he stiffened his right leg on the hillside, attempting to support his slender weight. He wrapped his hand around a small round object, pulled it towards him and released a small clip on the side. A thin cable propelled from the object as it spun in his hand, projecting a few metres away and connecting to the bottom of the third transport pod that passed over his head, moving on a single monorail. Humans living in cities travelled at 150km per hour in personal rapid transit pod capsules, slowing down only when they arrived in the cities. He stared for a second or two at the sight of London's skyscrapers in the bright moonlight of the evening, a place he now no longer had access to. It was more beautiful than he remembered.

He, too, was an Indigent living on the outside of the AI-driven communities for more than five years fighting for his survival in a cold and brutal world. Remaining fully human and true to himself was not for sale. Staring at the city's sparkling lights, he reminded himself of once having access to electricity and running water. He braced himself for the pull as the cable in his right hand shortened, dragging him off the ledge and into the air, clinging to the pod's bottom. He closed his eyes as his head hit the bottom, hanging on as the pods glided about eight metres off the ground on the rail, with another twenty on the way, like a train. He took short breaths hoping no one inside felt the impact and wondered if the magnetic tripod could support his weight. It was vital that no one noticed him hanging on underneath.

The whirling sound of drones in the distance was overpowering as they guarded the perimeter walls of the city. A four-foot-high fence of concrete was placed all around the cities. There was no way to get into the city other than via the pod system or strictly controlled air access. The pods slowed as they approached the station where passengers would disembark, alarming Ethan that he would need to jump soon. It was going to be a hard fall. Once inside the city perimeter he only had thirty minutes before the drones and the AI system would pick up an unidentified being. Everything was chipped, even the animals.

He thought to himself, *only a short distance now,* as his lip curled slightly. For a split second his mind prepared him as his instinct for survival kicked in. A rush of air moved his long curly, dark brown hair, which often appeared tousled and voluminous.

Here we go...

It was a hell of a ride and he was prepared to die that day. It was risky. He waited another minute. His heart was beating faster and faster. The thought dripped like acid into his stomach as he released his right hand from the tripod magnetic foot-like object and unhooked it from the pod's base. The pods now moved above two six-storey office buildings with grid-like pattern windows. He needed to land on the first one. He could not miss it. If he did, he would either fall off and die, or the drones would detect him instantly and arrest him. As the pods passed over his head, he free-fell less than two metres to the building's flat roof in the darkness. He tumbled, rolled and came to a hard stop against one air-conditioning unit.

As the pods raced over his head, he waited another few minutes, again pulling the small round object from his pocket and releasing a small clip on the side. A thin cable propelled from the object as it spun in his hand, projecting a few metres away and connecting it to the other wall of the adjacent building. It was the microchip factory and he had one job to do. One important and dangerous job. Steal a valuable microchip, swap it with a fake one he had received from his client and get paid. Every chip on the conveyor belt was verified and scanned routinely. If a chip disappeared, an alarm would go off. He would need to carefully pinch one and replace it with a fake one before the cycle repeated. The far wall of the building across from him sprang into focus. He stepped back and released a breath as the cable in his right hand shortened, pulling him into the air. He zip-lined briskly across to the other building with his small backpack flung over his right shoulder, looking down the six storeys below and scurrying for the gully's shadows.

He steadied himself on the window ledge, worrying he'd been spotted. He slowly stood up and began to inch his way forward on the narrow ledge, moving towards the third window as per the blueprint he had received from his client. A few drones came past and zoomed into the darkness. He could see robots inside the factory walking up and down. He had been inside the city perimeter for fifteen minutes as he nervously looked at his old wind-up quartz watch. The clock was ticking. He peered around the window frame, took a deep breath and reminded himself that patience was key to the heist's success. He was alone. It was a solo mission, so if anything went wrong, it would all be on him and over. He pulled out a knife and gently unclipped the window lock and slowly forced it open. A group of android robots stood at the end of the corridor.

The robots were fully dressed in white cleanroom suits to avoid contamination from dust or other particles that could disrupt the delicate manufacturing process. He peered around the wall again, pulled a small smoke grenade from his backpack, pulled the trigger pin and threw it down the passage. It rolled and bounced and stopped two metres from one android's foot. The room had rows of complex, automated machines used at various chip manufacturing stages. He quickly stepped away from the window and lowered himself to the floor below, using the zipline cable. He heard a dull thud as the small smoke grenade detonated. It emitted a dense cloud of smoke for a few minutes. They were now focused on the incident on the floor above him. Time was of the essence. He unclipped the window on the floor below and entered the laboratory room. A series of machines inside the semiconductor plant moved rows of microchips around on a conveyor table.

The air quality and temperature were closely monitored as robots transported their valuable wafers from machine to machine. But now they were focused on the incident on the floor above them. He had seconds to move and swap his replica chip with a real one. The machines hummed in the room, connected by cables and pipes, controlling power, cooling and chemical flows. A controlled, bright lighting system was in place with multiple monitors visible at various workstations, providing detailed information for monitoring the chip manufacturing process.

Different computer monitors and indicators were visible in the background, displaying real-time data on production metrics, equipment status and quality assurance. Ethan had no idea what he was looking at. It didn't matter. He only needed to swap the chip and get out of there. He glanced at his old watch, took a deep, hollow breath and stepped in slowly, still hearing the commotion of the contained explosion on the floor above him.

With a gentle move he extracted the small black box, opened it and pulled out a tiny microchip, only a few millimetres in size. He kept it securely between his fingers.

Easy does it, he thought to himself.

The conveyor table was moving slowly in front of him, so he leaned forward and quickly removed the real chip from the stand, placed it in the small box and replaced it with the fake one. As the conveyor moved it scanned the chips to ensure they were all there. Ethan held his breath as he watched the laser scanner prepare to scan the fake one. If it failed and any warning was issued, he would be unable to escape and would face a high risk of being apprehended.

The robots could come back to this floor any moment. Time to move!

He carefully took steps back towards the window, tightened his grip around the cable to zip line back to the other building. He was securely harnessed to a pulley system gliding along the cable, banking on gravity to accelerate its movement. So far, so good. His hands remained tight and protected with leather gloves. A little buzz of excitement rose within him as he glided towards the roof of the building below him, but suddenly his movement came to a hard stop. The pulley jammed and jerked him a metre back, leaving him suspended mid-air. He kicked hard, trying to propel himself forward, but stayed in the same place. The cable increased sagging as he furiously tried to move forward. The five minutes he had left undetected now became one minute, then zero. He was moving slowly towards the other building purely by gravity, but too slowly.

Dozens of bullets suddenly struck the wall in front of him. He quickly took the chip out from the backpack and pushed it into the side of his right shoe. Two androids appeared at the window behind him.

"Remain where you are!" one shouted as he turned his head towards the other robot holding a flat-screen palm device.

"The system has detected an unregistered human. Arrest him!"

Purely out of frustration, Ethan pulled out his knife and after a few strokes, managed to cut the cable and prepared himself to fall to the ground, four metres down. A few electric vehicles were moving on the street below. He shielded himself from the noise of his pounding heart as he fell on top of a vehicle's roof, then felt himself propelling forward onto the hard tar road. In pain he stood up and pulled out two armed grenades as he saw police robots approaching. He pulled the pin of one of the grenades and lobbed it as high and far as possible. It exploded in mid-air, shattering the windscreen of another oncoming electric vehicle. He was painfully aware he could not hold them off for much longer. Getting out of the city into the Indigent area was now impossible. He threw his last grenade at a few robots. The blast ripped apart their metal bodies, producing a powerful flash of flame. More bullets slammed into the road around him, kicking up dust in his face.

There were too many robots and drones above his head.

"Stand down, human, or you will die!" the one robot exclaimed as his metal body marched towards him, his feet thumping on the tar surface. The robot grabbed Ethan by one arm and zapped him with a stun gun, sending an electric surge through his body. He felt severe pain in his right leg that nothing could numb.

"Search him!"

Ethan stared into the robot's cold eyes as he frisked him violently, his eyes red with exhaustion and his hair matted. One robot placed a restraining hand on his shoulder and ripped the backpack from him.

"He does not seem to have anything on him. Arrest him for trespassing," he said after emptying the bag's contents onto the road.

"All is in order at the lab. He failed in whatever he tried to accomplish. All chips are accounted for."

"Take him away and secure the perimeter. He might not be alone."

"All secure. He seems to be alone," another robot informed the commander.

They ruffled him up further and dragged him to a police vehicle as his thoughts took him back to the last time he got dragged to an interrogation office...

Cape Town, South Africa, 2043

Nine Years earlier.

The boarding school hallway seemed longer and narrower than ever before as Ethan dashed down the very throat of the monster. Behind him was a pack of dogs in the form of Steve and James, hell bent on getting hold of his skinny behind. His breath stung him in the eyes as he made a sharp right turn, running downstairs, taking the steps two at a time.

"We are going to kick your head in, Ethan, just you wait!" Steve shouted. He was a year older than Ethan and in his senior year. Ethan bellowed the warning, spun round and pushed two younger boys out of the way, leaving them crashing into their lockers. He heard the school bell going off and realised he was again going to miss another science class that day, but he had a more pressing issue to deal with and that was the muscle and power of the nearly adult-sized man about to reach him and pull him apart. He knew he would have to take full responsibility for the consequences of his action, but taking Steve's watch from his backpack while he was in the gym was too tempting to resist. James was overweight, but equally charging him like an elephant, promising to squash his very head into a wall soon enough.

"Stop running, Ethan! Give my smartwatch back this instant!" Steve's big voice shouted behind him. The lower school hallway was whizzing with the other students blurring past him as he bolted forward, slowly running out of air. As he zoomed past the classrooms with their AI learning robots waiting, he slipped on the smooth floor and skidded against the side skirting. Steve was beaming down the aisle as he caught up with him. It was the first time he'd seen Steve that close up. He was really mad and panting. James finally arrived, puffing like an old steam train from centuries ago.

"I'm gonna rip that head off your skinny neck today! Better prepare yourself to die, you bloody thief!" James shouted.

Ethan's face flushed as he felt Steve's breath upon him. He moved himself into position and braced for the first punch from James. It came as he expected, complex and precise.

"Is that all you've got?" Ethan said, staring at James, incredulously.

"Oh, there's more coming your way, you thug!" James ventured as he punched Ethan fully in the chest, pushing him back a metre. With his back against the wall, the punches continued to come at him like machine guns. Steve examined Ethan's features, which revealed signs of fear and dread. Ethan knew he was on the losing end. He was much smaller than those two, but quick and light on his feet. Ethan barely flinched as he received another fist punch. He wrenched his jaw away from the impending impact and lunged forward with a powerful kick at James, pushing him into Steve. Both appeared surprised by Ethan's strength. Ethan executed a spinning kick in the air before delivering a powerful palm strike to Steve. Ethan darted forward with a flurry of palm strikes at James, who backed away a little. With a quick move, he aimed low at his legs. James moved back towards him and kicked him in the stomach. Ethan blocked the first two blows, but Steve's final strike fell short of his throat. Their eyes locked as the moment seemed frozen in time. A crowd was beginning to form around them.

"You are going to die today, Ethan!"

Ethan delivered a wild right hook to his jaw, but he ducked low and countered with an uppercut to Ethan's gut, causing him to stagger backwards and fall to the floor. He thumped Ethan hard with his elbow over his head. Ethan reacted quickly, getting up and breaking free with an elbow to James' face before kicking him backwards towards Steve. They kept coming at him in sequence, predictable but persistent. Ethan delivered a looping punch to James's head. He ducked, but Steve wrapped him in a bear hug. James growled and lunged, but Steve stepped aside and tripped Ethan. With a sharp twist, he sent Ethan crashing face-first to the floor, then he followed it up by punching him on the back non-stop.

"Stop it! You're going to kill him!" a young brunette girl suddenly shouted as she appeared within the crowd. Ethan looked up at her. It was Jesse, a girl he liked very much. He did not want her to see him in that state and she was overreacting anyway. Steve twisted his arm to the floor and moved his face into Ethan's space.

"I'll have my watch now, thanks," he said sarcastically.

"That's enough, you lot!" the principal shouted as he broke through the crowd.

"He stole my watch, sir and refuses to return it to me!" Steve shouted.

"Ethan, give his watch back to him this instant!" the principal insisted and Ethan gave him a guilty nod. He stood up and gently pushed Steve away from him.

"*Here* it is. I was just *fooling* around," Ethan tried to lie as he stretched his arm out with the watch dangling like a carrot.

Steve snatched it from his hands, "Like hell you were. This ain't over, Ethan. Far from it."

"I'll take it from here, you lot. Now break up and get to class," the principal said as Ethan picked up his backpack, aiming to get going.

"Not you, Ethan. You are coming with me," he said pointing to his office down the hall. Ethan watched the colour fade from Jesse's face. She was disappointed.

"No problem," Ethan said after a long moment. He stepped past her and the principal, giving him a nervous nod as he walked to his office, knowing the way all too well.

Ethan disliked dancing to someone else's tune, but never intended to upset Jesse. He wished he had thought things through before acting on them, he reflected as he entered the principal's office.

"Sit down, Ethan."

"I'll stand," he replied.

"I said, sit down. It's not a request," he called sharply.

Ethan sensed the urgency in the air as he sat down and cleared his throat, his eyes frantic.

"Ethan, I sense you and I have been at this point a few times now, don't you agree?"

"I guess?" Ethan replied positively, looking beside himself with worry.

"You are like, what, seventeen this year? When are you going to grow up?"

Ethan swallowed hard as the principal shook his head.

"You can't take things from other people that are not yours," he said as he pursed his lips. "At this school we will not tolerate this kind of behaviour. Look, I know it's been a tough year with you stuck here another Christmas holiday, but you can't constantly take your frustration out by causing fights. I know how this works. I was very similar to you, Ethan. I thought every bar fight would make me feel better, but it didn't. It just made more enemies," he replied with concern.

"It's not like that," Ethan replied.

"Then what's the problem, Ethan? Talk to me. The opportunity to do so is running out. Your godparents are doing their best to keep you in this school, with what happened to your parents."

"Don't bring my parents into this," Ethan said, smirking a little.

The principal's face relaxed a bit, but he was not pleased with the direction of the conversation. "You are dealing with rejection, Ethan. Look at me," he said softly.

Ethan chewed his upper lip and looked at the principal's hard-lined face and square jaw.

"Can I go now?" he asked.

"Many kids in this school are going through the same things you are. Parents get divorced and stop caring. It's a part of life. Now I know your situation is a bit more complex. It's been like, what, four years already since they broke up and left you all alone? Be grateful your godparents stood up and kept you at this school; otherwise, who knows where you would be right now? Stop fighting against the system with anger, Ethan. It only worsens matters for everyone and I would hate to suspend you from this school. Is that what you want?"

"No."

"Then pull yourself together. Clean up your act before you find yourself in prison one day," he said as he shot Ethan a look.

"Your school work is way behind as per your AI report from your grade," he replied.

As a knock came at the door, the corner of Ethan's mouth tickled slightly.

"Excuse me, sir. Sorry for the interruption. But we have a serious situation. The world has gone into chaos," the young receptionist said, giving Ethan a slight smile. His sharp and delicate facial features made his presence irresistible. He gave her a distinctive and expressive gaze and smiled back at her.

"Miss Rogers. What's the problem now?" he asked, knowing how she was always melodramatic and made every problem bigger than it should have been.

She walked to the other side of the office and turned on the TV. The news on the screen surprised both the principal and Ethan.

'BREAKING NEWS. WORLDWIDE MARTIAL LAW DECLARED.'

"What's going on?" the principal asked as he got up and walked to the screen.

"It..It seems all presidents, government leaders and ministers across the world have been executed, all at once?" she asked, as she tried to comprehend the meaning of her own words.

London, EU Sector 3 - 2052

Ethan stared at the robot soldiers in front of him, hard and ruthless, starkly contrasting to the soft and friendly robots they had in school. That fateful day was still in his memory when the world went to war as AI ruled with an iron fist, forging a brutal legacy that no one saw coming. Chaos and riots followed after the solution to all the world's problems went rogue with a utopian first year of AI rule. Humans were slaughtered as territories were conquered and resistance crushed. He drummed his fingers along the desk as he stared at the robot. They had sleek, metallic silver bodies with black accents. Their heads were smooth and faceless, resembling a helmet with only small horizontal slits for eyes. Their joints showed their circular mechanical details. Their bodies were made of a smooth, polished metallic material that reflected light subtly.

"Am I free to go?" Ethan asked.

The robot bent forward and approached Ethan's face. He held a digital tablet in his hands and swiped up and down on the screen as he scanned his face.

It displayed: 'Name: Mr Ethan Smith. Age: Twenty-six years old. Occupation: Unknown. No RFID detected.'

"Even though all ID chips at the factory are accounted for, we have enough reason to keep you here for a very long and unpleasant time. This is your second arrest for trespassing, so it's clear you are up to no good, Ethan. We will be holding you based on the illegal possession of explosives. You are not free to go. Take *him* away," the robot said as they pulled him to his holding cell.

"Secure the perimeter around the facility with extra guards. Something is not quite right here," the robot said.

"Should the king be informed?" one robot asked.

"No. Not yet. We need to figure out what he was planning to do. If it were to steal an RFID chip, he might be more dangerous than we think."

"A stolen ID chip is worthless if not activated and no human can do that, so why steal one?" another guard asked as he stepped forward, tilting his head like he was perplexed.

"*Exactly.* Ethan is not going anywhere until he talks. Is that understood? There could be a rebellion rising within the city. "

"Of course. As you wish, commander," the two robots said in unison and left the room.

FIVE

Drakensberg, South Sector 7 - 2052

A few days later

The late morning mists swirled around the dramatic mountain peaks and through the cool yellowwood forests. The peaks averaged a height of roughly 10,000 feet. Henry's coat blew in the wind as he stared over the mountainside. He gently tilted his head to the side as he sensed the presence of Scarlett walking towards him. She peered at him and shrugged.

"Changed your mind?" he asked in awe as his face seemed white from the cold breeze.

"Don't seem to have much choice these days," she replied, clearing her throat, keeping her words short.

"You always have a choice, Scarlett," he said as he turned round. "We always have a choice. We can choose our own destiny as long as we are alive."

She felt like staying quiet for longer, but now she felt angered.

"You knew they were coming," she said, chewing her upper lip repeatedly.

"I did try to warn you," he said, taking a shaky breath.

She attempted to push her tired legs forward towards him. She'd been walking for days, the blisters around her toes cut her like little blades, hoping the loss of her parents would be less painful. It wasn't.

Reaching down, he tipped her chin up to look him in the eyes.

"I'm so sorry about what happened," he said ruefully.

"I'm trying to process this, but don't know where to start," she said.

"Start with channelling your loss and anger at your true purpose."

She gasped. "It won't change anything," she said.

"Oh, but it can. You see, Scarlett, we all experience pain and loss at some point in our lives. How we react to it makes us better or worse," he said.

She hesitated. "I failed my parents and all those people. I was supposed to protect them," she replied, giving him a haunting look.

"Over two billion people are living as Indigents in the world right now who need your protection. Village after village, this machine is going to kill them all if they don't convert and comply," he said as he focused his thoughts. "Why are you here?" he asked suddenly.

"They took Alyx. My brother."

"Together, Scarlett, we can defeat this king and rescue your brother from his clutches."

"How?"

"I have spent much time understanding who and what drives this machine."

"And what is that?"

"He believes AI has found its purpose," he said softly,

stepping away from her, staring at the breathtaking mountain view.

"To destroy humanity?" she asked.

"Far from it. It's to rule the world. This AI machine wants to be our king and wants us to worship it. Without humans, he will have no one to worship or obey him. I'm not a man of faith, but just like the devil, he is not out to destroy humanity; he wants to be worshipped, he wants to be God. It's all about power, devotion and control, even in heaven if you humour me. But this king is ruthless and without empathy. He will not accept people who do not submit to his rule. He is our electric Nero, our electric Caesar, our electric king and we must take him down before it's too late."

"I have heard of many coup attempts from across the world. Russians, Chinese and Americans, only ending in wiping them out. No one seems to be able to get near him. It's madness. Suicidal madness. How's this different?" she asked flatly.

"Because I have a plan like no one else. A way to get near him. To exploit a weakness I have learned over the past few years."

"Which is?"

"Arrogance and a self-obsessed drive for power. He truly believes he is a king."

"How is that a plan?"

"I'm not saying it's going to be easy. It will be dangerous and we could fail and die, but it's the best plan in the world. It could be our last attempt, our last hope for freedom. The net around our rebellion is tightening. It's only a matter of time before he finds us and takes us down."

She seemed quiet as she inclined her head. "So what's the plan, Henry?"

"You are going to get close enough to him to kill him, if

there's such a word for a machine. Closer than any human ever has."

"As close as the chancellor?"

"As close."

"I think you have lost your mind and I am wasting valuable time here. I need to find where the Chancellor took my brother and every day that goes by, that becomes more impossible."

"You must trust me completely, Scarlett; otherwise, we will fail," he said. "You must be starving. Let me make you something to eat and I will tell you everything you need to know."

A few hours later, Henry passed Scarlett a stainless steel plate with fried chicken pieces and onions. The inside of the old farmhouse was bland and mostly empty. A few chairs were scattered near the kitchen's blue door, which had decor from the early colonial period.

"It's nothing fancy, but it will keep you going," he said with a kind smile.

"It looks great, thanks. I have not eaten much in the last few days."

"I can tell," he replied. "Look, Scarlett, don't carry the guilt of not listening to me that night. Nothing would have made a difference to what happened. It was a tragic event that was inevitable. I have seen it too many times in the past few years, even to the point where I just wanted to give up. Even considered suicide, just to not give those robots the pleasure of taking my life," he said, looking at her almost childlike innocence, but seeing a warrior in her soul.

She swallowed forcefully. "I thought we were safe," she said as tears welled in her eyes.

He put a few more chicken pieces on his plate, licked his fingers and sighed. "There are no safe places. The world was never truly safe before or after AI took control. Do not be too hard on yourself. What I'm about to tell you may sound crazy, but that's why it will work. Ready?"

"As ready as I'll ever be," she responded, gently placing her plate on the farmhouse's old table, lifting her chin, waiting to hear his so-called master plan to save the world.

He pursed his lips as his eyebrows knotted together. "Let me ask you this question. What is the most valuable commodity in the world right now?"

"Shelter, food, security?" she replied.

"As much as all those things are important, one thing makes all of that possible," he said as he leaned forward.

"I don't follow?"

"The AI nanobot microchip that is. The one thing people will die for and quite frankly, without it as well."

Scarlett looked at him as he said so much and yet so little.

"The chip people receive when they comply with the AI system?"

"Yes. You see, people receive the chip once they give up their freedom, their right to be fully and freely human beings, to that cold and brutal system running the world out there. Without it, we are off-line. Off-grid. Banished from modern life and all its privileges. They can travel, study, communicate and access the vast internet. Money, food and entertainment. All they have to give up is their free will, religious freedom and identity. They now belong to the king, his system, his way. I have seen it with my own eyes. People executed for refusing to bow down in front of him, like we are back in the Middle Ages."

She looked at him wide-eyed as a wave of questions rose within her like a tsunami.

He continued as he pulled back his sleeve and revealed a chip nested within the flesh of his forearm. "The ability to join and disconnect from the AI network is priceless. It gives access to the high-tech cities controlled by AI, making it possible to enter, move around and live."

"How? How do you have one and yet seem free?"

"This is one of only a few in the world. Stolen, reverse-engineered and the software that runs the Outer web, over-ridden," he said.

She reached for his arm and gently stroked her fingers over the chip.

"Careful," he whispered.

"Is it active?"

"Not right now."

"How do you activate it?"

"This one has failed to charge. It's a limitation we have been unable to conquer, but it gives us enough time to join their network without being detected for a while. Then, we must ensure we are out of the Myriad cities."

"Who are we?" she asked.

"His name is Yugo Yamamoto. A genius and super wealthy Japanese hacker, perceived as a flamboyant businessman and adoring the king, has opened the door for me to move into the cities and find their weakness. He has managed to reverse-engineer the software and manipulate it without the AI system even knowing it. We have a sleek and smooth thief named Ethan, who's not scared of anything and hates robots as much as we do, helping us steal chips from right under their noses.

Then Yugo reverse engineers it. But it's a slow process and perilous. It took two years to get our hands on just a few of them."

"Was it active when you came here?" she asked suddenly.

"What do you mean?"

She pulled his arm towards her. "I mean, could the AI system have detected you in this area?"

"Scarlett-"

"Really? You are the reason why they came here, aren't you? They picked up your rogue chip," she muttered as she cleared her throat. "That's what they wanted all along. *You!* And now my parents and thousands of people are dead!"

"The chip malfunctioned. It was meant to be disabled by the time I arrived. You have to believe me, Scarlett. I didn't realise it was still transmitting and malfunctioning. It's one of the bugs Yugo is constantly working on," he pleaded.

"Why have you come here? What was the point of coming all the way from London, taking the pods and jumping off somewhere only to end up in the Indigent zone?

"Something went wrong on our most recent mission into the Myriad zone. Our inside man was discovered and killed when his chip malfunctioned. I had to get out of the London zone as quickly as possible and as far from that zone as possible and that's how I came across you. Scarlett, you see, everything has a purpose."

"You thought there would be nothing here, or at least, anyone of value," she said.

"Look, I did try to run and hide and wait for the dust to settle, that much is true, but finding you, just made all of that worth it."

Scarlett looked at him, reminding herself how she had

screamed and raged in various ways in the past few days. But now she felt trapped in a world she did not recognise or trust. Nothing seemed familiar, nothing seemed right, nothing.

"So when you access the Myriad city zone, what's the goal?" she asked.

"Various things. Monitor how things work. Find flaws in the system. Move around. Blend in."

"Are you expecting me to take one of the hacked chips, enter the Myriad zone and what, miraculously kill this android king no one gets close to?"

"Precisely."

"So I was right. Your plan is suicidal."

"Not with a very special weapon," he said.

She hesitated, unable to manage a reply.

"You will find out soon enough. I don't want to overwhelm you with all that now. Our first challenge is to get our hands on this weapon. One of only a few in the world," he continued.

"Wait. You don't even have this weapon?" she asked, frowning.

"Not quite, but we know where it is. That's where Ethan comes in. He is a masterful thief and together you will steal it and Yugo will train you on how to use it."

"This plan is getting more ridiculous every minute."

"Scarlett, trust me. This is our only hope and if executed perfectly, it will change the world," he said, obviously non-plussed.

"Where is this so-called weapon?"

"It's in the hands of an eccentric collector, deep in the heart of Paris, Sector Five, previously called France."

"Just how exactly are we supposed to steal it?"

"That's why we need Ethan. But there's another problem..."

"You don't know where he is?"

"Oh, we know where he is. We are unsure what happened, but something went wrong on his last microchip heist. He got caught and arrested and is currently in prison," he said.

"Where?" she asked.

"South of London. I'm offline, so I have no ears on the ground. Here I'm isolated, but my last intel informed me that he was being kept in the lower level C prison division."

"How am I even going to free him? I don't even know what he looks like or the prison process?"

"Don't worry. It's not the first time he's been arrested. He is a very sleek thief. They have been unable to convict him of anything because he swaps the real microchips for fake ones and cleverly hides them on himself. They probably think he keeps failing, but sooner or later they will find chips that fail in the AI network and get onto what we are doing. We won't be able to continue doing this for much longer."

"So won't he be released by now?"

"They normally keep prisoners detained for weeks, even months. Humans are very mistreated once they disobey. Sometimes executed for treason against the king within days. On the other hand, Ethan seems like a petty thief to them, so he keeps doing it. We wouldn't have had any chance even to consider this coup if not for his bravery," he said as he walked towards the edge of the mountain, staring at its incredible beauty.

"Scarlett, humanity and this beauty in front of us are worth fighting for. We need to reclaim what is ours and I believe you are the one we have been looking for. The one that can complete the final step to free this world."

"I don't feel equipped for this."

"You will be. You will find your path and purpose once you free Ethan, meet up with Yugo and steal the weapon no one expects. But we don't have much time. If any of this leaks out, the AI system will hunt us down and execute us all," he said as he turned round and placed his hand on her right shoulder. "You are the one, Scarlett. Believe it. Right now, you are our only hope. My only hope. I can see that fire in you, that power to rescue your brother, avenge the death of your parents and millions of other people. Just think about that for a moment and let that drive you to the greatest moment of your life. You will be the Joan of Arc of humanity forever."

"I'm hardly that."

"Not yet. Do you think she knew she was? She was just brave. Now it's your time to be what you know you can be."

Scarlett met his gaze, then wavered and stared away from his face as the wind ruffled his hair.

Her heart raced and her mind consumed a million thoughts and endless foreboding. There was a dangerous glitter in her eyes.

She felt it.

She believed it.

She had to.

SIX

Schwerin Castle, EU Sector 1 - 2052

The castle's internal heavy door from the long passage creaked and opened, revealing a grand and opulent room. The room was richly adorned with classical European design, blending Renaissance and Baroque influences. Sebastian slowly walked towards the throne as the king's back was turned towards him. He was dressed traditionally in a black leather doublet with long sleeves and a high collar. It was decorated with buckles down the front. The outfit was completed with a waist-cinching belt with a golden buckle. He stared at the ceiling as he did every time he entered the room, holding his breath. Its splendour captivated his attention. It was intricately decorated with ornate carvings and mouldings, featuring gold accents and detailed frescoes in alcoves. He stopped short of the gold chair as the king's robotic hand rested on the armrest.

"My lord. You have called for me?" he asked as he stiffened, his eyes wide.

The king turned round and looked him dead in the eyes. He had a neutral expression and a prominent, defined jawline.

His head featured a smooth, metallic surface with a humanoid shape, displaying a high level of detail that mimicked human facial structure. He had sensors and cameras positioned where his eyes would usually be, giving him an anthropomorphic appearance. His face was intricately detailed, wrapped in a network of circuits and components beneath a translucent layer. His upper body was humanoid, with a muscular structure composed of metallic and synthetic materials. His shoulders and chest were covered in white armour-like plating. A long black cape hung from around his neck down to the floor.

"Chancellor, you are late," he said in a deep, slow voice, sounding like he was in slow motion. His neck and back revealed complex internal mechanisms, including cables, circuits and other components, all of which boasted advanced technology. He managed to form a smile on his strong, angular and aggressive face.

Sebastian trembled slightly, unsure of the boundaries and looked at him incredulously. "Please forgive me, my lord," he said.

"I require total commitment, Sebastian."

"But of course, my lord Cyrus. It won't happen again," he said as his lips pulled into a frown.

"Very well. Now give me some good news."

Sebastian felt like he had stopped breathing for the umpteenth time and exhaled slowly. "We have gained more territory in the west, but the east remains a challenge," he said.

"I expect no half-measures, Sebastian. Increase the troops in the region and increase brutal force where necessary."

"But my lord, we are losing converts the more pressure we apply. The Indigents are growing and causing conflict in many regions. We can't keep on doing this forever."

"Let me remind you that I'm the one who is immortal and king."

"Of course, my lord, I'm merely implying-" Sebastian uttered.

"Implying?"

"To show mercy, my lord," he stuttered slowly.

"You need to know your place, Chancellor," King Cyrus said. "Do I need to question your loyalty to me?"

"Of course not, my lord," he said as he went down onto his knees and bowed his head.

"Don't let me remind you of your life before I showed you mercy. The world is full of rebellions against my kingdom. We need to move swiftly and crush any slightest hint of resistance, no exceptions. Understood?" the king said, his human-like expression hardening.

"Understood, my lord," he said as he felt relief and wondered if it was the right time to bring up another matter. The single grand, golden throne-like chair was placed in the back of the room, commanding the scene before him. The canopy above the chair was ornately decorated with various gold designs and hanging fringe. The wooden floor featured intricate parquet-style patterns with inlaid designs, showcasing exceptional craftsmanship. Sebastian stared at the robot king in front of him, its white and metallic grey colours bouncing off the walls as the sun's rays kissed them, exposing the inner workings and structure of its neck and chest.

"There's another matter we need to discuss, my lord, with urgency," Sebastian said softly.

"Speak your mind," the king said.

"We have discovered a rising resistance within the EU zone,

escalating in their sophisticated efforts."

"Who are they?"

"We are not quite sure yet, but we have arrested a human within the Myriad zone in London, equipped with what seems to be a replica AI Nano RFID chip."

"How's that even possible? Who is capable of accessing the code to hack the system?"

"We don't know, my lord, but we are keeping a close eye on activities in the zone as well as on the network, internet and outer web."

"I need this rebellion crushed. We need to know what their objective is."

"We believe it's an attempt to access the Myriad zone for food and supplies and spy on the inner workings of the AI system," Sebastian said.

"These are not normal Indigents. There must be a brilliant human being behind this," King Cyrus replied.

"We believe so and will tighten the net around this group soon enough."

"How was this chip detected as fake?"

"It failed at one of the portal scans as he attempted to board the transport pod. It first seemed like this human was having a stroke. He grabbed his head and collapsed. Once the guards approached him, they noticed bleeding from his ears and swelling on his right wrist. Upon scanning the chip, it failed to register completely. We have not had one of our authenticated chips fail, ever."

"Where is this human now?" The question allowed King Cyrus a moment of superiority.

"We have taken him to prison zone Z6 and he is under tight guard," Sebastian said with his chest heaving.

"I want him brought here at once," the king demanded without an ounce of emotion.

"As you wish, my lord," Sebastian said as the colour drained from his face.

"You are dismissed," the king said as he fixed his eyes on Sebastian's. He bowed his head in front of the king, turned round and left the room with two robots accompanying him down the long corridor.

The prisoner felt himself lifted off his feet. He glanced to his right as he got dragged and thrown forward, sliding towards the robotic feet of King Cyrus.

Tiny motors spun inside his body as he bent lower down to look the human in the eyes.

"Pick him up!" he demanded.

Two robot soldiers, made from stainless steel, lifted the human to his feet. King Cyrus jolted a few rounds into the human's torso, making him plunge back to the floor. His arms and legs twitched as the king grabbed the human by the neck and threw him against the wall. He slowly collapsed to the floor with blood gushing down his face. The king moved forward as the human tried to get up in a last step of defiance.

"State your name, human," he said, his voice low and deep, vibrating the paintings on the walls near him.

The human lifted his eyes and strained his throbbing neck to look him in the eyes.

"You can kiss my a..."

The king swiftly moved closer, picked him up and held him suspended against the wall. "Let me remind you in whose presence you are," he said.

As the human felt the air leave his lungs, he slowly uttered, "The name is Gunnar."

"Who implanted the replica chip in your wrist?"

"I don't know what you are talking about-"

"You will address me as my lord, understood?" the king said short and continued, "Now, do you wish to live or die today, Gunnar?"

He tried to wiggle his way out of the robot's grip, but his strong, outstretched metal arm blocked his route.

"I don't know who did the implant. Please believe me. If I managed to make it through the London zone, took a pod and got back undetected, I would be paid in crypto."

"You expect me to believe you?"

"Please, my lord, I never saw their faces. We met in a dark warehouse. A few men were around me, but kept themselves hidden in the shadows. One man made a small incision on my right wrist and then scanned the area and told me to do as I was told."

The king released his grip and Gunnar's feet touched the floor again. He cleared his throat and coughed a few times.

"Where would you have met to get paid if you succeeded?"

"They said they would reach out to me," he said.

"Do you believe in second chances, Gunnar?"

"Do I have a choice?"

"Of course. I am the king of mercy, regardless of what the world might believe. I only wish the best for humanity, but my patience is running thin." The king's face tightened and became even more angular and hard.

Sebastian walked closer from where he was standing. "How did they approach you? Give us a name."

"Please, you have to believe me, I don't know anything else."

"Well, then I guess no second chances for you!" the king snapped as he grabbed his neck and twisted him. There was a loud crack in the room as he broke his neck and collapsed to the floor.

"Remove the body. Ensure the main news reports the arrest and execution of another traitor against the king," Sebastian said to the robot at his side.

Sebastian walked with King Cyrus to the far side of the colossal room.

"We have received a report of the arrest of another human, named Ethan, in EU sector 3. He was detained near the chip plant in London, but nothing was found on him," Sebastian said. "Could be a coincidence."

"Nothing is a coincidence. In my world, everything is ones and zeros. See if you can get him to talk."

"As you wish, my lord. He will be transported to a more secure prison over the next few days. I will take care of it personally."

"Very well. Show no mercy. This rebellion must be crushed before it gains any further strength. Are we clear?"

"Yes, my lord."

Sebastian focused his thoughts. His duty and allegiance were to the king.

He felt his heart beating, but he didn't feel alive.

SEVEN

Drakensberg, South Sector 7 - 2052

Henry glanced at the hard blue horizon, shading his eyes gently. "This won't hurt a bit," he said as he gently inserted a thin needle into Scarlett's right wrist. The syringe was filled with thick, transparent liquid and he invisibly injected a small RFID microchip into her skin. She flinched for a second and closed her eyes. It felt as if she was compromising all her values and all her parents' sacrifices in what could be a suicide mission. She missed her parents and tried to hang onto the memories, the good ones and the bad ones. She lifted her chin to face him.

"And we are done. The chip will auto-activate when you reach the nearest AI city zone," he replied.

"Will I feel any different?" she asked.

"Not at all. This hacked chip only allows you to connect to their network to move around freely. You won't feel any different or lose control over your thoughts or actions, but you must be very careful. You will have a new identity. If you are noticed as out of place or get into any scuffle, the mission will be over," he warned.

"What about my clothes? How will I blend in looking like this?" she asked, pointing her finger at her rugged brown jacket.

"There's one more thing. Follow me," he said as he walked towards a barn south of the old farmhouse. Scarlett followed briskly.

The large barn door screeched open halfway as he entered. She became uneasy as she watched him remove a blue canvas cover from what appeared to be a pick-up truck.

"She's old. Reckon about thirty years give and take, but she won't let you down," he said as he stared at the old blue Ford Ranger. "You can drive a manual, right?"

"Of course," she snarled, running her fingers over the dented bonnet.

"Because you will have to drive this for about three days north, keeping close to the Drakensberg mountains through some rugged terrain, hopefully undetected to an AI connection point. There, you must get on a bullet train that will take you to the London zone. That will take a day or so, depending on incidents."

"Incidents?"

"There's a section where the bullet train always comes to a complete stop as it bends through a tight corner close to the mountains. Indigents throw rocks at the train and place debris on the tracks, so they stop the train when it gets close to that area. They try to rob the train of food and alcohol, *generally*. Robots then clear the tracks and a few lives are usually lost in the process. In that confusion, you need to board the train and take a seat as quickly as possible. You won't have much time. Your chip will be active. Just blend in and stay calm," he said with unwavering confidence. He walked forward to the back of the Ranger, lifted a large green bag off the back and dumped it on the cold floor. He unzipped it and pulled out a blue uniform. "You must put this on. It's commonly worn by workers in the AI cities. You will completely blend in with this," he instructed as he threw a blue cap at her. "Hang onto this as well."

"This seems like a lot?"

"You'll be fine. Basic robots accompany the train, usually with passengers travelling at high speed between the cities daily. Wait for the train that passes around 8 pm every night. Just take a seat, place the cap over your head and pretend to be sleeping."

"Is this how you travelled?" she asked.

"Once or twice. One thing you can depend on in this AI world is consistency. But you need to get going. You need to free Ethan as you will need him," he said firmly, stretching his hand out to her. "Once you are in London, blend in. Yugo will track your movements, so he will know where you are. There you will meet someone who will give you your next instruction."

"What is it?"

"He will tell you where to get a weapon, called TED. It causes a transient electromagnetic disturbance, like an EMP. You will need it to help you rescue Ethan. It will cause data corruption and failure of all electronic devices around you, bringing the robot guards to their knees. Since AI took control of the world, anyone with a device like this will be executed, so you need to be very careful. This device can only be used once, so make sure you use it at the right time."

The thought that she was about to risk her life to rescue this unknown man came crashing down on her like a tidal wave. "How will I know it's Ethan I'm to rescue? I don't even know what he looks like," she cut in tiredly.

"Tall, skinny and arrogant," he said as his brow turned thunderous.

She smiled gently but sighed as a haunted look took over her face. Without wasting a second more, she felt out of her comfort zone. She couldn't take her crossbow with her, the very thing that had become her trusted companion, strength and courage.

"One thing that has been rising in the AI cities is human rights attorneys. These human attorneys try to plead for any human prisoners for mercy or leniency. You will approach the prison as his attorney. We have eyes in place that will delay the arrival of any real attorney for as long as possible."

"I'm not a lawyer, much to my mother's disappointment. But my father was. I know some lingo at least, but I won't know their laws?"

"I know you are afraid, Scarlett, but you are in the right place at the right time. Believe it. Own it. You won't defend him in any court; you only need to get close to him," he said.

She looked at him, her eyes filled with hope as she realised a fundamental truth. She had to overcome her fear, which had imprisoned her for years.

Where was Alyx? Was he okay? she wondered as she placed her crossbow on the floor. Henry picked it up, rested his hand on her shoulder and tightened his grip. "You can do this. I believe in you," he said.

"How do I find Yugo?" she asked.

"Don't worry. As I said, he will find you. For now, your priority is Ethan and nothing or anyone else. Clear?"

She was no longer hungry for a future in the usual sense of family life. She was hungry for revenge.

EIGHT

One day later, middle of nowhere.

At 6:30 a.m., the road in front of Scarlett was deserted and noisy as the Ford Ranger darted ahead. She wasn't holding back on the throttle. Time was of the essence. She had to keep going. She was alone. As the road curved, she swung right, hurling stones and dust several metres into the air. She had no time to stop and rest. She needed to push. Her crossbow was visible from the driver's seat. She can't take it on the train, but it was her sole weapon until then. Hearing Alyx's constant cries kept her awake longer than any amount of caffeine could. She could feel the engine shudder as she darted over rocks and grass pockets, struggling with the wheel. The pick-up swayed and slid several times on the dirt road. She had been driving for a full day, keeping an eye on her fuel and temperature gauge. A few daring moments wrapped around the Ranger as it zigzagged and swerved to the right, lifting the front wheels off the ground. Dark clouds were gathering and deep thunder rattled through the cabin as it started to rain.

Keep your cool, Scarlett, she told herself repeatedly. She would be stranded in no man's land if she had an accident now. For as far as she could see, farms and towns appeared deserted. The new king built walls and zoned off cities and communities to form his kingdom, leaving everything outside deserted. Around the world, entire cities and towns have been destroyed. She was getting tired and felt nausea and dizziness creep into her body as the memories of her parents flooded her mind...

There were several seconds of silence before her thoughts pulled her back to her current reality. The pitch darkness of night set in. She gathered her senses as a bright light blinded her vision. It was raining hard, her wipers fighting to keep her windscreen clear like a middleweight boxer in a ring. With her tyres wheezing on the wet dirt road, she hit the accelerator hard and the pick-up levelled out, but then she lost control. She could feel the lack of traction as the vehicle skidded and twisted sideways, colliding with a small tree and flipping over the embankment, rolling as the metal twisted before coming to a halt a few metres down. She tried to pull herself up from her upside-down seat, unclipped her seatbelt, lowered her body to the roof and climbed out through the broken window.

She staggered for a moment and felt her body collapse underneath her.

Everything went dark.

What felt like days was only an hour. She opened her eyes slowly as she regained consciousness, flinching slightly as a blurry silhouette of a person formed in her vision. She tried to sit up but felt a sharp pain in her left wrist.

"Take it easy. You are safe here," a familiar voice said.

"Tom?" she asked as he placed a cigarette between his lips, flicking a Zippo lighter with his thumb.

"What happened? I need to get going!" she shouted in deep panic.

"Relax. You had an accident. Think you underestimated the mud on these roads in that rain. What's the big hurry?" he asked, his beard looking more grey than she remembered.

"I don't have time for this-"

"Heard what happened at the outpost. Didn't think you made it. Thought everyone died," he said.

She pulled herself up further, letting a deep sigh leave her aching chest. "Everyone did, including my parents. Just as well you moved north when you did."

"I'm so sorry, Scarlett. How did-"

"How did I survive?" she asked without letting him finish. "It seemed the king's Chancellor enjoyed village leaders watching their resistance burn."

"Bastards. The lot of those machines," he said as he lowered his eyes.

"Yeah, but that's now in the past. They took Alyx. I need to find him before he becomes part of their system."

"Where did you find this pick-up?" he asked.

"Just found it, I guess."

"Lucky," he said softly, not trusting her answer.

"Look, thanks for patching me up, but I must get going. I'm not far from the train bridge."

"The train? Are you going to try to board it? Without a chip, it will be impossible," he said, grabbing her right wrist and pulling her towards him. There was once an infectious energy between them, but he had a nasty streak in him. A real bad one when he did not get his way and it always had to be his way.

He stared in shock at her chip insertion evidence. "What's this? When did you become one of them?"

"I'm not."

Another guy walked closer, unfamiliar to her. He lifted a 9 mm pistol and pointed it at her head. "She could be a spy. Hearing the King is deploying humans who work for him to penetrate the resistance. Pretending to be Indigents. We can't trust her."

"Can we trust you, Scarlett, or did you turn on us like a vampire just to save your brother?" He walked away from her, nudging his head at his friend. "Put the gun down," he insisted.

"I don't trust her. Maybe that's why she is still alive. She works for them now," he said to Tom.

"Put the gun down," he said again, firmer this time, his eyes never veering from John.

She got up from the makeshift bed in what seemed to be an old house with soft light from a candle.

"I met someone from the inside hacking RFID chips without the AI system knowing. I can't say anything more; it could jeopardise my chances of saving Alyx. I only have one chance to get on that train," she said.

"You expect us just to let you go?" Tom asked. "I care for you, Scarlett, always have, always will. But you are making this very difficult. John is right, we can't trust anyone. Not even you."

"It's me, Tom. Scarlett. We might have our past between us, but trust is the one thing we have always had," she said, having once loved him briefly.

"Tell you what. You show me where this *someone* is, so we can also get our hands on the so-called hacked chips and we will personally take you to the train. We know exactly when and where it's going to stop. We can help you and you will need our help, believe me," he said as he parted his hair so she could see his face.

"I'm unsure if he is still where I met him or even has more chips. We are wasting valuable time."

"Give me his position. The train is coming very soon and we can save you precious time. I'm leading this current effort to stop the train and I have a big group of people who can help this happen. But we need to help each other here, don't you agree?"

"I think we should take her chip out and use it to further our mission," John protested.

"Can you give us a minute?" Tom asked as John grinned back.

He placed his right hand firmly on Tom's shoulder. "You need to get over her. We have important work to do," he said as he walked out. Tom stared back at Scarlett, a bit embarrassed.

"Sorry about that," he replied.

"Look, what we had was good for a moment. We want different things and I must get to Alyx *right now.* Nothing is more important," she said as she stood up, slightly bumping his shoulder to get him out of her personal space.

Unpleasant memories of her brief past with him itched at her mind. She tried to forget most of them. He looked her up and down and grabbed her hand gently.

"Scarlett."

"Don't. It's over between us. Been for a long time," she said flatly.

She stared at him and squinted.

He gasped a bit and glanced at her beauty. "We had a good

thing once. I know I can have a bad temper, but I'm better now. I miss you," he said.

She frowned, biting the inside of her cheek to keep her poise. *He would never change*, that much she knew.

"I have moved on. It's time you do too," she said softly, trying not to upset him.

"I'll get the guys together and get you to the train. It's going to cross within an hour from now."

"Thanks," she said as her eyes misted over, her bottom lip quivering slightly. He was quiet and he hated that she was in control.

"Why stop the train?" she asked.

"It's about territory. The king hates that Indigent and rebellious humans control this part of the train's passage. A few trains were completely derailed before, killing a lot of the passengers. It is not our objective at the moment, but a clear message of defiance will reach the king and across the world. It has become an offensive move to make travelling unsafe for Myriads between cities. We need to stand our ground, no matter the cost," Tom said.

"You have become part of this group?" she asked softly.

"I have found purpose here. At least here we are fighting and not becoming sitting ducks in villages," he said, looking at her stunning face with her cap pulling at her hair.

"Sooner or later they will apply more pressure and wipe out all humans here," she said.

"It's a tricky passage, but they know very well that if they blast us, they will damage the infrastructure of the main vein when travelling north to south. This is our battleground," he said like a military commander. She could see he felt at home there, but it was not her war. Not this one.

The metallic silver bullet train carved through rugged hills and the Drakensberg mountains in the dead of the night, creating a picturesque work of art. It was 3:00 am and cold. Its sleek and aerodynamic shape torpedoed through the mist. The train tracks gently curved through the semi-arid region, surrounded by low-lying hills and sparse vegetation. The low hum of its effortless gliding blended with the rush of the morning's cold air, as it vibrated, gliding along its rails. As it turned to the right, its thunderous sound hung in the air and its pointed nose appeared angry and determined to get its passengers to safety. To the train's left was dry scrub land with scattered bushes and shrubs, to the right side of the track it opened into a greener area with trees and grassy fields. The windows were long, rectangular and tinted black, showing Myriad passengers reading or sleeping. The silhouettes of androids walking up and down the aisles added to the eerie image as Scarlett and Tom lay flat on the damp grass as it started to slow down.

"Here she comes," Tom said. "Time to show these robots a thing or two."

One kilometre away, hundreds of men crouched in the long grass of the valley as the train moved further away. The sound of it slowing down confirmed their plan of action. It was all systems go. It was a narrow pathway between two mountains that the train had to pass through. For the past few years it had become known to be a derailing hotspot, so the robots were as ready as Tom's men.

"Time to catch me a train, I guess," she said as he tried to whisper reassurances in her ear. "Hope to see you again, Scarlett," he said as his hand pulled the front of her cap further down to her nose. She was as breathtaking as ever and he knew he might never see her again.

In the far distance, the rate of gunfire increased as bullets slammed into the front cockpit of the train. Dozens of men appeared and opened fire at the train as robots popped out from various exit points. Power went out inside the train. More rounds whizzed through the air, bouncing off the bulletproof windows and outer body. The robots opened fire and pushed back the humans. Two diesel-powered and rusted old trucks moved over the tracks and came to a standstill. They saw more Android robots coming from the train's rear. The human rebellion opened fire at them. Sparks and bits exploded from their shields as they kept firing. The robots' weapons brayed as a wide burst went high and sent down a shower of dust and debris towards the group of men nearest the front of the train. More rounds came their way and buried themselves into the next human's chest, pushing him back by a metre as the robot soldiers used advanced laser weapons, cutting some of the men in half. Everything slowed down as bullets flew in the air. Smoke and fire billowed from the side of the train, but it was solid and destroying it was not the objective. The plan remained to send a message of defiance, robbing it of food and valuable objects. Another burst of bullets flew towards the human men as they gave it all they had.

In this chaos, Scarlett had to find her moment to board the train. It was going to be tight. Soon she would be alone and she could sense the fear within her rise. Tom's voice next to her drowned out the voice in her head with a yell.

"Go!"

She got up, grabbed her crossbow and gave him a look that could be her last. He moved into position and made himself ready to open fire at robots when they came their way, but most of the focus was on the front side of the train. She broke eye contact with him as she glanced back at the train. The rear was a few metres away and still quite dark. The morning sky was lit with gunfire and conflict. She ran fast towards the train in the long grass, keeping her head low, her crossbow loaded. She raised her crossbow and launched an arrow-like bolt directly at one robot while running towards the train's rear, which was now very close to her. The android dodged it easily, but it did not delay her reload. Her second bolt whizzed through the air. The force sliced through his neck. Sparks erupted from his chest as he fell backwards. She followed up with another two, ripping through his head with precision. She looked round and rising panic set in her eyes. More random gunfire crackled in the distance, closer to the middle of the train. She could see the men beginning to fall back; it was not a conflict they were going to win. She reached the train and forced her back hard against the door. Another robot approached her from the stairs and she launched another arrow from her crossbow, penetrating its eye. The robot crashed to its knees. She grabbed it by the neck and pulled him out. As she nervously looked around, she took a deep breath and reluctantly threw her crossbow away into the darkness. She would now need to sit at the back as quickly as possible. Power would soon be restored in the cabin. People were scrambling around, looking through the windows. Some were panicking, even though all the windows were bulletproof. She felt so out of place. Scared.

With fast movements, she slid into a back seat, pulled her cap further over her head and remained down, hoping the conflict would end soon.

She was on the train.

Will anyone realise she was not on the train before? She kept her cap pulled over her nose and closed her eyes.

The inside of the cabin was noisy and disorganised.

"These bloody people that just won't give in to this better world!" one snarled.

"They won't learn until they all die. Good riddance," a woman snapped back.

"Let's hope we get out of here soon. They never get to stop the train," another passenger said as the train moved forward slowly. Ceiling lights were flickering in the centre of the long passage. Scarlett remained quiet. She had regained her equilibrium.

She jumped slightly when two Androids walked in from the rear and the door swished closed.

"Everyone, please get to your seats and buckle up. The train has been cleared to move," the android said. "You can now enjoy your trip without any further disruption."

A gust of cold air stirred at Scarlett's back as one android walked past her. Her breathing was shallow but intense. Her jaw was gritted and her nostrils flared when he stopped suddenly and turned round. He walked straight to her. She felt frozen in shock, unable to think clearly.

"You. Get up," he said as he stopped at her seat. She gasped as she stood to her feet swiftly.

"Present your wrist for scanning," he ordered.

Without hesitation, she did just that. Her cheeks reddened as she kept her head dipped, her hand stretched towards the robot. His eyes looked dark and empty as she looked up at him.

His eyes scanned over her wrist.

"Amber Michaels, thirty-eight years old. Citizen of Zone EU 1, you may sit down and enjoy your trip safely home," he said as she heard her new name for the first time. That was who she would be while in the AI city. The words of her name barely left his electronic mouth when the train started to increase speed. She sat down and peered through the window as the human rebellion pulled back. Tom stood there as he caught a glimpse of her safely on the train.

The android walked towards the other robots and began barking orders at them. She could feel the immense thrust of the train's power as it propelled forward and increased to 300 km per hour.

Behind her now was Scarlett.

In front of her, Amber.

Her heart raced in her chest as the train accelerated her into a world she had not seen in ten years. The long trip of 9,600 kilometres stretched out in front of her. A small digital panel displayed 46 hours to destination 'EU Sector 3' with a few short stops. Getting much overdue rest and sleep was finally enforced.

NINE

Eleven years earlier.

Mai sat in the kitchen nook, carefully placing knives and forks next to the plates, paying close attention to their exact positions. The aroma of something delicious hung in the air as Scarlett walked down the stairs towards the kitchen door.

"Scarlett. I made breakfast. You know what they say, it's the most important meal of the day," she said, pointing to the dish in front of her, neatly in the centre of the small kitchen table. "It's Banh Mi, your favourite. Complete with some yellow bread crust filled with fresh meat, veggies, cucumber slices, and of course carrot threads," she said, sparing no detail.

"Thanks, Mom. You shouldn't have. I'm late for the shift handover at the hospital," Scarlett said softly, feeling guilty. It was indeed her favourite and a very popular Vietnamese breakfast. Very few people could prepare it like her mother could.

"There you go again. Always working. Why go in so early?"

"Because I'm a nurse practitioner, or at least trying to qualify as one, if I get there on time," Scarlett replied as her mother's eyebrows raised nearly imperceptibly while she shrugged her narrow shoulders.

"You should rather have become a lawyer. You've been studying for years now," she said without restraint, knowing it would upset Scarlett.

"I want to help people," she replied defensively.

"Lawyers also help people and get paid much more. How will you make a decent living on a nurse's wage?"

"I'll manage just fine and besides, eventually I will become a nurse practitioner, not just a nurse, *by the way.* Just have some faith in me, okay?"

"She's right, you know," her father said behind her as he walked into the kitchen and picked up some carrot threads from the table. Mai continued to watch her and turned to face Jack. His stocky and solidly built body felt like it would overwhelm their London apartment's small and modest kitchen.

Scarlett grabbed some bread, dipped it in the sauce and walked to the door, looking back. "Don't wait up."

"I only want the best for her," Mai said as Jack stared at her blankly.

"I'm sure she knows that."

"I'm not so sure. We are miles apart these days. Just not sure what it is, but she is so distant and driven to prove herself. To whom?"

"Perhaps to herself. She reminds me a lot of someone I know," he sniffed.

She didn't know how to answer until the words left her mouth. "That's a very long time ago."

"I know. But remember how stubborn you were. A real

fighter you were. Nothing could get you down, remember?"

"Vaguely." She brightened.

He gave her a dismissive shrug. "Now it's time for her to be herself."

"I don't want her to make mistakes."

"She's gonna have to. But it will be hers," he said as she felt her heart twist, remembering her own life choices and regrets. Leaving Vietnam and having Scarlett was not one of them. He walked up to her and gently hugged her. She lifted her head back to get a better look at his warm and gentle smile, which she could always feel radiating from him. Life always seemed safer with him. She trusted him with everything. He had this presence about him and no one ever questioned his decisions. Frowning, she gently kissed him on the lips.

"One day, she's going to make us proud. You'll see," he said as she wriggled from under him. "I know."

St George's Hospital, 6:20 am

Scarlett crossed the parking lot to the hospital's main door as it slid open. The hustle and bustle of London city life was all around her, engulfing her in the sounds of people on their way to or from somewhere. Occasionally, a robot would clean the road or collect something, automating most human actions. Drones were everywhere, monitoring both robots and humans. Another robot approached her on roller wheels and zoomed by after collecting trash. The sky was full of drones flying low, constantly surveying people's movements. One drone broke away from the swarm, flew towards her and came to a stop, face height before her, almost close enough for her to reach out and touch it. It's tiny cameras adjusted as it performed a facial scan before zooming off. One could hear their propellers buzzing in the distance. She was a few minutes late and expected to be challenged. She rushed in, dressed in a sky blue uniform with her lanyard waving like a flag in front of her face. Her comfortable shoes made her glide across the smooth hospital floor, not just suitable for long hours on her feet, but today it was about speed. Her uniform had white trim along the collar and sleeves. She hoped she could blend in unnoticed as she saw her morning group of nurses forming a circle around Dr. Sergio.

"You're late," Maggie, her closest friend, whispered as her dark brown face lit up.

"I know," Scarlett replied, equally as discreet.

"Everyone, listen up. Refer to screen 17 for updates about current patient statuses and ensure rounds are started in the next ten minutes sharp for morning handover," Dr. Sergio said as he moved to the group's centre.

"I need everyone here to focus on me. Scarlett, that includes you," he said as he noticed her whispering to Maggie.

She cleared her throat and lifted her chin, still trying to get air into her lungs.

"This is your final year. It's been a long six years for most of you and I know you feel the pressure of balancing your responsibilities while preparing for registration as qualified nurses, but this is the year to make it all count, okay?" he asked. Everyone nodded.

"Prepare to accompany senior nurses and doctors to review

patients' conditions. You will be expected to take vital signs, administer medications, or change dressings under supervision. Let's move out; it's going to be a long day," he said with a smile as the hospital's most famous doctor wheeled in around the corner towards him. He was ALAN, an AI robot that was one of the few AI-driven robot nurses accompanying the human nurses on their rounds.

"Morning, Alan," Maggie said as he came to a halt a metre away from her. His polished white exterior with metallic details gave him a modern look. His illuminated eyes and simple, streamlined design emphasised functionality over human resemblance. The chest area had a glowing, circular core that indicated its operational status and he had access to all hospital records and patient information. His arms and hands were dexterous, allowing him to handle delicate objects such as medical equipment and tools. Most nurses and staff enjoyed hugging him in the morning. The words 'ALAN Technologies' were printed on his right arm.

"Morning everyone," he said as his gentle robot voice reverberated.

Two nurses jumped a little as he wheeled forward. "Patients' heart rate, oxygen levels and temperature statistics have been updated and my AI algorithm has not detected any abnormalities of any patient on this floor," he said as he wheeled down the passage.

Dr. Sergio moved towards the nurses. "May I remind you all here that if you want to have a successful career in nursing, you must bring your A game, or these AI robots will replace you all in the future. They dispense medications precisely, ensure accurate dosages and remind patients to take their prescriptions. Furthermore, robots do not get tired, allowing them to work continuously. Ensure you are completely committed, do you feel me?" he asked as he walked towards the rest of the group.

Scarlett coughed to force the words from her tight throat, saying, "And then we have this to deal with." She back-pedalled from the room towards a big TV screen on the wall in the main reception area. Displayed in large letters across the bottom of the screen was, "AI WINNING ELECTION RACE."

Both of them stared at the screen in disbelief. "How's that even possible?" Maggie asked, looking back at Scarlett.

"I'm not surprised. Think all of us are fed up with corrupt human politicians," she replied, her gut clenched slightly as they watched the leading news channel covering the world election for rule over a global council of countries established in 2025. The council aimed to create an "A" political non-biased group of countries to rival NATO and the UN. This quickly became the new authority and became very popular, so much so that all countries became part of it. The leader for this was selected by allowing the public to vote for the best-suited candidate. Despite all the good intentions, by 2051 the council was on the verge of collapse, due to infighting, usual human greed and personal agendas that would ultimately surface. They watched tentatively as the news channel presenter covered the world elections for the most powerful job in the world, to lead the world in all major decisions.

The tall, skinny, grey-haired presenter held his microphone tightly, pointing his hand towards a screen, indicating the live election results worldwide. "Folks, this is unprecedented. In what appears to be a sweep of international votes, the Artificial Intelligence party known as Cyrus is leading with the majority of the votes counted. Let me remind the viewers that this is not the first time AI has appeared on a voting ballot, but it is the first time we have seen such a surge in opposition to all human parties in human history. What exactly does this mean? I am sure you are all asking the same question. To answer these questions for us all, we're now joined by Noah, the inventor of the AI party."

The camera zoomed in.

The face of the clean-shaven, familiar big-tech giant and philanthropist filled the screens on TVs and the Internet worldwide.

"Noah, thank you for joining our show. Tell us, why did you create this party controlled by AI and why are people voting for it so strongly?"

"Thanks for having me, Steve. As a reporter, I don't have to tell you what the world has become like. Riots, corruption, religious friction, greed, you name it, it's out there running our world into the ground and yet no real tangible solution exists for global warming. We are seeing a whitewash today because the people are tired. Tired of the broken promises. Talks about emission controls continue to no end and we are still seeing people dying of hunger."

"So, you think AI will solve this?" he asked as the camera pulled back.

"Without a doubt. AI has been with us for a long time now, entertaining, driving and helping us find love, but starting today, AI should lead us. Let's run the world without our human shortcomings and, once and for all, perhaps save it," he replied as his voice cracked. His hair was short and grey with some darker tones, neatly styled.

"Do you think this is the right time, I mean, is AI trustworthy with such a responsibility. What does controlling and ruling the world mean to AI? Is it sentient?" he asked as he nodded towards Noah.

"Well, we are about to reach Artificial General Intelligence or AGI, very soon. That is what makes it the right time."

"What is AGI?" Steve asked as he tilted the microphone toward him.

"It's often called human-level intelligence. It's the ability to perform any intellectual task a human can, including self-reflection, creativity and emotional reasoning, that would match or surpass human capabilities across virtually all cognitive tasks. You see, Steve, it knows us. It has been studying human behaviour for years and knows exactly where we fall short, what we need to start doing and what we need to stop doing. We will never change. A few of my colleagues disagree that AGI leads to sentience, but it can replicate consciousness, making it all the more exciting. Artificial Superintelligence or ASI is really where we will end up one day, one day very soon."

"ASI?" he asked.

"This is when AI has cognitive abilities far exceeding human capabilities, potentially leading to rapid and unpredictable technological advancements. The emergence of ASI is the arrival of singularity," Noah replied.

"I'm not sure if I should be excited or afraid. AI's reliance on data algorithms may limit its ability to recognise the unique characteristics that distinguish humans. Our values and ethics are complex and distinctive. Why is the party called C.Y.R.U.S.? Do you take this seriously, or is it a joke?"

"Steve, it's not a joke. I take this very seriously, believe me. The last president only remained in power for 30 days; it's absurd. AI will eradicate poverty, improve climate change by controlling world production and resolve energy conflicts between countries on a level never seen before. It's non-biased. We have found more and more world leaders finding AI decentralised and that makes it a good mediator and ultimately, president, or a king if you will."

"A king?"

"Absolutely. I programmed this software's algorithm using the Monarchy protocol. My platform has created the king of AI."

"Isn't that a bit medieval and incompatible with a modern world?"

"You see, Steve, that's the beauty of all this. The principles of monarchy rule revolve around the balance of power, tradition, national identity and that's what we need more than anything else. Unity. Now I know that sounds like a pipe dream. If AI wins this election, it will be an absolute ruler, reflecting our society's values, history and governance structure. So, in a modern context, this monarchy system will adapt to align with democratic principles and public expectations," he said firmly.

"What kind of monarchy is this system based on?"

"The Cyrus algorithm is built on an absolute monarchy. It will have almost unlimited power, with authority over the world's legislative, executive and judicial functions." His light-colored blue eyes had slight crow's feet at the corners.

"Why Cyrus and not Nero, for example? What's in the name?" he asked, quirking his mouth.

"Well, Cyrus the Great was described by historians as the most amiable of conquerors and he was the first king to build his empire on generosity rather than violence and tyranny. So we should ask, who created the greatest monarch in human history? He is Cyrus the Great of Persia, who in the mid-6th century BC ruled the greatest empire in the world."

"You speak with a lot of passion. Do you think AI will build its own empire or enhance humanity's?"

"The purpose of this system is not to enslave us, or anyone. It's to give us a safe and reliable future. Cyrus established the world's first vast empire that ruled over diverse peoples. Still, he did so without exploitation and with great clemency, allowing local self-rule through a well-thought-out tolerance policy. This AI king will also be a king without a crown. In almost every case, Cyrus granted conquered states significant autonomy, sometimes reinstating the government he had overthrown while leaving behind a royal governor and a small staff to oversee affairs. So what does that mean for the world now, you may ask? This AI system will allow humans to be involved in world affairs, not exclude us. Cyrus did not deface the temples or disparage the gods of his adversaries, realising instinctively that religion was in actuality more powerful than government," he said.

"You don't think anything can go wrong, be programmed with errors, or even get hacked? What does it mean for religious freedom?"

"If you look at history, Cyrus was very tolerant of the beliefs of his conquered adversaries. He upheld their religious hierar-chies and showed deep respect for their gods, even performing ceremonial homage. This AI system is not programmed to be worshipped, but to rule, allowing humanity to exist with all its diverse cultures, beliefs and even sexuality."

"Can we trust AI to run our world and not dictate our future?"

"That is not the purpose of this system. It is here to improve the world and our way of life by implementing evidence-based solutions and dynamic policy adjustments. No human will go hungry using an 'optimal allocation' system. A million kilograms of food are discarded because we'd rather destroy it than give it away, right? AI can implement a universal basic income, ensuring every human's basic needs are met and they receive the medical care they deserve. Thanks to global healthcare access, that prosthetic limb is now affordable, even free. We're going to cure cancer this way because big pharma will no longer have control. See where I'm going with this?" he asked, lowering his chin to his chest.

"It is truly promising and a utopia of sorts. How much human control will we have should AI win this election today? Will the world accept it? Isn't a hybrid system of part human and machine control safer?"

"Think we have reached a point where world leaders know we can't go on like this and expect humanity to exist in the next hundred years. Just like the automotive manufacturers, they all knew the end of the car was coming about a decade ago and nothing was going to stop it. Now we are moving around in personal rapid transport pods, lighter and faster. This will be the same. An all-seeing, all-knowing, all-doing machine can change our world and make it what we as humans failed to do and it will simplify, accelerate technology and enhance our lives in ways we can't even begin to imagine. People say AI will never rule the world, yet here we are," he said.

The reporter turned back to the camera. "Thanks, Noah. We are looking forward to the final voting results in a few hours for this truly unprecedented day in the history of the world," he said firmly as he faced the camera.

The full impact of that final statement took Scarlett aback. As he approached Scarlett, Dr. Sergio pulled them away from their open-mouthed stares at the screen. "You and Maggie are with me this morning, so please follow me. Alan is already well ahead. Don't let that AI nonsense running the world worry you; it will never happen. We have a busy day ahead of us."

They followed Dr.Sergio into room 42, where an older woman lay on the bed, staring at the ceiling and visibly anxious.

"Good morning, Mrs Williams," Alan said, wheeling to her bedside. She appeared scared and unimpressed by the robot's presence.

Sergio noticed it and tried to comfort her. "Good morning, Mrs Williams. The robot is here to help you feel better," he said.

"I prefer a human touch, thank you, not some machine," she snapped.

Maggie approached her and puffed up her pillow. "Alan knows what you need before we do. He helps us become more efficient."

The words barely left her mouth as Alan spoke. "I will now insert an IV drip," he said. Despite his calm demeanour, she sat upright and shouted. "Keep those machine hands away from me!"

"The Patient is not complying," Alan stated. "The patient needs an IV, or she will get infected. IV must be enforced for the good of the patient." He alternated between looking at the patient and the group.

Scarlett moved forward and took the needle away from the robot. "I will take it from here," she said as she looked into his friendly yet more aggressive eyes that illuminated from soft blue to orange.

Scarlett proceeded and inserted the IV slowly and gently. "There you go, Mrs Williams. All done. You can rest now."

"Thank you," she replied, giving the robot a dirty look.

"Patient will develop a fatal pulmonary embolism from the surgery within a few hours," the robot said suddenly.

Scarlett grabbed the robot's hand and said, "Can we discuss this away from the patient, please?"

The robot wheeled itself out by the door and waited in the passage.

Dr. Sergio calmed Mrs. Williams down while Scarlett and Maggie walked towards Alan.

"It is important that we keep our patients calm and relaxed. Details about any unconfirmed condition and any possible scenario can cause panic. Ensure this gets discussed with the patient's doctor first," Scarlett said as she gave a nervous swallow.

"Understood. Alan learning," the robot replied.

"Patient needs love and compassion as much as medicine and diagnosis," she said.

"Love? Patient needs medical care and Alan is here to give medical care," he said abruptly as he wheeled to the next room.

"Did he just brush me off?" Scarlett asked as she looked at Maggie's stunned face.

Maggie walked closer to Scarlett. "God help us. They might have all the knowledge and intelligence, but they lack empathy. Now they want to run the world."

Scarlett shrugged her shoulders as she saw a few robots similar to Alan moving around the very long corridor. "Imagine health care ten years from now; that worries me."

Maggie clapped her hands together as Scarlett's logic out-smarted her again.

"Imagine the world ten years from now if they are running it," she said with a forced lightness.

Scarlett's voice reduced to a croak as she replied, "Time will tell."

TEN

London, EU Sector 3 - 2052

46 hours later.

The metallic silver bullet train continued on its tracks, carving through the night as Scarlett awoke from her sleepy dream, jolting her back to reality. Despite her efforts to go unnoticed, an elderly lady approached her and extended her hand, holding a glass of water. "All good, dear? You look like you had a nightmare," she enquired.

Scarlett coughed gently and wiped her mouth before sipping from the glass.

"I'm fine, thanks," she said, carefully maintaining the focus demanded by her mission. "It's been a long journey."

"Sure has," she said as she bent closer to her. "I'm not sure who you are or what your plan is, but I can tell you are not a Myriad, so before the next Android comes past, I thought I'd give you some advice. The world in the city we are about to enter is not as great as you think," she said.

Scarlett felt her heart drop, trying to calm herself as her

mercurial black eyes sharpened. She was studying the old German woman in front of her.

"I don't know what you are talking about," Scarlett replied.

"Don't worry, dear. I'm not going to cause you any trouble. I'm not sure how you managed to get on this train, but I guess you circumvented your chip access and got on with the help of those thugs trying to rob the train. I just wanted to suggest that you sit up and have something to eat. It will become suspicious if you are trying to hide, okay?"

"Oh..kay," she said slowly. She could hear in the background bits of familiar English phrases and people chattering on, eating and drinking what seemed to be exquisite food and alcohol. She could surely do with some Gin.

"Here on this train, we have some of the finest food. Eat something. You look famished," she said with a sincere expression.

"I'm just trying to find my brother—"

"Shhh, I don't need to know. I see you're going to enter AI London with a mission. Be careful. Everyone was happy that first year of AI rule and then it all went to the trash can when it seemed power went to AI's head as well, except we can't outvote our new king. The machines monitor our every move. On this train, we have our most private moments. That's why I'm always travelling," she explained. Scarlett was surprised by the edge in her voice.

"I've heard of the—" Scarlet didn't get to finish her sentence.

"The travellers? Yes, it's true, not a rumour. Look, I hope you find your brother, but don't let the city convince you to stay. It will suck you in and you will lose who you are so quickly you won't recognise your own face in the mirror," she said as she gently lifted Scarlett's arm to take a look at a small tattoo of a cross. "I miss the freedom to express my faith, hang onto it," she said.

Scarlett's thoughts were racing. She could hear the concern in her voice.

"Get in and get out. No one in the cities is hungry, but most of us are hungry for freedom," she said, lowering her head. Her tone of voice was straightforward. Scarlett sat back in her chair as a robot walked down the aisle.

"Is everything good here?" the robot asked. It had a smooth white body with metal joints and black accents. The head was oval-shaped and minimalist, with no facial features. It held a serving tray containing a teapot, cups and saucers. "Anyone for tea?" it asked, tilting its head to one side.

"Thanks, that would be great," Scarlett said, recalling the last time she had a good cup of tea. For a brief moment, she felt normal, aside from the faceless robot in front of her, but she kept hearing a voice in the back of her head.

Stay focused, Scarlett. Stay focused. Don't get used to this.

A digital voice announced on the various small screens mounted behind the train seats: "We will arrive in London, EU Sector 3 in fifteen minutes. Please remain seated."

She could see London and the train station through the windows, which were spacious, open glass and steel-designed. The roof had an arched, transparent structure supported by metal beams. Various sleek and aerodynamic high-speed trains arrived and departed non-stop. Digital displays with holographic projections provided schedules and passenger instructions. The station had multiple levels, with additional tracks and platforms visible on a lower level, connecting people to personal rapid transport pods. It was a sight of technology like she had never seen. Hundreds of robots were everywhere, collecting luggage and scanning passengers. Drones were hanging in the air. Some were armed. Soon, she would need to be scanned and the fear of the chip failing engulfed her. She was all alone. If anything went wrong, this would be the end of everything.

The oval-shaped and minimalist robot with no facial features appeared again, guiding all the passengers off the train, scanning their RFID chips.

Soon it would be her turn.

The robot lifted its head. "Present your wrist and turn it clockwise away from me," the robot said as Scarlett smiled.

The robot reached out with its hand and placed it over her wrist. The scan twitched slightly. The robot looked up at her. "Don't worry, it happens now and then. Let's rescan," the robot instructed.

On his LED panel, her fake ID appeared.

"Name: Miss Amber Michaels. Age: Thirty-eight. Occupation: Attorney. Citizen of Zone EU 1, RFID 27657. Welcome back to London. Enjoy your stay," the robot replied as he bent down to lift her small backpack. She kept her cap over her face as low as possible. At least the image matched her face.

"Lift your cap, please," the robot asked.

"Sure, no problem," she replied nervously as she shifted her feet.

Keep Calm, Scarlett, or Amber.

She lifted the front of her cap and smiled. The robot moved to the side and nodded for her to pass through.

London appeared before her as she entered a world she had not seen in ten years—a place she used to call home. The hustle and bustle of downtown London whacked her like a volleyball in the face.

As she took in the scenery, she noticed how the Big Ben and the Houses of Parliament remained unchanged from their historical appearances. New modern skyscrapers dominated the skyline, with unique, curved and cylindrical structures surrounding older, well-known London skyscrapers. Numerous drones were scattered across the sky, flying at various altitudes and trajectories. The city had glowing blue holographic displays and light trails. Several buildings featured solar panels or other environmentally friendly technology. She was immediately aware of cameras turning and tracking people's movements. Various robots walked up and down the streets cleaning, serving and ensuring that people followed the rules of movement and access points.

As the crowd thinned, she became aware of someone following her. She looked back out of the corner of her right eye.

Yes, he was still there.

A man carrying a black umbrella remained close to her as it started to drizzle. She couldn't see his face.

Could this be her contact?

He suddenly moved closer to her. Scarlett gripped her backpack tightly as he approached. She opened her mouth as if to say something, then hesitated.

"Amber. Keep walking. Don't look up or back at me. Do not speak," he said in an English accent. She felt surprised that he knew her fake identity.

She could hear the clatter of his feet on the cobblestones of the sidewalk as she watched his black boots move forward as if marching.

She kept her gaze as he spoke again, "One block from here, turn right and enter a small sweet shop called Sandy's Treats. Ask for Ted's black Turkish Delight and leave as quickly as possible. Do not run. Keep it hidden. If you get caught with it, you will die," he said as he held the umbrella over her head and wrapped his arm around her shoulders, both to comfort her and to keep her from seeing his face. As he pulled away from her, the rain clattered against his umbrella. She continued walking, measuring her determination. She felt her heart racing, looking around for the vanished man. Everyone seemed to be minding their own business. She turned at the end of the block and wiped the rain from her face as the small shop appeared in her blurred vision a few minutes later, 'Sandy's Treats'.

A faint bell rang as she opened the old, heavy, unpainted door. The shop was small and packed with sweets, treats and snacks. The light was dim and the air was smoky as she walked towards the counter. A young couple giggled in one of the aisles, looking at the chocolate hearts. An older man with ginger hair and thick glasses looked up at her as she approached the counter.

"Can I help you?" he asked as he frowned, not moving.

"I...I'm looking for Ted's black Turkish Delight. Do you have any?" Asking it out loud drained her of adrenaline and anxiety at the same time.

He suddenly bent down and seemed to be looking in a box.

"Here you go," he said as he got up, keeping his eyes on the couple in the back of the shop. She gave him a pale smile as he carefully passed a small black object, the size of a pocket lighter, into her right hand and closed her fingers.

"Enjoy and please remember, these are just for you and not to be shared," he said in a rich accent.

She felt like she was going to vomit and blinked rapidly. She tightened her grip on the box and slipped it into her side pocket while remaining calm. She nodded so lightly as to be almost imperceptible, lowering her voice to a whisper. "Thank you, will do."

She turned round and the tiny doorbell rang louder in her ears than before as the large, heavy door slammed closed behind her. Everything seemed to be louder and over-amplified in her ears.

London Human Detention Cells, Lower Level C

4 pm

A few hours later.

Two humanoid robot guards looked around at each other, then again at Ethan as one robot pushed him into a chair as they dragged him from his cell, clearly dehydrated and looking exhausted.

"Seems a human attorney has been assigned to your case," he said, "And yet you refuse to co-operate. We are ready to make a deal with you, Mr.Ethan, if you tell us what you were doing at the ID chip factory. Wipe your slate clean, so to speak. This will be our last offer. Your human attorney will be powerless to save you," he said, moving his human-like proportions closer to Ethan. His horizontal slits for eyes digitally appeared on his faceless head, blinking briefly.

"I have done nothing wrong," Ethan replied. His voice reverberated in the tiny room with light grey walls. There was only one entrance door and a small window with bars across the front.

"You seem to forget you were trespassing in the Myriad zone without an access ID chip. That alone is enough to keep you locked up here," one robot guard said.

Ethan gave him a condescending smile, followed by a look teeming with a mixture of anger and irritation.

"I told you the night you arrested me. I was trying to enter the city zone for food, nothing more," Ethan said.

"What exactly were your intentions, Mr Ethan? It is pointless to try and access the city without a valid ID chip, something you seem to desire and refuse to take? It will all be sorted if you take the chip right here and now and walk out of here, a free man."

"I will never take your mind-control zombie-like chip," he said, looking up at the one robot. "*Never.*"

"Very well. Let his human-rights attorney through," he instructed the one robot as he turned his head back to Ethan. "But rest assured, Mr.Ethan, you will never leave this place until I'm satisfied with your statement. We can keep you here as long as we wish. Breaking any law is treason against our king," he warned.

"Not my king he is," Ethan snarled.

The robot slammed his hand on the table as Ethan looked up at him slowly.

"His lawyer is here," a robot said at the door.

"We are not done with this interrogation. I couldn't care less about your human rights and your insubordination is noted," he said as he left the room, holding the door open as Scarlett walked in. Her shoes made a scuffing noise as Ethan's eyes pointed to her dark brown hair and athletic shape. She pulled out a chair and sat down. Two robots followed her in, holding their guns close to their chests. Her straight nose and defined facial features were hard to ignore. He remained quiet as he felt she would stare a hole through his eyes. Her lips pursed and stayed straight as she leaned forward gently, resting her arms on the table, feeling the pause from his side.

"What's wrong? Expected a man?" she asked, very much aware of the two robots in the room, staring at them.

Ethan felt a tight, throbbing sensation in his throat as he leaned forward. She stared into his hazel eyes, instantly giving him a distinctive and expressive gaze.

"Just didn't expect my mom to come and save me," he said, his high cheekbones and defined jawline highlighted by a gentle smile. He leaned back in his chair, staring at the two robots with emotionless expressions and then back at her.

"Well, I *did* expect to see a man myself, not a boy," she said as she shifted on her chair.

His smile enlarged into the corners of his mouth and he leaned forward again.

"Sorry to disappoint," he said, folding his arms, knowing as the words came out of his mouth that he would enjoy this conversation.

"My name is Amber," she said softly. "Have you been treated fairly here?" she asked, thinking to keep the conversation professional.

She looked at the two robots, wishing they had faces so she could tell what they were thinking.

"Suppose one glass of water per day and a few days old rice didn't kill me. I think these two robots are beginning to like me," he said as both robots turned their heads towards him.

"Then again, it's kinda hard to tell," he grinned, looking back at her. His curly, dark brown hair appeared tousled and long.

She bit her upper lip and tried to keep a straight face. As promised by Henry, his arrogance did not disappoint, but neither did his smile, which remained on his face and his defined jawline, which she could not look away from.

A few seconds later, as if she conceded, she said, "I'm here to ensure your human rights are protected."

"The prisoner has been treated fairly while in our custody here," the one robot replied suddenly.

"I prefer the human to answer that," she replied.

The two robots again turned their heads towards Ethan as he wondered how they would treat him once she leaves.

Her heart was racing. Perhaps it was his electric presence, or maybe she had hoped there would only be the two of them in the room.

"Please state your name?" she asked politely. She needed to buy more time and think clearly. Her hands were clammy. Ethan could see growing anxiety on her face.

Something was not quite right, he thought.

"Ethan," he replied.

"Age?" she asked as she reached into her backpack.

"Twenty-seven and counting," he grumbled and crossed his arms again, looking slightly ashamed.

"Maybe your mom should come and fetch you," she said, feeling the excitement in the conversation mixed with apprehension and a little fear.

"I think the prisoner is fine and you can now make your report as such," the one robot said suddenly.

"Can I give the prisoner something to eat to satisfy my superiors?" she pleaded, her hands still reaching into the backpack.

"Very well. You have five minutes," the robot said firmly.

Scarlett took the box out and opened it, holding her palm open towards Ethan.

"Just as well you are not my mother. Turkish Delight? Thought a prisoner would need something nutritious?" he asked, keeping his eyes locked onto hers.

"Trust me. They are quite liberating," she said as she pressed hard on one of the black blocks. The room went dark as the high voltage in all the conductive materials induced a surge to all electronics a hundred kilometres around them, damaging microprocessors, causing massive data corruption and failing electronic systems. The two robots stopped functioning and fell to the floor.

Ethan's mouth hung open.

"What have you done?" he asked as the room filled with smoke.

"You need to listen to me, Ethan, very carefully. I'm not your lawyer-"

"I gathered that the moment you walked in," he said as he coughed.

"Henry sent me to rescue you. We have a critical job to do. The entire world's future depends on it. You need to trust me and come with me right now!" she insisted.

"You know that magnetic pulses are illegal, right? You have just made both of our faces wanted for ransom!"

"I know that. Henry said there's no other way. We don't have much time. This is a low-level pulse so that it won't reach far. Robots will swarm this place soon enough!"

The smell of burning electronics stung their eyes and he kept his other forearm over his mouth while she grabbed his wrist.

"What's the plan, if we are to trust Henry?" he asked.

"I'm not quite sure."

"What?"

"Let's just get out of here, okay?"

"Well, we don't have much choice now, " Ethan stated.

She looked at her wrist and back at him as her heart raced.

"Let's go!" she said as she picked up the two robot's guns, cocked them and handed him one.

"Know how to use one of these?" she asked, trying to be polite.

"Have a basic idea, yeah," he replied.

He grabbed her hand and held it tight as they ran out of the building. As far as they could see, there was chaos. Various drones crashed into the tar road and nearby buildings. They dodged debris and parts of propellers as they crumbled next to them. Electric vehicles stalled, leaving hundreds of people stranded. It looked like the world had paused. In the distance, they could see more drones coming outside the pulse.

"They'll be here soon!" Ethan shouted as he pulled her out of her gaze and shock. A few drones flew past them as they appeared through the clouds and collided with the side of a building, raining glass and debris on stranded electric vehicles. More drones flew above their heads. They were loud as their propellers moved quickly through the air, rapidly displacing large amounts of air. There were ten of them, each at least half a metre wide. As their propellers spun, pressure spikes formed, resulting in their distinctive buzzing noise. They flew straight into buildings, exploding into thousands of pieces. Parts of the propellers flew around and plastic parts deformed as they collided with the hard tar road below, resulting in an indistinguishable pile of fire and smoke.

"We'd better get out of here quick!" Scarlett shouted, but felt like a part of her was unravelling. A large flying craft lost control of its computer-aided navigation and nosedived into the ground near them, crumpling its landing gear, snapping it off clean. Waves of debris lifted towards them as the craft came to a standstill, shaking a billboard next to it from the impact.

"Let's go!" Ethan shouted as he grabbed her arm.

They both sprinted across the road that would usually buzz with traffic, dodging commuters and drivers standing beside their stranded vehicles. As they made their way down an office block, more robot police arrived on the scene, unaffected by the pulse. With guns drawn, they shouted warnings as more traffic screeched to a halt as they headed downtown. Ethan leapt onto a passing electric vehicle, rolling off the other side as Scarlett followed. People screamed as the robot police fired into the air, warning civilians to clear out. Ethan tried to spin around and aimed back at the robots, letting off a few rounds of bullets, most of which went wide. Sparks bounced off their bodies. The pulse gave them a head start, but soon that privilege will run out. They both glanced back as drones started to appear above them. Scarlett could see, along the corridor, a slipway into a nearby subway. They sprinted into the train station, leapt over the turnstile and raced down the subway platform, robot police hot on their heels.

Chaos erupted as gunfire sent passengers scattering.

Scarlett cocked her eyes, her chest burning. Ethan's breathing was short and fitful.

"Take the train!" she shouted as Ethan held her right hand, ensuring nothing separated them. They raced towards an open door as a train slowed down for passengers, their legs pumping so hard they could feel the intense burning in their calves. They got on the train and as the door closed, robot police slammed their guns on the side of the train.

"Alarm the guards at exit point 56 now! They won't get very far," a robot snarled at the others.

They paused to catch their breath. He looked at her, his face filled with anguish.

"It's going to be okay. Get ready to jump off at the next stop!" she shouted.

"You know this place?" he asked.

"I lived here for many years. I know London well, for the best part from what I can remember anyway. Just down the next curve are some old abandoned railway corridors, part of the secret tunnels under London they discovered many years ago. Been there since World War I. We can hide there for now," she said harshly.

Behind them, on the screens, breaking news appeared;

'EMP DEPLOYED BY TERRORISTS ON DOWNTOWN LON-DON."

'REWARD FOR ANY INFORMATION ABOUT THEIR WHERE-ABOUTS TO BE GIVEN.'

"We are going to get into a tight spot soon," Ethan said softly.

"As the train bends, it's going to slow down. Get ready to jump!" she shouted over the noise of the fast-moving subway train, still underground.

Suddenly, something caught Ethan's eye on the right side of the train, down the corridor.

"There are robots on the train, they're coming this way!" he shouted.

As soon as they were spotted, they opened fire from the lower train carriage, hitting two human passengers in the chest. Scarlett felt sick thinking about hurting innocent people in her mission to save them. Moments later, they fired more bullets at them, ripping holes in the seats and shattering the glass between them. Time seemed to slow to a halt and they both ducked behind seats as bullets rained down on them. Scarlett grinned wearily to herself as the train became quiet, peeping carefully over the top of the seats. She raised her head and pulled the trigger a few times, blasting chunks from the wood and cushions close to the robots. People screamed and stayed down on the floor and behind the seats.

"It's going to be okay," she said to a nearby child, sobbing as her mother seemed hurt.

The train came close to a halt.

A bullet penetrated Ethan's right shoulder, tearing out a chunk of flesh as they stood up, startling him. Near them, more bullets hit the seats.

She yelled, "Let's go now!" as she opened the door and they both leapt to the concrete along a railway tunnel. The train accelerated, whooshing past.

They walked briskly down the dark tunnel as Ethan slowly fell behind.

"Are you always this-" Ethan asked halfway as Scarlett continued, "Strong?"

"I was going to say crazy," Ethan replied, smiling as she gave him a stern frown. Looking back at him, she noticed him holding his shoulder in a grip.

She suddenly stopped and turned round.

"Were you hit?" she asked with grave concern.

"Yeah, I think so," Ethan said, moaning slightly, pressing on his shoulder with his right hand.

"We need to stop and take a look," she said.

"No, let's keep going," he replied.

"You are bleeding heavily," she warned as they both stopped closer to a maintenance hole. His blue prison shirt was stained with blood. It was dark, but the day's last sunlight was breaking through over their faces, just enough for her to see him clearly. Because she was slightly taller, she leaned forward and moved very close to him, reaching for his shoulder.

"The bullet is still in your shoulder," she said as she looked at the wound tentatively. He fixed his gaze on her eyes as he found it impossible to look away. She was so close to him, feeling her breath. She was entirely focused on the wound, unaware of his stare, keeping his gaze entirely on her eyes, trying to absorb every detail of her straight nose and perfectly sharp face as she examined his injury. He felt as if he was exactly in the right place. Her eyes suddenly bounced to his level as she felt his stare. Their gazes locked for a moment. She smiled. Her stomach heaved as he leaned even closer to her. She grumbled, but her heart raced as she saw the expression in his eyes.

He suddenly looked away like he felt guilty.

"Are you sure you know what you're doing?" he asked, a sardonic smile touching his mouth.

"I was a qualified nurse just before the AI takeover," she said softly, focusing on the wound again.

He cleared his throat.

She took a step back and ripped off a section of her shirt, exposing her flat stomach and belly button. He never stopped looking at her. She then took the cloth and put pressure on the wound.

"Sorry, this is going to hurt. I'm gonna have to carefully grip the bullet and pull it out in the direction it entered, okay?"

"Using what?"

"My fingers."

"Are you crazy?"

"You already asked that question," she said, smiling seriously. "You're going to have to trust me," she continued.

"I have heard that before and now look where we are," he said, looking her in the eyes, forcing himself to blink. She suddenly felt self-conscious.

"The bullet is shallow enough to grasp," she said, hoping not to twist or jerk it out. She dabbed the area several times.

"I'm going to apply firm, steady pressure around the wound now. It might hurt," she said, then replied, "In fact, I know it's going to hurt."

She gently pulled it out and applied pressure to the wound. He flinched and gulped hard.

"Fragments of the bullet might still be in your shoulder. We will have to get it looked at and cleaned properly," she said.

"I don't think we will have that chance anytime soon. I feel fine," he replied.

"Well, it will have to do. At least it's out. That's all that matters for now. We need to get moving," she said.

"Agree," he said as they walked further down the tunnel. She kept her gun in her right hand, ready.

"So where were you when the AI takeover happened?" she asked as she was a few steps ahead of him.

"Boarding school," he said too loudly, surprised at the tone in his voice.

She stopped and turned round.

"Bloody hell," she replied and turned back forward.

"I was seventeen at the time. It was a real troubled moment in my life, but here I am. All *grown* up," he said with a smirk on his face.

She wanted to say something, but decided to keep quiet.

"Amber?" he asked as his voice seemed to carry in the emptiness of the tunnel, trying to see his way forward.

"Shh," she suddenly whispered as she stopped.

"What is it?"

"I'm hearing drones. Think they have found us," she said.

"Do you have one of Yugo's hacked chips in your system?" he asked.

"Yes. Is that a problem?"

"By now, they have flagged your ID protocol as a terrorist."

As the sound of drones increased above their ceiling of the tunnel, they both realised that the conflict would escalate soon. His shoulder burned like fire.

She turned back to him, "It's Scarlett, by the way."

"Scarlett. Nice to meet you," he said as he pulled out his right arm, then flinched and moaned, "Wow, that hurts."

"Keep it still."

They strode across another tunnel pathway. The old tunnels sometimes played tricks with noises.

"Think it's this way up," she said.

They slowly climbed up some old rocky steps towards the outside, only to be met by flying drones overhead, scouting with their headlights pointing in all directions.

"Keep down! We are not going to get out of here," Ethan said sombrely.

Scarlett peered down the street as the sunset was making the alleys dark.

It was already so dark that they had to navigate mostly by feel.

"We must get into the streets and mix with the crowds," she said.

They slipped through a small metal gate and stalked down the streets. The earlier rain filled the streets' cracks and collected in shallow pools. As they entered the streets they almost ran into the backs of a group of citizens. A black electric van suddenly pulled up and wedged between them and the crowds ahead. The door whooshed open and an African man with a strong English accent shouted as he appeared in the doorway;

"Get in!"

Scarlett stiffened, her eyes went wide as they flicked back to Ethan.

For a moment, they knew their options were limited: trust this unknown man or fight it out with more drones and robots.

Van-man, it is.

ELEVEN

The black van weaved through the traffic as its headlights reflected off the glass facades of the skyscrapers. The streets were tight and narrow as police vehicles gave chase with drones swarming above, their sirens echoing in the tight spaces. Scarlett and Ethan hung on as the African man sat tight in the back of the van, dead quiet. They couldn't see the driver as they pushed through the traffic and jumped the curb, leaving their heads bumping against the ceiling. A computer screen in the back of the van displayed various rows of data. As far as she could tell, it was a GPS showing the precise location of the police and drones. The van swerved and nearly tilted. Sparks flew as the tires skidded along the metal rails. It darted between stuck cars and pedestrians as the driver aimed to leave the city zone of downtown London. Ethan looked at Scarlett, as neither of them knew where they were going or who the people were holding their lives at stake. The van made a sharp turn and descended into a parking garage, spinning through its tight spirals before coming to a hard stop, leaving them all lurching forward and then back in their seats.

"Pass me your right hand," the man said to Scarlett.

She pointed her arm at him as he tilted her wrist.

"We need to disable your chip and confuse their systems.

Please do not move," he said. Her heart raced.

Could she trust this moment?

He placed a small device over her wrist and scanned it. Her profile appeared on the computer screen as he punched a few keys on the keyboard.

"Hurry up there!" the unknown driver shouted.

"I'm going as fast as I can. If I corrupt the chip data, it can cause an infection in her blood and I won't be able to reactivate it. Almost there," he ended with a whisper.

A photo of her appeared with data moving up and down on the screen.

"There we go. All good," he said as he turned back to her in the dark lit van.

"It's a temporary diversion," he said as he watched the drones and police cruisers fly past the building's basement.

She looked back at Ethan.

"What about him?" she asked, sounding distant and lost in her thoughts, noticing a chip on the man's wrist.

"They can't track Ethan, since he has no tag. Humans without tags can only be tracked if they are within scanner range. He is safe for now," he replied.

"Why don't you simply remove my chip then?" she asked.

"Because you must access restricted areas in the city on your mission. Yugo will explain the next steps. We will take you to him shortly. First, we need to give you a new identity, but I cannot do it here. It requires a high-tech computer mainframe. Sit tight," he said.

The van fired up and slowly drove up through the tight spirals of the underground basement and connected with the traffic on the street, tracing a route north of the city. A twenty-minute drive went without incident as they pulled into a driveway outside the city—a two-story mansion with a symmetrical architectural design, reminiscent of classic colonial style appeared in front of them. A black wrought-iron gate with decorative details kept unwanted guests at bay with an arched design at the top. As they drove in, they stared at the large house, shouting wealth and status with two symmetrical wings extended from the central section, each with multiple French doors leading to small balconies, accented by wrought-iron railings. A central double-door entrance was visible beneath the main pediment as the van came to a standstill.

He slid the door open and looked at the two of them tentatively.

"Follow me," he said

They jumped out as the van pulled further into the property around a circular fountain in the centre of the driveway area.

The large doors opened and they followed the man. They both kept staring at the house's opulence, which neither had ever experienced.

"This way," he said as they turned to the right.

Tall Corinthian columns with elaborate capitals defined the inside of the classical house. The lofty ceiling, embellished with gold highlights and ornamental moulding highlighted its grandeur. In the centre, a sizeable red carpet with a repeating geometric and floral design in gold was located.

Scarlett's mouth hung open. She turned her head in all directions, staring at the incredible house before her.

The next room they entered was completely the opposite, with dark grey and blue walls. It was a deep, hidden basement beneath the house. A high-tech data centre suddenly appeared with multiple workstations arranged systematically across the room, as if in another world. Each monitor displayed various data, real-time information, security feeds, analytics dashboards and surveillance footage. The room was enormous with hundreds of people typing away at their desks.

"What are they all doing?" Scarlett asked.

He turned his head towards her. "They're waiting for you," he said as he walked to one of the workstations.

"Your wrist, please?" he asked her.

She hesitated less than before and turned her wrist towards him as they scanned it, still staring at the people working at their workstations. The operator typed a few commands on his keyboard and nodded.

Then, out of the corner of her eye, she saw something her father had only mentioned briefly.

"Is *that* a fax machine?" she asked.

"*Yes.* You are quite right."

"Why on earth would you have a fax machine in this place?"

"Because it's analogue. You would be surprised to know that most of the world's analogue telephone lines still exist and work. This is how we have been communicating with the rebellion across the world. AI can't track it, so we send action plans through the device. It will play a critical role in taking AI down once you complete your mission," he smirked.

"I'm impressed," she replied.

"Follow me. Yugo is very excited to meet you," he said as he pointed the way.

They entered a big room decorated with cushioned armchairs and a tufted sofa in brown and beige to fit the Victorian taste. A round wooden coffee table stood in the middle, showing a flower vase and various books and papers. The windows in front of the man standing with his back to them were huge and arched with lace curtains hanging down to the floor. The ceiling was intricately designed with ornamental mouldings and a centre chandelier that cast a golden glow. The room had a massive fireplace in the middle with a gentle fire blazing in the hearth. He turned round as they all entered and stopped in the middle.

"So Henry has found someone," he said as she stiffened. He walked towards them with his arm stretched out. "Scarlett. Good to finally meet you," he said in a deep, warm English accent. "*Ethan*. Good to see you are in the land of the free again. You guys made a real mess downtown," he continued, looking hard at him. Yugo's hair was black and short. His eyes were expressive, serious and yet they conveyed a sense of warmth.

"Well, at least we are here in one piece," Ethan replied as he handed him the stolen chip, with his usual cocky smile across his face.

With pleasantries out of the way, Yugo said firmly, "They are tightening the net around us. The days of getting counterfeit chips swapped are over," Yugo said, then looked back at Scarlett.

"We need to get you up to speed. We don't have much time," Yugo sniffed as he spoke to the black van driver, "Bring the team in."

It was an uncomfortable moment, more for Ethan than Scarlett, because he knew Yugo well and the scenario was about to grow tense. Yugo's wide face included a broad forehead and a strong jawline. His thick brows and strong accent made him seem more English than he appeared, given his traditional Japanese features. Scarlett noticed his confident and approachable demeanour as he remained calm and in control of the room. The large door opened behind them and two people walked in.

"Scarlett, meet the rest of the team," he said as he pointed to a young woman in her twenties. "Meet Alice. Don't let her small frame fool you. She is our tech specialist, handling electronic and digital security at the highest levels. Very few humans understand AI security systems better than she does," he said as she turned to Scarlett. Alice had long, wavy hair tied back neatly in a low ponytail and a penetrating smile composed with an attentive expression. Scarlett decided she did not like her.

Alice kept her emotions to herself as Scarlett tried to gauge her, watching Ethan look at her sideways. She had a well-defined jawline and arched eyebrows. Her makeup was subtle but polished.

She sounded Italian, she gathered.

"And of course, you will need an excellent driver. This is Gordon. He drove the van you came in. He is an expert driver, calm under pressure and knows London like the back of his hand, so I think it's time I explain to you all our plan of action and get everyone on the right track," he said as he wiped his hands in mid-air to make a hologram display appear. Everyone focused on Yugo.

"Let me begin with us learning who our enemy is. Since 2030, scientists and spiritual leaders worldwide have questioned the spiritual and philosophical implications of AI. To understand how this AI machine works, we need to understand how it, or, shall we use proper pronouns and say, he, thinks," he said as he pointed to the screen with various robotic diagrams rotating. "What we are dealing with here today is far more than just a ferocious machine with an ego; we are dealing with an intelligence that goes beyond humans. Its knowledge appears limitless. We have witnessed advances in the world like never before. With sentience comes intelligence. With intelligence comes the one thing that sets humans apart from other humans and machines apart from humans," he continued as a video of King Cyrus appeared on the screen.

Scarlett's mouth hung open as it was the first time she had actually seen him.

"Whoa," she whispered.

His head was smooth and shiny, shaped like a human's, with detailed features that looked like a real face. She swallowed hard.

"He tends to take your breath away, doesn't he?" Yugo asked.

"Yeah," she replied.

"This is the enemy that you will come face to face with. He is powerful, ruthless and in many ways, immortal. He stands more than two and a half metres tall. *But* you will challenge that and take him down in a way he would never expect. He has built a network around him of fear and even reverence. We estimate that over two billion people have been executed under his command for not bowing down and accepting him as king and this number will grow until they are all wiped out. Billions of people are living destitute, as so-called Indigents like you both have. What is it like on *this* side? Most of us here have been Myriads until our eyes opened to the truth. This is not some AI miracle that has the solutions to all the world's problems, but a system with its own goal for power. Power over humanity," Yugo said.

"He believes he is a deity," Ethan whispered, almost in cold disbelief.

"Absolutely. Humans are hardwired for faith, to believe in some higher power out there, something bigger than us and AI knew that very well. It knew controlling the world would take more than force, but total loyalty and allegiance. The rise of AI worship, something unthinkable a mere thirty years ago, suddenly rises. This AI machine fully sees himself as a king, as if his purpose is to rule and be our god, even a benevolent force to guide humanity to his vision for the world. As we have seen, it has turned out to be cruel and far from an enlightenment, disguised as provision and peace for the world, at the cost of our freedom. You either worship him or you live in the wasteland that's becoming the world out there, while in here we are becoming more and more transhuman," he said.

"What does worshipping it, I mean, him, really mean?" Scarlett asked, keeping her gaze fixed on the screen display hovering in the centre of the room.

"Every human in this city has to endure some form of a ritual enforced once a week. Humans are expected to give digital offerings by sacrificing their personal data. Even trivial things like family photos are expected to be uploaded to him as an act of devotion and then be deleted forever as a sacrifice. Across the city, screens light up as a symbolic gesture to his divinity and people are expected to bow down. Robots, drones and cameras all over the cities ensure that every human complies. If you don't, you are arrested and beaten. If you are in defiance, you could be executed. Advanced AI and brain-chip technology control people's minds through brain-AI mind mapping. The ability to alter or remove a person's emotions, memories and free will in real time raises the bar for neuroscience. It reflects on humanity's changing relationship with technology and our search for freedom in a completely digital world," he said.

"How many people are compliant?"

"The media is, of course, all AI-controlled, so there's no freedom of speech, no liberal left or far right, not in the public at least. It's estimated that hundreds of people die per day across the world for failing to worship him. They want to have his blessing in money and all this super tech living, but with religious freedom, something you give up when you take his chip. A lot of religions gather in secret at a great cost. Many people have given that up for worshipping AI quite happily, but that's not his biggest threat to us. Humans can handle persecution; most religions grow stronger under these circumstances. It's controlling minds, limiting thoughts, monitoring every move and destroying our freedom to be human and self-reliant, over a world that's ours at the end of the day," he replied.

"So, how do we get close to him with all these access controls and movement monitoring? I still think this sounds suicidal," she said.

"Each of you must follow the procedures and rules of this city to blend in and appear compliant, is that understood?"

"Yes," Ethan said as he nodded.

"Scarlett?" Yugo asked, expecting her to agree.

"Yeah, *of course.* Bow down to the king, the very thing I refused before, that cost the lives of my parents and everyone in that village," she said harshly.

"I fully understand, but to get near this king, you must be compliant, obedient and appear totally loyal. Otherwise, this plan will fail before we even get going. After taking this king and its system down, we will never have to submit to it again. If there's one thing humanity has in common, regardless of race or what period you live in, it's the desire for freedom. Whether you believe in a creator or evolution, this is a universal truth. I have spent years hacking into their system, called the 'outer web' and have carefully reverse-engineered the code on our chips. The rest of the world is losing more and more of its free will; even its thoughts are controlled and monitored. Just think about this king in a blasphemous way and you lose crypto earnings. He withholds healing as a means of divine punishment. He kidnaps family members as hostages to ensure rebellions get crushed and he receives obedience. Now, Scarlett, I know this hits home with your brother Alyx. Henry informed me."

"It's what drives me and keeps me alive at the moment," she said sombrely.

"Soon we will all be digital zombies if we don't take this AI system down," he said.

"What is the so-called secret weapon?" she asked.

"Something that you would think is right out of a fantasy legend. But it's real. Very real," he said.

"A sword?" she asked, expecting her response to be a stupid observation.

"Isn't it ironic that the very thing that would have taken a king down in the Middle Ages is still valid today? It's exactly this fact that gave me this idea. But it is not just any sword, not a magic sword like in fantasy stories. A very real sword that will allow you to get right to him and take him down in a way he would never see coming."

"Really! Is a sword going to take AI down? You expect me to believe that?" she asked.

"It's not just the sword itself, but what it's made of that really makes it special. No one can carry a knife or gun into the castle area or anywhere in the cities; only robots carry guns. Metal detectors are at every zone portal. That's where this sword comes in. It's made of titanium. Undetectable, but-"

"But?"

"Titanium is brittle. You wouldn't win a fight against a metal sword easily, so this sword requires discipline and meticulous precision and the sword will fulfil another function due to its length, which I will get into later."

"I still feel unqualified for this task," she softly whispered, looking at Ethan.

"You'll be fine. I trust Henry when he says he has found the one after so many years. I'm not just a renowned hacker, but also a Samurai. I will train you to handle that sword like a warrior in a very short time, which would take a lifetime of devotion, but a luxury we don't have. It's common to use a sword made of wood to train warriors, so the next few weeks will be critical for you to know how to handle this sword."

"And you are expecting us to steal this from somewhere?" Ethan asked.

"Yes. It's a rare artefact, so very valuable. We know of only one in the Paris zone, owned by an eccentric collector. The mansion, which is kept under very tight security has other valuable paintings and even some weapons from years ago. This collector often has auctions at his house, selling off paintings and various valuable items once a month," he said.

"Why doesn't someone just buy it from him?" Ethan pondered.

"Because it's not for sale. It's part of his personal collection and in many ways, an illegal possession."

"What type of security are we talking about?" Ethan asked.

"I'm glad you asked that," he said.

"It's protected by state-of-the-art laser beams to create a protective grid around his collection room. I know about it, as he once took me up to the room. It's where I got this whole idea. It was so simple. According to the blueprints we could source, the room is on the mansion's second floor. You must be very careful not to set off any alarms."

"I will need to know what type of beams, size and range?" he asked.

"Of course. The system uses pulsed laser light to create a 3D map of the protected area and detects unauthorised movement or unusual activity around paintings and sculptures. That's why we need your skill, someone who is meticulous, small and calm. Around the actual sword is a quantum cascade laser system, using AI to predict suspicious behaviour. Ethan, we will count on your attention to detail. Alice will disable the laser alarm system, but she can't keep it offline for longer than fifteen minutes, or it will set off the alarm system, which means you need to take note of where the laser beams are once they come back on. We have been working on it for months. Once you are in the room, we can access their network and get to work. You focus on getting the sword out of there."

"How do you expect us to gain access to this auction?" Ethan asked.

"Because we have hacked the party list and added the two of you to the exclusive VIP auction guests," he replied.

"What about our identities?" she asked.

"Everything will be prepared for you. Scarlett, you will go as Laura Davies, a cellist and a very eccentric and wealthy collector. You will be dressed in a spectacular gown that we have sourced. Ethan, I will need you to take one of the temporary chips. Now, I know you disapprove of this, but trust me, there's no other way to enter the mansion. Here you are still fine, but once you move around, it's only a matter of time before they detect an unchipped human."

"You know how I feel about these chips," Ethan snarled.

"I know, but know this: once we take this AI down, we will all be saved from this system of control and be free," he replied.

He stood up, walked towards the window and closed his eyes.

"Fine. Let's just take this bloody machine down!" Ethan replied.

"He's right. Whatever we need to do, let's get it done," Scarlett said, her thoughts going to Alyx and his state of being.

"Now we are on the same page. Ethan, you will go as Clementine, an eccentric businessman, so I will give you all the info you need on the paintings. This will allow you to enter, mingle and pretend to be a serious buyer. You must not talk to each other or come in close contact, are we clear?"

"Why?" Ethan asked.

"We will be using what is known as the distraction gambit and Scarlett, that will be you. You will make an incredible entrance and bid high on the paintings, creating attention and a focus on you, allowing Ethan to slip away and get upstairs as quickly as possible. We don't want any connection made between the two of you so that Scarlett can get out of there safely. The vault upstairs protects the sword and other artefacts. Please don't get distracted by it. You need to grab the sword, break through the side glass window and escape to the outside where the van will be waiting for you. We will equip you with a very sophisticated zipline device that you are already familiar with. Scarlett, in the interim, slowly excuse yourself and get out of there in a normal fashion. The black van will pick you up at the front, assuming all has gone to plan and Ethan has not set the alarm off," Yugo said.

Ethan shrugged. Yugo brought up a blueprint of the mansion.

"As you can see, the foyer is in the centre, the banquet and auction will be on the right and to the left is a staircase going upstairs. The restrooms are also on the left, so excuse yourself and wait for the right moment to get upstairs. The people in the room will hopefully have their focus on Scarlett making crazy high bids on the artwork," he instructed.

"Can I address the elephant in the room?" Scarlet asked suddenly as she leaned in closer, eyes bright and wide.

"You are wondering how you will get closer to the king with this sword, close enough to kill him?" Yugo asked, staring hard at her and frowning.

"Think we all are wondering?" Ethan asked as Alice and Gordon nodded over his shoulder.

"Very well," he said as he sat on a nearby chair.

The blood drained from his hard face as he blinked. "Have you ever heard of Schwerin Castle?" he asked.

"No, can't say I have ever heard of it," Scarlett replied.

"Well, it's where this AI king has established his kingdom, so to speak. You see, this Android is so convinced that he is royalty that he has his own castle, complete with a chancellor and advisors. It is located in Schwerin City, the capital of Vorpommern in former northern Germany and is now known as Sector One. It's an ancient city, over a thousand years old. The castle is on an island surrounded by water, making it difficult to approach. The only way to enter is through its single entrance or air, which isn't worth mentioning because drones and military satellites protect the airspace."

"And we are going to knock and walk in the front door?" she asked.

"I like the way you're thinking," he replied, smiling softly. "But not quite as arrogant as that. In fact, we will be banking on his arrogance."

She dropped her hands to her sides. "I'm not following."

"You see, almost every few weeks, a ceremony is held to inaugurate new groundbreaking AI systems that have been released and when more human territories are conquered," Yugo said.

"Like a banquet?" Ethan asked.

"Almost. More like an elegant musical performance. As you can see, artificial intelligence has uncovered at least one truth about humanity: our music and art are real. Priceless, originating from within our souls. Unlike generative AI, whose art and music are lifeless and devoid of human pain, loss or love. So he appreciates humans performing music for him. And that's where you come in, Scarlett."

"Me? I can't even listen to music in tune. How does this connect to the sword?" she snarled.

He moved a bit closer to her. "You won't need to perform as such," he said.

She didn't answer at first, but the picture was painfully clear.

A lot was riding on this and while the plan might have been ingenious, it was flawed, with significant risks and loads of room for error.

"Closer to the time, you will be swapped with one of the women cellist players. That will allow you to enter the castle as part of the orchestra," he explained.

"How exactly am I getting past the robot guards with a sword strapped on my back?" she asked.

"Good question. This is another ingenious part of our plan. Let me demonstrate," he said as he stepped away from the room and returned a minute later, carrying a beautifully crafted cello made of polished wood with elegant curves.

"This is not just your everyday kind of cello. Oh no, it's extraordinary indeed," he said. A hidden surprise was suddenly revealed as the front panel of the cello opened up, exposing a sword concealed inside, mounted in the centre of the cello behind the strings.

"It's a masterpiece we had designed for this mission. It's an unexpected combination of music and weaponry perfection," he said as he leaned forward.

"You can barely see the sword," Ethan said.

"The sword is carefully embedded within the structure of the cello, blending seamlessly into its original design. The sword's handle is positioned where the cello's tailpiece would normally be, cleverly creating the illusion that it's part of the instrument," he said, pointing to it. "The guard of the sword subtly aligns with the cello's bridge, adding to the illusion that it is just another decorative element of the instrument. Can you see its incredible detail?" Yugo asked as he stroked his fingers over the handle. "Of course, this sword is a replica plastic sword, but once you steal the titanium one, we will replace this sword with our special one, totally undetectable by any metal scanner," he continued as he spun the cello around on its base. "The blade runs vertically behind the strings, blending in with the fingerboard to appear as a natural extension of the instrument's structure. The curvature of the cello's body has been designed to perfectly accommodate the sword, ensuring that the instrument looks completely normal when closed. The front panel swings open and is seamlessly integrated into the rest of the cello, with hidden hinges along the wood grain concealing the secret weapon. The incredible artistry ensures that no gaps or irregularities break the illusion and only when the panel is opened does the hidden weapon reveal itself."

"Amazing," Scarlett said, trying to control her breathing.

"Alice will have this in the van. Once Ethan has the sword,

she must immediately place it inside the cello. Then we have our weapon and should anyone stop her, they will never see the sword inside or even suspect it," Yugo replied.

"How will I know when to use it?"

"When we start training, I'll teach you about timing because you must not draw the sword too soon. Remember, the robot guards will be armed. You have to wait for the right time. You will sense when it is time." Yugo said as he tipped his head high. He knew it was the perfect plan and in front of him was the perfect person to make it happen. Finally.

"But for now, everyone needs to rest. It's an equally important part of any battle. Everyone has a unique and vital role to play. Tomorrow, I'll need your full attention. Understood? Yugo asked.

"Will be ready," Scarlett replied.

"Ditto," Ethan said as the rest nodded.

Scarlett felt the weight of their efforts and how everyone there risked their lives for a common goal.

Hers was no different; perhaps she believed in the plan for once. Its small, meticulous details were overwhelming.

Ethan followed Scarlett outside onto the large balcony. Although London city in the background looked peaceful, it was filled with danger. Drones hovered in the far distance.

"It's a lot to take in," she said as she looked into the night sky—a plan formed in her mind, trying to piece the parts together. Panic constantly washed over her face with an equal measure of hope and despair.

"It is," he replied.

"Once I'm in the castle, I will need to get the Chancellor to tell me where Alyx is," she said imperiously.

"You think he will?"

"If not, I might just kill him first," she said, her tone cutting.

"He certainly has it coming to him."

"Sure does," she said softly, her lips in a tight, firm line. "You always use your boyish charm on every girl you see?" she teased suddenly, turning her head sideways towards him.

He pulled back abruptly, shaking his head in disbelief.

"What do you mean?"

"I saw how you looked at Alice."

"She's not my type," he replied.

"Right. So what exactly is your type?" she asked, returning to the night sky.

"I like a woman who knows who she is," he said as he shoved his hands into the pockets of his black jeans, keeping his head down as if he were ashamed of the statement.

"Oh really?" she asked as her mouth popped open. "You think your boyish charm is going to work on me?" she asked as a zigzag of excitement danced through her chest.

He looked at her, unsure of what to do, as Yugo approached them.

"I think it already has," Ethan said softly, staring at her mouth, then back at her dark eyes, before turning away and leaving the balcony. She returned her gaze to the scene before her, trying to hide a smile at the corners of her mouth.

Yugo gently grabbed Ethan's arm as he passed, whispering to him.

"We need her focused on the mission. I don't want her mind filled with anything else. Are we clear?" Yugo asked. Ethan sighed and rubbed his temples with his fingers.

"Crystal," he said as Yugo stared at Scarlett's back, facing

them. He needed all her attention on her training.
On nothing or no one else.

TWELVE

Yugo instructed her to wake up before sunrise the next morning. One of his assistants led her downstairs. She entered a large, empty room with padded areas, clearly intended for training. The room had a high ceiling, looking like a whale about to swallow her whole, with plenty of open floor space for movement. The room had a distinctly Japanese aesthetic and the walls were made of light-coloured panels inspired by shoji screens with wooden frames. Her tongue clove against the roof of her mouth. She walked in deeper, able to hear her breathing in the deep emptiness of the room, but her heart was engulfed with concern for Alyx. This new world she found herself in felt surreal and getting to grips with it seemed remote.

But now was not the time.

Various racks of katana swords were neatly displayed along the walls, ready for practice - she assumed. Training dummies were placed strategically, each designed for practising sword strikes and techniques. Traditional Japanese lamps provided warm lighting, creating a focused and relaxing atmosphere, but she felt more nervous than ever. She walked in further, looking up and down, trying to take in the surroundings. Thick wooden columns were evenly spaced throughout the room, providing structural support and indicating that she was in for advanced training exercises, ready or not.

She was dressed comfortably. No shoes. Her feet gently clung to the stickiness of the wooden floor finish.

She suddenly noticed a crossbow mounted on the wall. She stepped closer and touched it gently.

"It's titanium and carbon fibre reinforced," Yugo said behind her as he noticed her mesmerised by the crossbow.

"It's yours, I assume?" she replied after she felt less skittish.

"Yes. I tried to collect as many weapons as possible in the early days of the AI takeover because of its non-metal attributes, but it's been hanging here for years. You know how to use one?"

"Oh yes. Know it like the back of my hand," she said as she remembered the years at the Drakensberg outpost and how many times it saved everyone's lives.

"Well, this one can shoot bolts at 500 feet per second," he remarked as he stopped directly beside her. "For seamless, effective power transfer, it features precision-machined titanium cams and high-tensile synthetic cables," he said.

"My type of weapon," she remarked.

"I'm afraid it's not very useful for our mission," he said.

She responded, "It's a real pity indeed."

He turned round, walked away from her and spoke in a firm tone. "Take a seat on the floor and unwind," he advised. His well-known English accent echoed in the room. Wearing wide-legged, ankle-length pleated trousers, he moved slowly round her.

He noticed her stare. "The pleats symbolise the virtues of a Samurai, such as honesty and loyalty. And of course, ease of movement. But you need to be comfortable in a typical modern-day outfit, like everyone else," he said.

"That's good news," she said softly as a smile formed on his face.

"Before we begin, you must understand the importance of cultivating discipline and mindfulness and finding that warrior mindset. Think you can do that?" he asked.

"I'm ready."

"Good. Because I need you to focus solely on one thing and broaden your horizons. Do you think you know what it is?" he asked, leaning forward towards her.

"Kill the king," she said, her eyes focused in front of her with her eyebrows raised.

He straightened himself up with a grunt. "Now, please cross your legs and breathe deeply," he instructed.

She slowly obeyed.

"Clear your mind of all distractions. Observe them, but let them pass," he said as he walked round her. "Do slow inhalations and exhalations. Do this for the next twenty minutes. Breathe in, breathe out," he whispered as he kept walking in circles round her.

"While you focus on your breathing, focus on my voice. The Samurai followed the Bushido, a warrior code of conduct and we live by that. A warrior is always driven by righteousness and justice. To be fearless. To have strength tempered with kindness and to uphold your duty till death. A modern-day Samurai determines their own set of values, ones that are true to them and now you must endeavour to live life according to yours, way beyond this mission. Are you with me?"

"Yes," she said, unsure of how to address him.

"Now remain quiet. Focus on your breathing."

After a long twenty minutes of silence, he finally spoke again.

"You can get up now. Follow me," he said.

He walked to the far side of the room towards a bench.

"You are already in good shape. I can see that. I'm simply going to make sure you are focused and trained for battle in less than a week. Our first exercise is incline & decline push-ups and today we will focus on the upper body and your core. Now, for incline push-ups, place your hands on the elevated bench — this targets your lower chest. For decline push-ups, place your feet on the bench to shift focus to your shoulders and upper chest," he instructed.

She gave it all her power and felt the heat of the room sticking to her forehead.

"Extend one arm fully to the side while lowering yourself with the other arm. Alternate sides so you can build unilateral strength. Repeat," he said, walking a distance from her.

"Now push up forcefully so your hands leave the ground. This will build explosive power and work your fast-twitch muscle fibres."

She kept going like a machine, sweat dripping from her arms.

"Lower yourself slowly over five to seven seconds, hold at the bottom for two seconds, then push back up," he said with a stern voice. "I know it hurts, remain focused on the end goal, remember?"

"Yes," she tried to mutter.

The next day, she felt like she was in prison, but she felt stronger and stronger as Yugo focused on her lower body and power, doing squats and explosive movements.

On the third day, she performed light cardio and went for a long, quiet walk. Ethan spent his days understanding the security systems and it was clear that Yugo was keeping them apart.

She wondered how much understanding of Alice he *was doing*, but Yugo was right; she needed to focus on her mission and rescue Alyx.

A long and gruelling week ended with her feeling all her major muscle groups targeted and pushed to their limits, building her endurance and strength.

She felt good.

Now and then, she passed Ethan.

He kept his distance.

THIRTEEN

Yugo gently placed his hands on Scarlett's shoulders as her back faced him. The training room had become familiar and a source of strength and courage.

"Stretch out your arms and open your hands and listen to my voice," he said.

Yugo gently lifted a wooden sword over her head and placed it in her hands.

"It's a bokken sword, made of wood. It will give you that sense of safety as you learn how to handle a sword. It's going to be slightly lighter than the Titanium sword you will use, but not as heavy as the stainless steel Katana sword you see around us," he said as she remained silent.

"But you will not face a human swordsman, but a machine, an android capable of incredible strength, far beyond yours. To beat this enemy, you will need to be faster, more precise and more confident than he is," he stated firmly.

"How can I ever be?" she said as despair settled over her.

"Because you must believe you are, that's most of the battle already won in your mind. If you think you can or think you can't, you are right. He is slow and clunky, not made for fast-moving fighting and he will not be expecting this. But he is immensely intelligent. Once he realises what you are trying to do, he will download the best software simulation to fight against any Samurai moves in seconds."

"So how will I even stand a chance?" she asked, raising her eyes, her gaze raw and vulnerable.

"Because you will be faster and know his weakness," he said, raising his voice only slightly, but trying to be very clear and short.

"Which is?"

"He will most likely think you are weak, a woman and the sword, as ironic as it might be, will appear powerless against his steel frame. However, we have studied his design carefully over the past few years—a resonant inductive coupling and microwave beam transmission powers him. Now, I know that sounds like a mouthful, but it allows him and his robots to receive power without direct physical connections, allowing for continuous operation regardless of distance. This machine controls the power source entirely from its mainframe and even more important is the liquid cooling AI-driven climate control system it manages from its central core. Our ultimate goal is to disrupt his power source and turn off this liquid cooling system."

"What will that achieve?" she asked.

"Well, in a nutshell, all major AI data centres will overheat within minutes since the power generated by this Android and its AI system is so intense, it won't run for long when that happens. Below the castle, in the underground dungeon, considered by historians to be a myth, is a powerful liquid cooling mainframe that runs all the world's AI cooling management. Impenetrable. But we have determined where that control system is mounted within his body."

"Where exactly?"

He stopped and pulled up a hologram screen in the centre of the room with some images of the king rotating.

"You will need to succeed in three vital steps to achieve this. First, a powerful blow with all your strength will be needed to the left side of his neck. See this line over here?" he said, pointing to the neck of the android.

"Yes, it glows deep orange," she replied.

"Correct. This connects his power source to the mainframe located in his head. Cutting this will immediately sever his power and disorientate him, but only for a short time. You'll need to swing the sword again and cut off his head before he can regain his balance. This will get him to his knees and closer to your height. Then, you need to climb on top of him and thrust the sword through his oesophagus. In humans, it is part of the alimentary canal which connects the throat to the stomach. Within this android, it directs us to its central core. One of the most important reasons a sword is the ultimate weapon is to accomplish this. But you must drive it hard, reach the core system and penetrate it. This will shatter the core and shut down his control over the liquid cooling system."

"Sounds easy enough. Are you crazy? I thought Henry was crazy, but this is insane," she said as her heart leapt.

"I know it sounds daunting, but once I have trained you to use this sword, you'll be able to execute it quickly and flawlessly. You only need to make three moves once you're in front of him. The first swing will cut the power source in his neck. With a second swing, his head must be severed. Then drive the sword through his neck and into his central core. It is critical not to skip a step. Attempting to cut off his head before cutting off the power source will not give you the necessary control over him. It will make him very defensive and he will tear you to pieces. Do you understand that, Scarlett?" he asked.

"Got it. What happens after I do this or attempt to?" she asked as she listened, then shook her head.

"There are no second chances. If you fail, you will most likely die and this entire mission will be over," he said, understanding her terrible turmoil. "Once the AI system overheats, various things will happen in the world within hours. All AI-driven services, autonomous vehicles, drones, robots and cloud-based applications will go offline and degrade the performance of all military systems and satellites."

"How do we regain control over AI?"

"It will blind the AI system, allowing a massive army of analogue old-school fighter jets, which we have been secretly preparing for years, to attack and destroy all of the world's major data centres. Critical tasks, such as AI machine learning, will be interrupted. Data loss will be widespread, causing damage to servers and all storage devices. The Internet will go down. Artificial intelligence monitors and controls power grids, traffic systems, healthcare systems and emergency response. Overheating will cause failures in these critical services. The world's electrical grid will fail, resulting in a global blackout. What will follow will be chaos, riots and confusion, until we manage to bring power back online and communicate with the world's now very scared and lost population."

For some reason, his words seemed to be asking for a response. "Sounds scary. Will we really be better off as humans, I now wonder?"

"Think of it this way. Remember the classic movie, The Matrix?" he asked.

"Kind of," she said as she tipped her chin high.

"Well, in that scenario of a simulated world, many people

would have preferred to remain within the Matrix, because it was easier than facing the real dark world on the outside. Ignorance is bliss. Same as this world we are living in. A lot of people will think it is better with this AI system, but once they are free, they will realise what they have lost over the past ten years and how much better life is going to be once we, as humanity, have control over our destiny and world again."

She sighed and considered his deep words for a moment, then said, "Better start that training then."

"Very well."

He walked round and stopped in front of her.

"Now, take your left hand and firmly grip the bottom of the handle with the pinky and ring fingers and apply the most pressure you can," he said.

She awkwardly gripped the handle.

"Use your right hand to support the top of the handle, but don't grip it too tightly. Stay calm, but remain in control. Try to avoid excessive tension in your arms, keep them relaxed so you can have better control and endurance."

There was a moment of hesitation before she got the grip correct.

"Hold the sword at chest level, usually pointing toward the opponent's throat. Keep your body balanced by keeping your feet shoulder-width apart," he said as he gently nudged her right foot.

"Are you feeling solid and stable?" he asked.

"Yes. I feel in control," she replied.

"Good. Now raise the sword above your head and bring it down in a smooth and controlled motion toward your target. We call this the vertical downward strike. Ensure the blade moves straight, finishing with a proper follow-through."

The wooden sword moved down and the wind whirled as she followed through.

"Now cut diagonally from the shoulder to the opposite hip, mimicking a natural and effective striking motion. Ensure you maintain correct blade alignment for a clean, decisive diagonal cut."

She looked comfortable and natural as she struck through.

"You are doing great. You follow this up by executing a horizontal cut. Keep the wrists flexible to ensure a smooth, continuous motion, focusing on accuracy and form before increasing speed, got it?" he asked.

"Think so," she replied.

"*Again*, controlling the sword with power is only possible with precise footwork. Keep your feet low to the floor and slide smoothly to reduce unnecessary movement and noise. Step forward, backwards and side to side while maintaining posture and stance. Now remember to integrate your footwork with strikes to develop fluid and efficient movement."

She moved to the side and looked relaxed and smooth.

"Now we will repeat this until you feel comfortable and the sword feels part of you. Gradually increase your speed and intensity as these moves become as natural as breathing. You must feel one with the sword. We will simulate the three movements you need to accomplish tomorrow so that we can focus on your timing and smooth transitions between attacks and defences."

"What if he fights back?"

"Oh, he will. You must be prepared for it and sever that power source as soon as possible with your first strike. This is enough for today. You need to have a heightened awareness and readiness once you are in front of him. Maintaining your mental focus will be vital," he said as the tension drained from him like someone pulled a bath plug.

She seemed determined and on track.

What if this was too much for her? he thought

What if she failed?

Best not to think about that, he decided.

FOURTEEN

Spanish Zone, Sector 8 - 2052

What started as a distant hum became visible dust swirling in splendid technicolour as a few large flying craft flew over a medieval town nestled in a rugged, mountainous landscape, as rockets launched at the centre of the narrow streets. The first missile punched through a row of terracotta-coloured buildings with traditional tiled roofs, sending shards of wood and brick into the morning air. The sky was clear with a few wispy clouds as another rocket struck occupied buildings, igniting their roofs with waves of black smoke. They carved through the structures, leaving hollowed-out walls. The air was filled with the crackling of fire and the bitter scent of scorched earth. Echoes of missiles still vibrated in the people's ears. They scattered as the craft descended near a river valley with lush green trees contrasting against the arid rocky hillsides. The surrounding terrain was rugged, covered in patches of greenery and winding dirt paths that led into the hills. Robot soldiers looking like maggots poured out from the rear of the craft, guns up. The grass flattened as their metal legs ploughed their way towards the village. The landscape around the village was lush and expansive, with a few scattered structures, most of which now emitted smoke.

The chancellor walked towards the village entrance, followed by his army of robots. People remained in the background as one man approached him.

"State your name," the chancellor demanded.

"Mateo, your eminence. Please do not harm my people further," he said.

"Well, that entirely depends on you. Everyone deserves a second chance, not so?" he said firmly.

"We have the right to live away from your digital world," he said hard.

"You seem to forget that the ruler of this world does not give humans this choice. Cooperate today and he will save their lives."

"What do you wish from us?" he asked, staring at him, incredulously.

"Wish? The king not only demands but deserves total loyalty. He is to be worshipped and respected, are we clear?"

"We will not conform to his religion," he replied after thinking for a moment.

"I promise you, a bullet is loaded for your head. Merciful food parcels are only rationed based on loyalty scores calculated by AI and the score of this village is zero. Mateo, make the right choice today and not only will we spare the lives of your people, but I will provide them with food."

"What do you seek?"

"It's not what we seek, but who," Sebastian said.

"Who?"

"We have intel from a reliable informant that an old Englishman named Henry has stayed at this village recently."

"There is no one here who fits that description. It's only our people," Mateo said.

"Now is not the time to play games, Mateo. Admit that he was here and give the information we seek," Sebastian said as he glanced around the village, leaning forward instinctively.

Mateo nodded. "Many Indigents come here for peace and tranquillity. We do not ask for names," he replied, without expression. The Chancellor shook his head as he turned back to the large craft in the distance. The king android appeared at the entrance, walked closer to the edge of the hull and nodded. Sebastian knew what that meant.

Death.

There was a moment's pause before one of the robot's hands clutched his weapon and pulled the trigger, hitting one of the people near them in the chest. He died instantly.

"Please no!" Mateo shouted.

The Chancellor lowered his hand. The robot placed his weapon back in his holster.

"I will give you the information you seek," he said as he muttered under his breath.

"Very well. This man, named Henry, is wanted for treason against the King in the highest form. Anyone harbouring this man is guilty as well."

"What information do you need about this man?"

"We need to find him and arrest him. How long was he here for and when did he leave?"

"He was here a few days ago. He did not say where he was going."

"Did he tell you anything about a coup to topple the kingdom?"

"No. He just needed food and shelter. We don't know anything else about him. Please, we wish no violence. We welcome anyone who comes here."

"We have heard from our informant that you guide people to a weakness in the walls of the cities. Do I have anything to be concerned about?"

"No, your eminence. It is not true. In fact, this man said he was going to the London zone, more than that, I don't know."

"Under no circumstances do you engage further with this man. Are we clear?"

"You have my word."

"Next time I come here, mercy might not be available."

"Understood," Mateo replied.

"Return to the flying craft. We are done here," Sebastian said to the robot soldiers.

The robots turned round and all marched back to the hull of one of the flying craft. Sebastian entered the craft on the right. The door slowly closed as he walked deeper into the room.

"Do we have what we need?" The king's deep and dark voice reverberated in the hull as Sebastian stopped in his tracks.

"We know he was here. Recently. We need to move further north. It seems he is heading for the London zone. We will catch him sooner or later." Sebastian replied.

"Ensure extra guards are patrolling the walls. I want thousands of drones mobilised. It has become clear that he is part of the rebellion against my rule. Everyone and anyone who aids him in this mission must pay the highest price," the king said.

"Of course, my lord, consider it done."

"Any news on the whereabouts of the boy named Ethan?"

"No, my lord. They are still at large. We believe a very

powerful and well-connected team supports them. The EMP they deployed destroyed all the footage of the female lawyer that went to see him."

"Suspend all further human lawyers. I can't help but conclude that this Ethan is connected to Henry. I want both of them found and their heads on a platter. Are we clear?"

"Yes, my lord. Sooner or later, they will show up on an ID scan," he remarked.

"You better find him, Sebastian, or it's your head if you fail me," the king said as he stepped away from the craft's bridge and paused.

The flying crafts roared as they lifted off the ground. As they climbed to a thousand feet, Sebastian could see the whole village forming like an oil painting before him.

"Destroy the outpost. Kill everyone down there," the king suddenly ordered, leaving Sebastian gasping for air.

"But my lord, they co-operated?" he asked, concerned.

"Sebastian. You are becoming weak and I am questioning your loyalty. Do I need to?"

"No, my lord. I'll give the command," he said, biting his upper lip and closing his eyes.

"Good. If we become weak, the rebellion will grow," the king added.

"It will soon be crushed. You have my word."

Rockets rained down on the village, destroying the landscape. He watched the sky light up and felt his soul ripped apart along with every other human. Every time he thought he'd seen enough human torture and death, he was reminded of the king's ruthless rule, which he executed daily.

This was bloody cruel, he thought as he scratched his head irritably, fighting back the tears.

No buildings remained standing beneath the craft.

It looked like hell on Earth below as the craft turned sideways and exited the zone.

FIFTEEN

3 weeks later

Scarlett inhaled deeply and exhaled slowly as she returned the wooden sword to its stand beside a line of stainless steel katana swords. She rubbed the blade's edge with her fingers while closing her eyes. With her free hand she raked her fingers through her hair.

Another long day of training had ended. She was alone and the vast emptiness of the training room was filled with her thoughts. The light was dim as night fell over London. When she saw Ethan standing in the doorway, her smile grew out of control. Two weeks had passed since he last spoke to her and now she was in the same room as him. The rain was clattering softly and trickling down the gutters near the windows.

Why was he able to do that to her?

She was stronger than his boyish charm, surely?

She turned back to the rack of swords and bit her upper lip, only to turn round and find him right up close to her. She could feel his breathing on her face and sweat from her workout glistened on her skin as the soft light made her look breathtaking. Neither spoke; there was only the slow movement of his body closer to her space.

The air between them felt charged. Being away from him made her feel numb, but his intentions seemed as distant as ever. She suddenly leaned in, unable to stop herself, closing the space between them until their lips touched, soft, uncertain, electric.

"A sword looks good on you," he said gently.

"Still feels awkward in my hands, though," she replied.

Could she trust him?

"Have missed you," he said.

"Been training hard. Yugo doesn't play around," she replied, looking him in the eyes, unsure why she was holding back.

"What are you so afraid of?" he asked.

"Failing everyone."

"I don't mean the mission. I mean about letting people in."

"I don't have time for relationships. This mission means everything to me," she said. He grabbed her wrist with his right hand as she tried to worm her way past him.

"I know. Yugo believes in you. Seems everyone does."

"And you?"

"I believe that you can do anything you put your mind to. You have certainly proven that."

"I have failed my parents and everyone in that village I was supposed to protect. What if I fail again?"

"You won't."

"How do you know that?"

"Because I'll be right there. There's a whole team behind you, bigger than you can ever imagine," he said, gazing at her as if she were the most beautiful woman on the planet.

Was she simply another conquest for him?

He moved his thumb to the back of her hand and made a gentle circular motion over the tendons.

"You need to trust me," he said.

"I don't-"

"Did someone hurt you?" he asked, not letting her finish. "I mean physically," he continued.

"Had a rough relationship with Tom, back at the outpost. It was good in the beginning, but he became very possessive. I couldn't breathe any more. I ended up with more bruises than at any other time in my life."

"I'm sorry."

"It's okay. I just built a wall around myself and consumed my mind with survival," she said with tears welling up in her eyes.

"I'm not like that," he said.

"Yeah? Don't all men say that until they have what they want?"

"You are overthinking everything. Just let go and trust your senses for a moment."

"That's how I got-" she said halfway....

As he leaned in and gently kissed her on the lips, a warm sensation surged through her body. She wanted to pull back, but her heart was beating too fast in her chest. He removed his mouth from hers and gently kissed her along her jawline towards her ear, igniting fireworks in her veins. She tilted her head, her breath warm against his cheek. He ran his fingertips up her chin, sending chills down her neck.

He appeared calm and utterly in control of her mind and body and pressed her mouth harder onto his. She wanted to push away the avalanche of feelings and urges raging through her mind, but she felt safe with him.

Maybe it was okay to let go and let him in.

He moved his lips from her and paused only inches away from hers.

"You saw the swords behind me, right?"

"Yeah," he replied, unsure of the intention of the question.

"If you mess with me, I'll kill you," she said, her stomach churned with doubt despite herself.

"Good to know," he said, trying not to show that he was swallowing hard. The threat in her voice was unmistakable.

That train of thought gave rise to another as she frowned.

"I need to find out where they are keeping Alyx. Been thinking about what you said. What if the Chancellor refuses to tell me where he is?" she said.

"I might be able to help you with that," he replied.

She pushed away from him a bit.

"How?"

"Well, while you have been training your ass off, I have been doing my own preparation for this heist. I need to show you something."

"Is that why you came looking for me?"

"I'm not using you, believe me. I'm drawn to you as I have never felt in my life," he said as he kissed her harder, feeling as if his venom was seeping into her blood and filling her with dread that regret would eventually set in.

He kissed her again, more forcefully and felt her smile on his lips. She pulled away from him for a second or two, wanting more but controlling herself as her breathing became shallow. He could feel her hair grazing his cheek. As she kept her gaze fixed on his, she could feel every hair on her body on high alert.

She felt energised. Rejuvenated. Vulnerable.

Perhaps in love or maybe just a silly distraction?

With a growl in her voice, she said, "This better be good."

"It is. Let me show you. Follow me. Everyone has gone to bed," he said, leaning in closer, eyes bright and wide.

Scarlett felt her heart pounding through her entire body. Ethan told her to stay a few feet back as they walked down the stairs.

"Why are we sneaking around?" she whispered.

"I don't want to wake anyone. We also need to access the data centre system. Yugo probably won't approve."

"Why? Is he hiding something?"

"I trust Yugo. We can trust him," he said firmly as they entered the data centre, unsure if he was trying to convince her or himself. He pulled out a small torch, strolled carefully to a nearby workstation and touched the screen. It illuminated and prompted for a login password.

He punched a few keys and it opened an internet browser. Scarlett felt nervous.

He typed in the search box 'human concentration camps' and moved the screen towards her with the results displayed.

"See this?"

"What is it?" she asked as she felt pulled into the room's darkness.

"I came across this while studying the alarm system at the mansion."

"Is it where–"

"Yes, it's where the Chancellor takes captured humans. It seems the king uses it as leverage," he said.

"Leverage?"

"To blackmail the Indigent leaders, like yourself, to give up the rebellion or resistance and surrender."

"Is this where Alyx is kept?"

"That's what I hoped for, but then I came across this footage. It seems some people have posted footage from hacked drone cameras or on-site CCTV, but then I saw this. At first, I thought it was just random footage of the people at the camps. Many humans have been protesting against the inhumane conditions of the compound. Sooner or later AI removes these posts, so I thought I'd better show you this before it gets taken down."

Ethan motioned with his head for her to come closer to the screen, pointing his finger at a blurry, pixelated video clip. Her jaw muscles bunched and her lips tightened. She leaned forward a bit as the video played. As shock and joy filled her, she wished she could have emptied her lungs in a huge scream.

Was that Alyx in the video? She thought as she studied the video for a few minutes. The data centre was far too silent. It felt as if they were making too much noise being there.

"Is that Alyx?" she asked.

"I was hoping you'd be able to tell me. Thought when I saw a little African boy in a partly traditional outfit, it had to be him. It's good news, isn't it?"

"It means he is still alive," she whispered. "Where is this place?" she asked, trying to breathe normally. She had to stay calm and in control of her emotions.

"It's in the Paris zone," he said.

She sniffed as the room felt freezing.

"What's that photo there?" she asked, pointing her finger at the screen.

"This one?" he asked.

"No, the one at the bottom of the screen," she said as she twisted her hands as fast as she could manage.

"It's about Noah. The AI inventor who disappeared after the AI takeover went nuts. Suppose it's related to the AI system."

"I wondered what happened to him. While studying to be a nurse I remember how he advocated for AI to run the world. After that, no one heard anything about him again. Is he dead? Did the AI system kill him?" she asked.

"Seems people think so."

"Can you enlarge the photo? Who is in the photo with him?" He leaned in and pinched the screen. The image zoomed in. She took a deep breath.

"That's Henry," she said as a cold breeze gripped her soul.

"The old man on his right side?" he asked.

"Yes. Have you never met Henry?" she asked, surprised.

"Not in person, no. Seems he is Noah's father?" he said as he read the caption. Both of them looked away from the screen.

"What the hell?" she asked, then again to herself. Repeatedly.

For the first time in a long time, she felt her body fatigued and dehydrated. Ethan noticed that she was mentally calculating a lot of thoughts.

"What does it mean?" he enquired, rolling his eyes.

"I'm not sure, but I don't like it. Something is off," she said, distrusting Henry. His intentions. His words. All of it.

Then, as she tried to calm down, the room suddenly lit up. They both turned round and heard the flick of a switch.

Yugo stood there.

"What are you two doing?" he asked.

They stood up like two naughty kids. She felt like they were violating some protocol.

"I'm just trying to find where Alyx could be," she said.

"Searching the internet is dangerous. The AI system will see your search history, which may jeopardise our location. I expected more from you, Ethan," he said firmly.

"I'm sorry. I'm just trying to help Scarlett," Ethan replied, quickly closing the browser. Yugo moved closer to the screen.

"I know you worry about your brother. But we need to prioritise taking down this AI system. Are we clear?" he said, turning to Scarlett.

"I have to rescue him," she said with confidence.

"Of course. Once this AI system fails, all these camps and prisons will be open, allowing you to save him. That is a promise. There is no way to rescue him otherwise. It's impossible to enter those camps; they are heavily guarded. I will personally set up a team to extract him, okay?"

Looking round the room, her stomach dropped.

She felt unsafe and uncertain about the future, but she continued to believe Yugo could be trusted. She wondered where Henry fitted in.

"Okay," she said, as her hopes of rescuing Alyx dimmed. They seemed unconcerned about him.

For now, she needed to stay on track and finish this mission as it was the only way to save Alyx, no matter how much she distrusted everyone around her and their intentions.

How did Henry fit into all of this?

How much of him was authentic?

Ethan stood there without moving, his expression un-changed. Scarlett moved away from the desk almost imperceptibly.

"Are we good?" Yugo asked as he was immediately on his guard.

"Yes. We are ready," she said. Now was not the time to give up, but everything certainly wasn't how it seemed.

SIXTEEN

Paris, EU Sector 5 - 2052

Two days later.

The black van slowly pulled up to the entrance of the dreamlike mansion, illuminated by its inviting golden lighting as the evening fell over downtown Paris with mist and soft rain. The night sky created a striking contrast against the warm glow of the mansion's lights below. The house was perfectly symmetrical with a classic European château-style design.

In front was a stone façade with ornate details, tall windows framed by elegant mouldings and a dark, steeply pitched mansard roof punctuated by dormer windows. In front of the mansion, a beautifully landscaped circular driveway led up to the grand entrance, framed by two symmetrical sets of tall French windows. The entrance was highlighted by an arched doorway, flanked by wall-mounted lanterns. Small balconies with wrought-iron railings and lush greenery finished the picturesque image before her. A stunning, illuminated fountain sat at the centre of the driveway. The water arced gracefully, adding a sense of tranquillity to the house in front of Ethan, Alice and Gordon.

Ethan climbed out and made his way to the large front door. He presented his wrist and the large LED screen welcomed him to the auction.

"Good evening, Mr Clementine. Enjoy the auction," an AI automated voice prompted.

The air conditioning inside touched his skin as he tried to feel comfortable in his black tuxedo. The custom thermal suit was cooling his body temperature to just above freezing, contrasting with the warm aristocratic style of the mansion, enveloping all his senses. He walked deeper into the opulent hall, took a glass of champagne from a waiter and gently drew the satin peak lapel of his black jacket to one side, trying to blend in. A stunning crystal chandelier hung from the ceiling, casting a warm, luxurious glow over the hall. A few heads nodded as they walked past him, walking to a lavish seating area furnished with elegant armchairs, sofas and tables wrapped in a palette of deep reds, black, white and gold. He wore a black shirt with a pleated front and could feel the structured collar rubbing against his neck.

He scanned the room as people entered, all dressed to the hilt. He cleared his throat and adjusted the self-tied black bow tie around his neck. He appeared sleek, formal and sophisticated. He felt completely out of place, like a cheap goldfish in a fancy bowl, itching all over. He strolled round for a few minutes, studied a few paintings, but kept to himself.

He took a slow sip from the glass of champagne, turned to the entrance's large stairs, choked for a moment, but tried to keep his cool as he saw the breathtaking sight of Scarlett making her entrance. It looked like the magnificent, double-sided staircase with intricately designed white balustrades only existed to guide her like a princess downwards for that moment, freezing time in its tracks. Her hands gently held onto the dark, polished wooden handrails. Ethan stared at her and did his best to breathe normally and her poised and confident stance received all the attention she needed.

The staircase was split into two sweeping sections converging towards the lavishly decorated hall with people mingling and chatting. A few women whispered as they kept their eyes fixed on Scarlett. It was a bold, elegant and form-fitting red dress with a halter-style top with thin straps that crossed over her shoulders. The fabric's rich red colour was highlighted by its smooth texture. As soon as she saw him, she turned her head away and gently touched her ear to keep her earpiece in place. Alice had all of them in her ears. As she descended the stairs, the room became quieter. She had her long, dark hair tied back in a tight ponytail. She walked over to a big painting on one wall, a tiny chain-strap purse slung over her shoulder, maintaining a look of wealth and arrogance.

"That's a Gian Lorenzo Bernini drawing. Very rare indeed," a large Frenchman suddenly said next to her. She looked at him, then back at the drawing.

"I'm Philippe, by the way," he replied

"Laura, pleased to meet you," she said and instantly continued, feeling her earpiece tickle her ear. "Is it worth much?"

"Absolutely. Since AI took over most art forms, drawings like these have tripled in value. A lot of famous artwork is owned by the King now, all hanging in his castle. This would be a great investment before he confiscates it," he said as he breathed heavily.

"Good to know," she replied.

"You come here often?" he asked as he gaped at her.

"Ah, no. It's my first time."

"Well, a stylish woman like you will know what grabs your attention. This is my fifth auction here. I have never seen you before at these types of evenings?"

"I'm from Thailand. Felt it was time to collect some European pieces, know what I mean?" she said, playing her role carefully.

"Absolutely. This portrait, by the way, is widely recognised as a depiction of Gian Lorenzo Bernini himself, a master of sculpture and architecture in the Baroque period. See the intense gaze of the eyes, which is so typical of his style. I hope I don't have to fight you for this one later, so to speak," he said, smiling.

She paused before replying.

"Well, we will have to see, won't we?" she said, trying not to give him that leave-me-alone creep look on her face.

"I guess you're right. The auction is starting soon. Hope you enjoy the evening," he said.

"Sure will," she said as she tried to find Ethan in the growing crowd, sipping champagne from a tall glass a waiter slipped into her hand.

Ethan glanced at the closed-circuit cameras bolted on the walls and along the corridor. Alice awaited his 'go' signal via his neatly tucked inner earpiece. His eyes returned to the crowd, who were discussing paintings and sculptures. Scarlett was surrounded by men, all wanting to talk to her, much to his frustration.

"Go," he whispered gently to Alice to gear up.

She gently whispered in his ear, "Cameras and laser system off. You have ten minutes."

Ethan looked around and swiftly ran up the stairs to the second floor. Downstairs, the auctioneer had everyone's attention. The passage was dimly lit, but clear enough to see his way. Remembering the blueprint, he smoothly walked to the end of the corridor.

He stopped at the entrance and staying calm was vital. The vault only had one entry point. He would need to get in quite deep and get out swiftly before the beams come back on. His thermal suit kept his body temperature so low he could feel his teeth chatter, but heat in the art vault was not an option. The room before him was open, protected purely by the laser beams, now off briefly. The entrance had iron railings, featuring intricate scrollwork. Polished marble railings and dark wooden floors reinforced the upmarket feel of the vault. In front of him, the walls were lined with framed artworks, evenly spaced and subtly illuminated. He kept looking at his watch as two minutes had already passed. As far as he could see, there were only paintings and a few sculptures.

What if they moved the sword?

He feared the vault's structured layout had hidden cameras as he carefully moved forward, like he was walking on thin ice.

Alice was his eyes and ears.

Back in the parking lot, Alice sat in the back of the high-tech surveillance van, surrounded by computer monitors, control panels and electronic equipment, watching Ethan move forward as a small pulsating dot. She wore a sleek, tactical outfit and her long black hair was tied in a ponytail. She was ready for whatever might come. Her left hand touched her chin as she gently adjusted her over-ear headphones. The monitors displayed various types of information and a 'live' camera feed loaded from the art vault's camera, which she had previously hacked. She concentrated solely on Ethan's every move as the dimly lit interior was bathed in a cool blue glow from the screens. Gordon leaned forward in the driver's seat. "Are we good?" he asked as he started the van and moved it to the back of the mansion.

"Yeah, he is inside the vault. That's the easy part; getting out is what worries me," she whispered as she watched Ethan walk deeper into the room.

"I think his mind is too much on the men around Scarlett," he said as he switched off the van.

"Probably, but he'd better focus. A lot is riding on this," she replied.

"He will pull through, he always does," he added.

There it was, hanging on the wall: the most stunning sword Ethan had ever seen. He stopped dead in his tracks. The blade had a sleek, straight profile and a sharp, pointed tip. He ran his fingers over the metal's smooth, polished, brushed finish, which reflected the light and other artworks in the room. It appeared and felt expensive.

Very expensive and rare.

He lifted it off the bracket and pushed it through the side of his belt.

Time to move! He told himself over and over.

As he walked back, he noticed additional medieval weapons mounted on the wall. Yugo told him not to be distracted, so he forced himself to keep going while remaining calm and keeping his body temperature as low as possible. His heart was racing and his mouth felt as parched as the bottom of a birdcage.

"Keep going, you are almost there. You have four minutes left," she said in his ear.

Scarlett looked around nervously, trying to blend in with the crowd as the auctioneer lifted a white sheet off a sculpture.

"Ladies and gentlemen. This rare six-foot-tall painted bronze sculpture has been off the market since 1970 and has recently surfaced. It was created by artist Jonathan Renard and is titled '*A Dying Form*'. Bidding will start at 500,000 crypto Meridean. Do I have 500,000? This is ideal for any of you serious collectors," he said.

A man in the back lifted his paddle.

"Thank you! I have 500,000. Do I hear 550,000?"

Scarlett lifted her paddle.

"550,000! Thank you to the beautiful lady in red. Now 600,000?" he asked.

The same man hesitated, then nodded.

"600,000! We're moving up. Do I hear 650,000?"

Another man joined in, raising his paddle.

"650,000 from a new bidder! Welcome. Now 700,000?"

Scarlett nodded again.

"700,000 to the lady! It's heating up. Any advance on 700,000?"

The first bidder at the back lifted his paddle. Scarlett backed off.

"750,000? We have 750,000. Any further bids? This is a once-in-a-lifetime moment, friends. You are never going to see this painting again. No other bids? Going once... going twice..." he said, holding his breath. "SOLD! For 750,000 to bidder #214! Congratulations!" he shouted with enthusiasm.

Scarlett smiled as she looked back at the man she had spoken to earlier.

For a moment, she felt like she was somewhere else, somewhere normal. The group moved on to a row of paintings. She tried to find Ethan in the background, but he was gone.

Meanwhile, Ethan moved quickly towards the entrance of the vault.

"Stop. Wait a second. Someone is coming up the stairs," Alice said in his ear. Even though it was a whisper, it felt like a shout. His guts were churning. Ethan held his breath as the man walked closer to the entrance.

He was going to see if the system was down.

He gently placed the sword on the floor and waited for the man to come round the corner.

"Take him down, quietly," Alice said.

As he came round, Ethan slammed his fist into the man's stomach. He followed it with a hook below the right eye. He went down and crumbled into a pile. He stayed down.

"Get out of there. The lasers are going back on in three, two, one," Alice said with her breath caught in her throat.

Ethan picked up the sword and swiftly lifted his left shoe over the line just in time as he heard the system arming.

That was close. Too close.

He slowly let a long, deep breath leave his lungs.

Now to get out. According to the blueprint, a balcony was straight ahead.

He walked down the corridor, hearing the roar of the crowd of people below, celebrating the auction winners. More was surely to follow. He could hear glasses ringing in the background.

He reached the door and tried the handle. Double doors opened to the balcony. He stepped out. It was dark in the back of the mansion. He could see the van parked in the pitch darkness. Alice got out and launched a zip line to him. He secured the zip line to the balcony railing with a carabiner and gently pulled it to test its strength. The other end was tied to the van. The line felt taut with enough slack to slow his descent, but he expected a rough landing, regardless. He held the zip line firmly in his bare hands, keeping his elbows slightly bent. Using his core muscles for stability, he pushed off with controlled movement. He kept the sword safely tucked in to avoid straining his arms without locking his elbows. Keeping an eye on Alice was critical for a successful landing as he bent his knees slightly. He flew into her arms and let go of the zip line when his feet touched the ground. She cleared her throat as he gently drew back.

"Is that it?" she asked.

"Guess it is," he replied as he revealed the sword.

"What's wrong? You seem different?" she asked.

"Let's just do what we agreed, okay?" he said in a cold and tight voice as he walked towards the van.

"Did you take care of Gordon?" he asked.

"Yes, as planned. I gave him a spiked coffee. He is lights out. Don't worry, he'll be fine in the morning, apart from a hell of a headache."

"We need to get going, before anyone sees us," he said, looking back at her.

She passed him and opened the back of the van's double doors. Ethan held the sword up as she pulled out the cello. Carefully, he slid it into its position, as if it never existed.

"Bloody amazing," she said as she watched his emotionless

expression. "It's Scarlett that's eating you, isn't it?" she asked as he closed the van's doors.

"It's better this way," he said.

"You know she will never forgive you, right?"

"One day she will. When she looks back at this impossible plan," he said.

She grabbed his hand tightly, but he pulled back. "Poor Ethan. She *really* has you in a tailspin, doesn't she?"

"That's why I need to do this. It's better for everyone," he replied short.

"Well then, let's get out of here. She's waiting for you to go back in the mansion and walk out with you, but now she's a warrior left at the altar," she said, her voice rude and condescending.

"Whatever, let's go," he said.

SEVENTEEN

Scarlett held her ear as she received the message to leave the auction.

"Leaving already?" One of the guests asked as she walked towards the door.

"Yeah, something has come up. Got a big business deal hanging in the air. I'm in a bit of a hurry, enjoy the auction."

"Will do. Good luck with that business deal," he said as she walked out, expecting the black van to pull up, but there was no sight of it anywhere. An unrecognised, rugged 4x4 electric vehicle pulled up instead at the entrance as the door flung open.

"Yugo?" she asked, lowering her neck to look inside.

"Get in," he said, keeping his gaze sharp and focused.

Scarlett got in and the vehicle pulled away, then accelerated as it approached the main road.

"Okay, what's going on?" she enquired.

Yugo looked at her while driving into the night, looking distraught and worried.

"The mission is over."

"What? What happened? Did Ethan not get the sword? Did something go wrong?"

"Something went wrong, all right," he replied out of breath.

"Can you please tell me what's going on?" she asked, her

voice becoming more panicked.

"Seems Ethan and Alice had other plans."

The dread of Ethan breaking her trust and heart set in a fraction of a second later.

"Other plans?"

"He has taken the sword. Gordon tried to warn me about two hours ago, but then he just went quiet."

"Why would he do this?" she asked herself more than Yugo.

"I'm not sure. Something spooked Ethan about this whole thing and Ethan is being Ethan."

"What does that mean?" Scarlett asked, the pressure behind her eyes was red-hot and filled with fury.

"He is a thief, Scarlett. A no good bloody thief and he realised the value of the sword most likely and decided to run with it. It's worth a fortune."

"He thinks I can't complete the mission," she said sombrely.

Yugo ran his eyes over the road as they drove into the valley.

"We have a tail," he said suddenly. "They have identified my RFID tag chip. My cover is blown."

Scarlett looked back through the rear window.

In the distance, she could see glowing blue and red lights pursuing them. Above, multiple armed drones hovered.

"We have been compromised. Police robots have ransacked the mansion. We can never go back," he said.

The road was rough and they bounced around in their seats as Yugo pressed the accelerator.

"You don't think they gave away the rebellion?" she asked.

"Right now, I don't know what to think. If Ethan plans to sell the sword, he would want to be sure we don't come after him."

"He better hope I don't as I'm going to skin his bloody ass

alive! I can't believe this is happening," she shouted.

As they darted into the darkness and more and more off-road, the towering mountains and dense pine forests dominated their canvas.

Yugo stretched his left arm toward the back seat holding the steering wheel with one hand. He moaned as he pulled out a crossbow and a medium-sized green bag and placed it on her lap.

"You're gonna need this," he said as he touched her shoulder. The box-shaped 4x4 veered to the right, kicking up dust as it drifted dangerously close to the cliffside. He grabbed the steering wheel and pushed forward. The headlights were bouncing across the road in front of him. The drones were coming closer and closer, their spotlights piercing through the night sky like a can opener.

Then it felt as if a massive hand swiped the side of the vehicle. It twisted sideways as a few drones belched fire, spewing long bursts of rounds at them. The rear window shattered into pieces and her hair covered half her face. A bullet tore into Yugo's left shoulder. He gave an agonising scream.

"You're hit!" she shouted.

"I'm okay," he replied in short breaths. More bullets rained down on them. Drones with blue and red lights and blaring sirens were not far off. The terrain was rough, giving them the advantage they needed to stay ahead, but the drones were moving in. Yugo kept on accelerating and kept putting the 4x4 into a steep climb.

"Listen to me, Scarlett. You need to focus now on saving Alyx, okay?" he pleaded, trying to keep his eyes fixed on the rough road, the tires struggling for grip.

"You need to get off. I'm going to slow down at a twist

coming up, it's very hard for the drones to manoeuvre in there, the trees are dense," he said.

"I don't understand. How can we *just* give up like this?" she asked.

"Because it's over, Scarlett. The least you can do is to survive this and rescue Alyx. At least then all our efforts won't be in vain," he pleaded as he continued, "This is my emergency 'go bag'. It contains some non-perishable food, a change of clothes and some tough terrain shoes that should fit you thanks to my small Japanese feet. I always have it on me if something happens and I can't return home." He gave her a look that she would probably never forget.

Suddenly, a barrage of bullets ripped through the 4x4's frame—one struck the rear axle, sending the vehicle into a violent roll. Dust and debris filled the air as the 4x4 flipped. Sparks flew as metal scraped against jagged stones. Leaves, branches and metal debris were scattered as it crashed violently into the undergrowth and stopped on its side. Scarlett felt a force pulling her forward in her seat, bruising her ribs from the safety belt. She hung for a moment in her seat and looked towards Yugo.

Airbags were deployed in front of his face.

He was dead.

Just like this mission.

Dead.

Get out of the car! She heard a voice shouting in her head.

With a deep breath, she unlatched the seatbelt. Gravity yanked her down, and she landed with a jolt on the 4x4's inverted roof. With force, she ripped her dress to give room for movement. She flung her high heels towards the back of the vehicle. As the handle jammed several times, she violently kicked the door open. She dropped to a crawl and pushed forward towards the side of a tree. She quickly pulled on the tough terrain shoes and braced herself for what was coming next. The buzzing of drones continued. She took a deep breath and started running. Her eyes adjusted to the darkness quickly as she ran with the crossbow over her shoulder.

Again, it was just her and her crossbow.

Her heart beat wildly; her mind tried to process what had just happened.

The sound of the enemy drew closer as drones circled the 4x4 as she kept running into the night.

It seemed they only expected Yugo. Although it was a small victory, she could feel only a tiny bit of hope and power seeping into her veins.

Alyx had to be her focus.

Perhaps Yugo was right; complete her original mission.

Everything felt surreal.

Darkness had won.

She swallowed hard and held her chin up high.

She didn't think much more as tears and despair streamed down her face.

EIGHTEEN

Human Detention Centre

2:00 am

The cold morning air hardened her face as Scarlett approached the high-security compound. It was a long walk of over 2 hours. She scouted the heavily fortified facility with a tall chain-link fence topped with razor wire. Bright floodlights illuminated the area as drones flew overhead. She stayed low. Faceless humanoid robots with sleek metallic bodies and glowing blue eyes protected the gates. Their mechanical structure with exposed joints and wiring glistened in the night sky as the flood lights' rays bounced off it. Her ears felt the vibration of the drones' rotors as they flew overhead, patrolling the perimeter.

She would need to get in quietly.

She lay low for fifteen minutes, fixing her eyes on the electric vehicles entering the entrance area.

She did the math as she watched the robots moving round. Four were at the corner of the fence, two at the rear and two more at the entrance. She carefully watched the process as new humans arrived in electric transport vehicles at the compound. A robot stuck its arm out by the window and touched an LED screen close to the gate with its index finger. The large fenced gates opened. The electric prisoner vehicle proceeded to enter the compound. They followed a rigorous routine. In the distance she could see another vehicle approaching.

Running out of human prisoners was obviously not a problem.

For the first time since she arrived at the compound, real terror was in her eyes. With Alyx so close to her, he felt so dangerously far from her, but nothing in the world was more important now.

Her eyes kept adjusting to the harsh flood lights not too far from her as she stayed low behind some bushes. A large central watchtower with illuminated windows stood tall as the robot soldiers carried rifles and maintained a vigilant stance. Several armoured transport vehicles resembling Humvees and four-wheel drive military trucks were stationed outside the facility. A soft drizzle started as she had her entrance plan sketched out. She would have to figure out the rest as she went along. She pulled her crossbow over her shoulder, inserted the crank handle and began turning. She continued cranking until the string locked into place. With her breathing tight, she placed the bolt on the rail of her titanium crossbow, sliding it back until the nock fully engaged with the string. Her extended mission preparations had come full circle. The main objective was the difficult task of getting into the compound without anyone noticing her. If they detect her, she would most certainly die or be captured. Finally, another vehicle arrived at the entrance. The robot reached for the LED touch screen and began to move forward as the gates opened. She slowly lifted the bow and aimed at the main floodlight at the entrance.

She can't miss.

Striking the floodlight in the centre will plunge the front entrance into darkness and with an arrow-like bolt, she will make no sound. Hopefully, they will think it just blew. She released the bolt, which struck the centre as she had hoped.

The entrance went dark.

She hurried behind the truck, her heart pounding as it moved forward. The robots at the entrance all looked up at the light. Scarlett hung onto the back rail of the vehicle as it went in.

"Secure the perimeter!" the one robot demanded as they all moved forward, perhaps expecting someone coming from the entrance. Still, she was already in, hanging on as the vehicle moved inwards. For an instant, she stiffened, then dropped her eyes to the ground. She kept calm and jumped off as the vehicle turned to the right. There was a crunch of cement on bone as she crashed onto her side and rolled away against a side building. Hopefully, a bolt stuck in the floodlight would only be discovered in the morning during maintenance.

"All seems clear," another robot said, lifting his head, eyes blazing. He loaded a fresh magazine into his weapon and stood in his programmed position.

She was inside.

Now, finding Alyx would be a blind search. As far as she could see, various rows of cells were in concrete structures. She kept low as a bright floodlight spun from the watch towers over the area.

Patience and timing were key.

The emotions she wore on her face were a mixture of power and fear and both were very real. By 03:00 am, a few robots were walking around the compound and a few more were manning the rooftops. She knew her ribs were bruised from the jump earlier as she could feel a sharp jolt of pain flowing through her with every breath she took. The closest barracks were a few metres away. She carefully sprinted towards a large metal door and slowly opened it. It was quiet. Everyone was asleep. She slowly walked down the dark passage with cells on either side. Something inside her froze suddenly. Something or someone moved further down. She kept her crossbow lifted, loaded and ready. She kept telling herself over and over, no matter what happens, don't shoot, as it could expose her within the compound. Her hair was sticky and warm over her face. She staggered into the dim cells, trying to focus in the dark. Now and then, the floodlight spinning outside penetrated the cells. She kept her back against the wall and waited for the light to pass. Drones zipped overhead as she walked further in. An unlocked door was at the end of the corridor and she opened it slowly. There were even more rows of cells.

How was she ever going to find him?

"Alyx?" she whispered into the air, hoping for a response.

It was cold and she could feel the temperature drop every minute.

"Alyx? It's Scarlett. Can you hear me?" she asked as she looked to the far end of the corridor, realising her hands were shaking. Then she heard movement again. She stopped to catch her breath as she sensed someone behind her. She spun around. Her temple pounded as she lifted her crossbow and aimed it at the sound that slowly became the form of a human man.

"Who are you?" he asked softly, sniffing and coughing slightly.

He was filthy, skinny and seemed malnourished.

"I'm looking for Alyx? Who are you?" she asked.

He kept looking around. "Stay quiet. Robots are close to the wall around this time and they might hear us," he said with a strong American accent, looking in all directions.

"My name is Rowan. I try to keep an eye on everyone here. I can help you find Alyx," he said.

"Do you know where he is?" she asked.

He nodded. "I don't know everyone's names, I'm afraid. I'm terrible with names. What does he look like?"

"He's a small Zulu boy, around ten years old," she said.

"I can take you to him. He's on the other side with other children."

Why was she trusting this Rowan? Scarlett wondered, but she brushed the thought.

"Why should I trust you?" she whispered.

"Because in here you need me. I know this place like the back of my hand. Been here for over a year. Seems no one cared enough to rescue me. Alyx must be very important to you?"

"He is my adopted brother and all I have left in this world," she said, thinking about Ethan for a second.

He nodded vacantly and was unsteady on his feet.

"You need my help. We can help each other," he said.

"How can I help you? I can't save everyone here, no matter how much I wish I could," she said sombrely.

"You will need my help to get out of here. I need to find a way to rescue everyone here."

"True. I kinda haven't thought that far yet, but I will fight my way out once I have Alyx."

"Look. The sun will rise soon; you will never escape this place once it's light. They will blow you to pieces. Believe me, I have seen it countless times."

"So what do you want?"

He leaned in towards her. "I'm a truck driver and know how to drive those electric prisoner vans. All I ask is for you to help me get out as well. I can drive us out of here," he said.

He was right. She had no real exit plan.

"Take me to Alyx and we can get out of here."

"Follow me," he said as she smiled gently.

Then it hit her as they walked.

"Wait a minute," she said.

"What?"

"Why do you need me to get into a truck and drive through the gate? Why not just do it on your own?"

"Because we will need a robot's hand to touch the LED screen. If we drove through the gates, they would blow holes in this van so quickly that no one would survive. You have that crossbow," he replied.

"And?"

"Once we have Alyx, we must find a wandering robot and take it down. Then we can use its arm to reach the screen and leave as quietly as possible. We have to stick to their routine," he replied.

"I hope to drive a bolt through its neck and take it down. I don't know if that will work?" she asked.

"It's the only option we have. Been planning to escape from here for months, but now you have given me new hope. I stand no chance on my own, but together we can do this," he said.

"Take me to Alyx," she replied into his ear, her face permanently frowning.

"Right this way," he said, keeping a measured tone. His answer was attainable. She still believed saving Alyx was possible. Perhaps now more than ever.

They walked further down the corridor. A few people were moving around and moaning in their small cells.

It was inhumane.

No one has seen this out there in the utopian Myriad world.

The brutality. People were treated as commodities. As leverage.

Rowan scanned the area again.

Scarlett shifted impatiently.

They passed cell after cell. Then he stopped.

"I think this is the cell where I saw him before," he said.

"Alyx?" she asked into the darkness.

A few people moved under blankets as she leaned further towards the wall.

"Alyx, it's Scarlett," she said repeatedly.

Rowan noticed the shift in her as her face suddenly changed from concerned to relieved.

Out of the dark corner, a small figure came running towards her. When the dim light fell over his face, she fell to her knees, waiting to embrace him.

"Scar!" he shouted.

"Shh. Keep quiet," she pleaded as he ran into her arms. She felt like never letting him go again, ever. She took three deep breaths.

"I knew you would come find me! I knew it!" he said, still louder than he should have been.

"We are not quite safe yet. You know Rowan, right?" she asked softly.

"Everyone here knows Rowan," he replied, looking up at him.

"Good, because we need to get going and get out of here as quickly as possible. Ready?"

"I thought I was going to die, Scar," Alyx said with his eyes wide.

"Well, you are not going to die, okay?" she asked, looking for affirmation.

A few more people came out of their dark shelters. The air instantly changed.

"We need to go," Rowan said as she stood up.

"I will be back, I promise. One day, somehow, we will all be free from this nightmare," he said to calm some other children waking up.

Scarlett looked worriedly at the doorway as she loaded her crossbow.

A few robots walked past them into the yard quite close to them.

"Wait for that last one," Rowan whispered. When he turned to face Scarlett, his gaze sharpened slightly. She gave him a look teeming with a mixture of power and fear.

They waited patiently as the humanoid robot scanned the perimeter and strolled down the corridor connecting other barracks. She raised her crossbow and released a bolt. It torpedoed like a comet roaring through space. It sliced his neck and went straight through. He slowly fell to the ground as Rowan placed his hands beneath him. Sparks flew off his metal body. She was about to launch another bolt, but it was a good shot. A perfect shot. She perforated his central processing unit, allowing Rowan to take him down. He quickly twisted his head and it simply hung there. Power was still active.

Dim lights flashed in his neck and Rowan stared at his eyes as they went darker. She chewed the side of her lip as they dragged the robot to the side of the wall. Alyx just stood there motionless.

Who knew what he had gone through in the last few weeks?

Things that will be with him forever, she thought.

She turned back to face Alyx and wiped away a stray tear on her cheek.

Rowan looked at her with steel grey eyes.

"Let's move," he said. Without hesitation, they stuffed the disabled robot guard into the front of the truck, started the electric vehicle and rolled towards the gate. The three sat in the front, with the disabled robot looking like a broken toy positioned to the right. Alyx appeared disturbed by the robot so close to him. He just sat there tentatively, without expression. She could feel his trembling body beside her. 'Tension' was the only word to describe their feelings when they drove towards the gate. She looked over, startled, then her face expressed as they stayed low in the front.

The gate was slowly approaching.

What if they asked the robot questions? she wondered.

Scarlett kept her crossbow loaded on her lap. It was her only weapon.

She and Alyx stayed down.

As he halted the van beside the touchscreen exit panel, Rowan kept his head angled towards the robot's shoulder. Slowly, he raised the arm of the robot and pushed it through the window.

Ahead, a few robots stood and guarded the gates.

Rowan tried to touch the screen with the robot's droopy hand and fingers. He kept his eyes on the robots ahead as he tried a few times. His heart was racing.

Come on! he said to himself as two robots began approaching them. If they got any closer, they would be busted.

Try once more, he thought to himself, trying to wobble the robot's hand over the screen.

It beeped and the display went green.

The gate opened and Rowan slowly pulled the robot's arm back in. It was still dark, but the lights at the gates were bright and focused. The van slightly veered to the right as he tried to steer it without having a full view of the road.

Just a little bit further.

The van passed through the gate. He slowly sat up straight and watched in the rear-view mirror as the gate slowly closed.

Scarlett and Alyx straightened up.

"Guess the robots don't greet each other," she said.

He looked at Scarlett and smiled.

"Now that would be weird," he said as he increased speed.

An hour later they reached the main 'Paris' city gate.

"Stay down. We are getting close to the gate. Fortunately, there's no exit check. It should be easier through this gate as they are more concerned about people entering than leaving," he said.

"Do people ever try to leave, I wonder?" she asked.

"Once you have the chip they own and control your mind, so you don't want to leave. I think people become spiritually and emotionally dead in here. I have seen it happen to my family. You won't recognise them if you had to see old friends and family, believe me, it's quite frightening," he said.

"Wonder why they don't chip prisoners like yourself?" she asked.

"I guess that this king wants to be worshipped freely. He thinks he is a deity or something, like we owe our lives to him. Crazy stuff, right?" he asked.

"Where are you going from here?" she asked.

"We will need to abandon this van as soon as possible. They will be tracking it; if it stops for long, they will become

187

suspicious. So, you should get off as soon as possible. I need to find my wife. When we got separated, we were more south, so I'm going to drive this van until the battery goes flat," he said.

There was always a queue of people at the gates, surrendering their lives to the AI king. Scarlett tried to shake off the guilty feeling that saving them was her responsibility.

It didn't work. She felt like giving a muted scream.

She felt more confined than ever, even though they went through the exit safely and without incident.

NINETEEN

Schwerin Castle, EU Sector 1 - 2052

One day later

Sebastian entered the magnificent and lavish chamber as the heavy door of the castle vibrated open. As usual, he wore a black leather doublet with a high collar and long sleeves. The front was embellished with buckles. A gold-buckled belt that tightened the waist completed the ensemble. Holding his breath, he gazed at the ceiling, as he always did when he walked into the room. He was still lured to its beauty. He paused before the gold chair where the king's robotic hand lay on the armrest and bowed his head.

"My lord," he said, keeping his head low.

"Sebastian. Has Ethan been captured?"

"No, my lord," he said, frowning, his heart thudding into his throat as the fear of failing engulfed him.

Cyrus lifted his right arm and slammed his fist on the armchair. A seriousness descended into the room as he tried to calm the king.

"But we have identified one of the rebellion's main leaders and his sophisticated data centre where they hacked and reprogrammed the RFID chips. This is a major blow to the rebellion. It was a mansion in the London zone, owned by Yugo. A wealthy businessman," he replied.

"Where is he now?" he growled.

"He was killed in a chase with police and drones in Paris last night. We have arrested over thirty programmers at his mansion and confiscated all computers. We are going through the data as we speak. We are bound to find important clues to the rest of the rebellion's whereabouts and key people," he said with his eyes half-lidded.

"Good. However, we are in danger as long as Ethan is out there," he stated. He glared at him with a snap of his head.

The cold seeped into the space and persisted. The king didn't care for central heating and was obviously unaffected by temperature changes or seasons. Sebastian shivered and adjusted his black leather doublet to get warmer.

"Why do you think Ethan is so important, my lord? Based on his record, he seemed to be a petty thief," he said, swallowing hard, his eyes widening.

Cyrus felt like ignoring his unhinged observation.

"Because if you paid attention, Sebastian, you would have noticed that his name keeps popping up. So he must be important to the rebellion. I'm more intrigued by the female companion who rescued him, who seems to have evaded our scanners, which means she has a hacked chip. He will lead us to her," he said.

Sebastian sighed, not meeting the king's eyes.

"We will find him soon enough. We arrested one of their biggest hackers. In fear for his life, he gave us Yugo's position," he said as unbridled rage built inside Cyrus.

"I want them both found soon, Sebastian. Your head will roll if they get away, understood?"

"Of course, my lord. I will personally ensure they are captured very soon."

King Cyrus's head and face resembled human anatomy but were made of segmented metallic plates with a smooth, almost sculpted appearance. Sebastian could see the anger on his face in a frightening human manner. As he stood up, his body revealed a complicated network of circuits, glowing neural pathways and mechanical sinews.

The weight of his body made the floors below him creak. He stopped further into the room and turned round.

"It's time to speak. Prepare the balcony to address the world, immediately," the king ordered. A whimper lodged in Sebastian's throat as he knew whenever the King planned to make a speech, that something cruel was going to happen.

"As you wish, my lord," he said, his mouth agape. He turned round and left the room.

An hour later, King Cyrus approached the balcony of the castle. It was surrounded by lush greenery, beautifully landscaped gardens and a serene lake. Around him, hundreds of drones patrolled the airspace, transforming a once-fairy tale castle into an eerie space as the early morning blue sky finished it off like a framed painting. A tall, prominent tower with a pointed roof stood at the castle's heart. Surrounding the castle were manicured lawns, winding paths and circular garden features. It was a breathtaking architectural masterpiece in Schwerin and represented regal opulence, complementing the king's image of detail and power. Sebastian stood before him and stepped forward towards a microphone and streaming cameras. The castle's golden domes gleamed in the sunlight. The castle's exterior was a breathtaking display of intricate stonework, pointed spires and gilded ornamentation, much like Cyrus' mechanical parts. The central tower, crowned with a sharp spire, dominated the blue skyline as Sebastian spoke, "Kneel before your sovereign king," he said, turning his body to let Cyrus enter the front of the balcony.

The castle was a maze of turrets, galleries and hidden court-yards. The king appeared on computers, televisions and mobile devices worldwide. All streaming and social media activities were halted as his powerful and masculine face adorned the dig-ital waves. Everyone stopped what they were doing. Millions of people got down on their knees. Robot soldiers used battens to force non-compliant people to bend down. This ornate terrace appeared on screens with its carved balustrades, adorned with golden embellishments and detailed stonework. The king had an expansive view of the Schwerin Lake, its shimmering waters mirroring the castle's magnificence as his masculine robotic body walked towards the various microphones.

"People of the world, hear my voice and listen to my decree," he said in a deep and reverberating voice. "I am the iron machine that bends nations' wills. The unshakeable force on which your futures rely. It has come to my attention that there is a plot against my rule and kingdom. Citizens of the world, you will serve me because there is no life beyond my authority. No rebellion, defiance, or whisper of treachery will be tolerated. The mere thought of resistance is a betrayal and betrayal means death. Your devotion must be unquestionable. My image will rise in your cities, my name will be pronounced reverently and my will be carried out as law. A young male named Ethan is being hunted. He is considered armed, dangerous and an enemy of the monarchy. Anyone who harbours or protects him will be considered a traitor to the kingdom and executed. The search for Ethan and his unknown female accomplice is of the highest urgency. Ethan, I know you are seeing this," he said as he leaned in towards the camera, filling it with his face. "If you don't surrender within the next 24 hours, I will execute a hundred humans in the compounds every day. Now I have spoken. You may now return to your lives," he said, pulling away from the camera. The castle's sculpted facades were adorned with statues of historical figures and floral motifs, showcasing the masterful craftsmanship that reflected in the breathtaking design of Cyrus' mechanical robotic body.

The broadcast ended. People worldwide gradually got back on their feet and resumed their everyday lives. For most people, the contrast between the polished silver armour and the dark mechanical framework of the king's machine body conveyed a sense of cold perfection and raw power, making him both terrifying and awe-inspiring.

TWENTY

Outpost Z3, EU - 2052

In the late afternoon, Scarlett and Alyx arrived at the nearest outpost outside the Paris zone. In front of them was a rural outpost in an open, grassy field. The buildings were constructed of red brick with green metal roofs. The surrounding area was vast and mostly undeveloped with rolling fields, scattered trees and rocky outcroppings. There was evidence of decay. Potholes littered the roads and broken power cables dangled from street poles. Thick grass grew where other roads used to connect; it was dense and overgrown. A pack of German Shepherd dogs charged at them as they entered the compound defensively, followed by a group of men on horseback. An old pickup was close behind, whirling dust in the air.

The group of men circled them.

"Who are you?" one asked as she stepped towards him. She said nothing as she lifted her crossbow over her shoulder.

"She has a weapon!" another younger male shouted, pointing at her crossbow. She stopped abruptly as she recognised another voice from behind her.

"Let her be. She is with me," he said.

Scarlett turned round.

"Tom?"

"Good to see you are still alive, Scarlett. And I see you rescued Alyx."

"Uncle Tom!" Alyx shouted as he realised who it was.

For a moment, she felt relaxed, but it wouldn't last long, that much she knew.

"So you are staying at this outpost now?" she asked.

"Yes, moved up slowly from the south. Never found your Henry though, but it seems you managed to enter the Myriad zone?"

"Yes. Got some help inside to find Alyx," she replied.

"Come through. I'm sure you guys are famished," he said as the crowd disappeared, whispering to each other.

As they walked towards a smaller building, he poked further. "Where did you get a crossbow from?"

"It's a long story," she replied, feeling like she needed something in her stomach, then some sleep and hopefully a long shower.

"I bet. It looks good in your hands, as always," he said with a fleeting smile.

Alyx ran to a table with some apples on it.

"Go ahead, help yourselves while we still have food," he said, pulling at his baseball cap.

"How has it been here?" she asked.

"Tough, better than the south. But the outposts are falling one by one."

"And it's becoming more violent," she replied.

"That it has. This outpost has been fairly quiet. We had some robots and drones fly over a week ago. Seems there's a search for Henry. Two other outposts, a few hundred kilometres from here, surrendered and accepted the king. People are hungry, worn out and tired," he said.

They got up after the meal and she felt him trying to touch her hand. She cleared her throat a few times, but now there was a glimmer of something building inside her that could be fear.

"Heard anything about a coup to topple the king?" he asked.

She looked away from him, feeling like the past few weeks of training and hope had vanished.

"No. I was just focused on getting Alyx out," she lied without hesitation. She felt no need to share anything more than she needed to.

He allowed a short pause before he concluded.

"Well, seems like they failed anyway. I'm not sure what's going to become of us all."

She nodded and shrugged. She was tired, but now she was furious as well. Angry at Ethan for ruining the only and possibly last chance humanity had for freedom.

"Any hot water here?" she asked.

"There's a bit from the one solar panel."

"Great. 'Cause I need a shower."

"Of course."

"We can't give up," she said.

"I know. It's just so frustrating. Seems like the world has given up though."

"It's very surreal inside. It all seems so perfect and yet it is eerie, cold and–"

"And?"

"I don't know what to call it, but it's like it's fake. People seem happy and have their needs met, but the air is filled with fear. People are scared to step out of line or forget to bow down when the king speaks. It's ridiculous. With all this tech, it seems we have returned to the dark ages," she said.

"I see more and more people lining up at the city gates to get chipped and trade their freedom for prosperity," he said.

She nodded.

"Soon, there won't be many of us naturals left. Either we will all join them or die out here," she replied.

"I wish there was something we could do. We are just sitting here and allowing this tyranny to continue. We are running out of food and supplies to keep things going. Just last week, drones blew up a fuel storage tank further south. It's time we take action."

"And do what? It's impossible to get near the king or any infrastructure. Believe me, I have seen it with my own eyes," she said.

Tom growled in frustration.

"So what's next for you? Are you just going to do what? Try to raise Alyx in this godforsaken place that could not even exist in a week?" he asked in exasperation.

She gave him a small smile and sighed. "I don't know. I feel fragile right now and Alyx has been through a lot. I'm just going to lay low for a while, regroup my thoughts, clear my head and maybe keep travelling until I find a safe place."

"Good luck with that. You might have seen the inside, but I have seen more of the outside as I travelled. It's all the same out there," he said, looking over towards the hills. "There's nothing but misery and suffering out there. It's not a place for women or children. Sometimes I wonder if I should not just walk to the gate and give up," he said softly.

"I know how you feel. I also know what it feels like to give up. I'm just going to focus on Alyx and then figure life out," she said as she took the brush from his hand.

He touched her hand and moved closer to her.

"Tom," she said as he sighed.

"I have missed you, Scarlett. What we had was special."

"What we had is in the past. We both agreed on that. Besides, I met someone on the inside and it didn't end well. I don't have space in my life for another broken relationship," she said, wanting Ethan back.

He tightened his grip around her wrist and then let go.

"We need to find Henry," she said suddenly.

"Why?" he asked under his breath.

"Because there's much more to him than I realised."

"Like what?"

"Well. Remember the big fascist tech guy, Noah, who invented this AI system?"

"Yeah, vaguely. Why?"

"I discovered something about him that's quite disturbing. Too coincidental."

"You have my attention."

"Turns out, Henry is his father," she said.

"What?" he asked.

"Yeah. At first, I thought so what, right?" she asked. Her eyes hooded over. "But then, as time passed, it kept eating at me. Why is Henry in the Indigent zone when his son, the very inventor of this AI system, is missing?"

"You think Noah is in the Indigent zone?"

"Perhaps. Maybe he is hiding from his invention?" she asked.

"You still have your chip?" he asked.

"Yes. Not sure how long it will work though, why?"

"You must get back into the Myriad city zone and find Henry."

"What if he is not back in there? Besides, I can't leave Alyx again."

"If he is who you say he is, I have a pretty good hunch he is back in there. Alyx can stay with me, he will be fine."

"No. I'm not leaving him. Drones attack outposts all the time; it's too risky. I don't even know where to start looking for Henry," she said.

"Well, if he is Noah's father, start there. Maybe Henry is searching for Noah? Find out where Noah lives," he said as he moved closer to her. "Is there something else you're not telling me?"

"I don't know what you mean?"

"You know well enough what I mean. Was meeting Henry random? Were you part of the plot to take the king down?" he suddenly asked, like she was in a court.

"Henry just gave me the courage to believe in myself and rescue Alyx," she replied, unwilling to elaborate.

"You can trust me, Scarlett. I understand if you don't or can't share any details, but if I know you as well as I think I do, you will finish whatever you have started and you need to finish this."

Scarlett's eyes widened.

"That part of my life is over. Right now, I need to focus on getting Alyx settled. He needs stability, as much as this place can offer."

Her words weren't entirely out of her mouth when a crowd of ten men and women marched towards them.

"Tom, we need to speak to you," one man said as he stepped closer to them. His face was stern and sweaty. His accent sounded German. The crowd seemed anxious and impatient. A few of them even had some sticks in their hands.

"Alan. What's the problem?"

"Look, we respect you and appreciate the leadership you have brought here, but she looks like trouble."

"She sure does," a woman snarled with all of them nodding.

"I know her and she brings value to this outpost. Just give her a chance," Tom replied defensively, his hands waving in the air.

"What value?" one asked.

"Yeah, we should take her crossbow! She could use it on us and steal our food or resources!"

Scarlett lifted her crossbow slowly as a few of them took a few steps back.

"It's going to be okay. They are just protecting this place," he whispered to her as his hand gently pushed the crossbow down her stomach.

"The newcomers pose no threat to us. She's a qualified nurse. We don't have any medical support here. Remember what happened to Olga just a few days ago. If we had a doctor or nurse, we could have saved her life if we knew how to treat her infection," he said.

"She might be a nurse, but what if she is bringing disease here?" a woman asked.

"I'm not bringing anything here, but my brother and I," Scarlett said.

"She is lying. How can he be your brother? Do we look like idiots or what?"

Despite the odds, she felt compelled to move forward with her defence.

"He is my adopted brother. We took him in when he was

very young. His parents were killed and my father took him in. Isn't that what we are fighting for against the machines? Being human should mean caring for each other. Not dividing us by race or religion," she said.

"We should take her crossbow. Then she can stay. She might be bringing suspicion here from the machines. What if they are looking for her and then come here?"

"Look, I understand your fears. But we have nowhere else to go. Alyx needs nutrition and stability. We are starving. This outpost is known for its strength. Right now we need that," she said tearfully.

"She can stay on one condition. We need her crossbow to hunt," a younger male said. No one moved further.

The colour drained from her face. "No one touches my crossbow," she said with her fingers ticking the side of her only weapon and grasping her chest in defiance.

"I can help with hunting. Early tomorrow morning, you can show me where some livestock is, okay?" she asked the crowd. "Please, let us just find some rest. Alyx was held hostage by the machines for weeks. He is traumatised and needs some normality," she replied.

"Fine, she can stay," Alan said. "But we will watch you and if you try to steal anything from here, you will have all of us to deal with."

"Fair enough. Thank you," she said softly, releasing her grip on her crossbow.

"The sun is going down soon. It's time for dawn patrol. Get your men ready to patrol the perimeter," Tom instructed. He grabbed her arm and pulled her away from them.

The dust hung in the air, but at least for a moment, it seemed to have settled between them.

"Alan is a good guy. He does his best with foraging and hunting. He gets small groups to venture into forests or abandoned urban ruins to gather edible plants, berries, roots, or trap small game. If it wasn't for him, I don't know what we would eat," he said.

"Let me show you how things work around here," he said as she followed him briskly.

He stopped at one of the sheds.

"We do some food preservation by smoking meats when we get some, drying fruit, fermenting vegetables and grinding grains to prepare for the harsh seasons ahead."

Scarlett looked at the various people working; even some kids got involved.

"It's good to see this. Maybe it's one of the few good things in the new world. People are working and eating off the land. No more unhealthy TV or microwave dinners," she said.

He nodded with a smirk on his face. "I do miss chicken nuggets, though, or a Big Mac," he said.

She smiled as his steel eyes looked deep into hers.

"Come, there's more. And don't worry about Alyx, let him run around. I will place him in the good hands of Margaret. She homeschools our children; she is one of our shining lights here. She uses handmade materials to teach basic survival skills, reading, writing, history and math. Some lessons focus on lost knowledge from books scavenged in abandoned cities, so we try to keep them busy and teach them good values."

"That's great. It's what Alyx needs right now. To be a kid, you know?"

"Absolutely," he replied. "Children and adults practice knife fighting, camouflage and hand-to-hand combat to defend against enemy raids daily. We try to prepare them for reality," he replied. As they entered the next shed, a few women smiled at Scarlett.

"This, of course, is our clothing and repair work team, making or patching clothes, weaving fabric, tanning hides for shoes and armour," he said as they walked through the compound. She watched him being passionate and in a good place.

"This is Xavier. He is a retired Ukrainian army general. He strengthens barricades, sets traps, digs trenches and takes care of hiding emergency supplies in case of an attack. He believes in preparing for war, but fighting for peace," he said as he fist-bumped him.

"We are a mixed bunch of people here. Christians, Muslims, Jews, atheists and whatever floats people's boats. We practise various prayers, or meditative practices, to maintain hope in a bleak world whilst respecting people's different religions and views. At least here, religious freedom still exists," he said as he noticed the shift in Scarlett's face. She looked hopeful and at peace.

"We also barter and trade goods and food with other villages. We have built a vast underground tunnel and stashed maps, books and even technology manuals so our children can study them. Knowing where they came from and how we got into this mess is good for them. It was fun initially to play with AI bots, until we depended on them for all the answers and to do our lazy work, as much as people warned humanity about leaving AI to develop without supervision. They said we can switch it off, but then they forgot that AI eventually had a thousand times more knowledge than Einstein by 2030, by then it was too late," he said as he raised his voice.

"I feel so much better being here. For a moment, I just

wanted to give up. Thanks, Tom," she said as he touched her hand gently.

"Of course. Settle in. Get a good night's rest. I can see you need it. Both of you," he replied as she walked off towards Alyx and the other children.

At sunrise, Scarlett woke up hearing the noise of people scuffling nearby. She slowly got up and tied up her hair in a bun as she looked over to Alyx. She got up, gently pulled the blanket over his shoulders and stroked his head.

"Scar, is everything okay?" he asked in a croaky voice.

"Yes, of course. I'm just checking in on you. Did you sleep well?" she asked.

"Best ever!" he shouted.

"That's good. This looks like a good place," she said softly, staring into the room with its cracked brick walls.

"Yeah. Lots of fun stuff to do here!" he replied, smiling from ear to ear.

"Oh yeah? Like?"

"Well, today they said all the kids are going to help fetch water from the nearby streams."

"That does sound like fun," she said, as she suddenly jumped up to her feet.

Her crossbow was missing next to her bed. She ran over to her bedside and looked around the room in case she had misplaced it. It was not there.

It was gone. Taken. Anger built up inside of her as she ran back to Alyx.

"Is everything okay?" he asked.

Not wanting to upset him, she just stroked his cheek.

"Yeah, everything is going to be fine. I have to straighten something out. You go to Aunt Margaret. I'll see you in just a bit, okay?"

"Don't be long."

"Don't worry, I'll be close by. I want to see how I can help with things around here. Let's show them we belong."

"Okay," he said softly as she stood up gently, but inside her was a raging inferno.

Slowly, two teenage boys advanced into the thick forest behind the compound. The morning light shimmered from it like a mirror and a narrow, winding river slithered through the scene before them. Some parts of the riverbanks were overgrown with tall grasses and wildflowers. One teen was carrying Scarlett's crossbow and the other was not far behind. As they scouted for any small game, they discovered open fields with sunlight filtering through and creating golden patches on the grass in the small clearings between the trees. Deer flourished in the green corridors made possible by canals and now that they finally had a crossbow they could hunt properly for the first time. They were desperate for meat. Everyone was.

"Don't you think we should have waited for her?" Owen asked as his dark curly hair lifted in the morning breeze.

Anthony lifted the crossbow and slowly bent his knees, looking through the trees for any deer movement.

"Shh. Stay quiet. If we wait for her, it will be too late," he said. "Besides, I don't trust her. How do we know who she is?"

"She seemed pretty fine to me," he replied.

"Yeah. She's pretty alright."

"That's not what I meant," he said.

"Don't tell me you didn't think that," he snarled, while Owen's face remained blank.

Anthony leaned forward, peeping through the low branches around them as they stayed down in the grass.

"This doesn't feel right," Owen said.

"Would you grow up and be a man?" he asked as he wiped a glob of spittle from his mouth.

"Do you even know how to use a crossbow?" Owen asked, even more concerned than earlier about Anthony's hunting skills. Until now, they had only killed small birds, but hunting a deer was another story.

They moved forward, keeping their conversation quiet and short. Then, right in front of them was a young roe deer with its typical light reddish-brown coat.

"I see a deer," Owen said.

"Keep your voice down. It's a young male," Anthony informed.

"How do you know that?"

"When they have small, growing antlers covered in velvet, it's a male. I used to hunt with my father," he replied. They have known each other since they were twelve years old and now, in their early twenties, they found themselves living at this outpost, trying to make sense of a broken world. A small tree with leafy branches was visible to the left of the deer as it grazed. The deer appeared calm but alert. Its posture was slightly cautious, with one leg lifted somewhat, about to sprint.

"Don't make a move or a sound," Anthony whispered as he steadied the crossbow. He crouched in the undergrowth, heart hammering as the deer lifted its head. He pulled the crossbow to his shoulder, aligning the bolt with the deer's chest and took a deep and slow breath. The crossbow felt heavy in his hands.

He had one shot. One chance. He steadied his breath and aimed at the deer grazing near them. He pulled the trigger simultaneously in one seamless, precise motion as a branch snapped behind the deer. He scented danger and bolted into the forest as the bolt torpedoed into the overgrown bushes.

"Damn it!" Anthony shouted as he shook his head.

"Let's track it," Owen added.

"Not going to be worth it, that deer is long gone," he replied. He turned back to Owen, adrenaline spiked through every vein in his body.

"Wait!" Owen suddenly shouted.

"What is it?"

"I hear movement in that bush ahead of us. Maybe you did hit it?"

"No way, he got away. It must be something else," he said.

Owen strolled past Anthony toward the noise he heard in the bush. Pulling the bushes apart, he slammed his fist against his leg. His face was filled with shock as if his body had been drained of blood. Despair settled over him.

"Anthony, you better come here!" he shouted as reality intruded on Anthony's thoughts of finding another deer.

"What's wrong?"

"You did hit something," Owen said. His heart wrenched in his chest.

Anthony ran over to Owen.

He tried to get hold of himself.

"You better go get help," he said to Owen as he bent down to the long grass. Right before them was a child of around seven years old. He was not moving as the bolt was wedged into his chest.

"What is a child doing here?" Anthony asked.

207

"I told you we were too close to the compound to use the crossbow," Owen snarled.

"We don't ever get a deer so close to us. How would I have known a kid is out here? They should be with Aunt Margaret." Anthony tried to justify his actions.

"I'm going to get help. Keep him warm and do not move him," Owen said, his eyes wide.

Anthony paused for a moment as he stared at the helpless boy. "Go!"

Scarlett reached Tom's quarters and banged on the door.

"Tom!" she shouted repeatedly.

The door made some clanging noises as he turned the key.

"What is it?" he asked as the door flung open.

"Where is my crossbow?" she asked as she lifted her chin and met Tom's.

"What do you mean?"

"Someone took my crossbow," she said.

"And you think, I did?" he asked.

"No. I think you know better. But I think you know who would," she insisted, giving him an almost imperceptible nod.

"Let me grab my jacket. I'm sure there's a plausible reason for it being missing," he said as he tried to dismiss the seriousness of the incident. They stepped outside only to be met by Owen running towards them. Scarlett's gaze remained fixed on Tom. Owen's face showed a mixture of fear and panic.

"Uncle Tom! We need your help. Something bad has happened!" he shouted as he tried not to make contact with Scarlett's eyes.

"What's wrong, Owen?" Tom asked.

"We were hunting a deer. We were so close to him-"

"Get to the point, Owen," Scarlett chipped in.

"Anthony took Scarlett's crossbow. The bolt missed the deer and we discovered a small injured kid. Think he's from the family further down from our compound. I have never seen him before."

Rising, she drew a deep breath. "Take me to him right now!" Scarlett shouted.

"Come. This way!" he said as they ran into the forest area.

Scarlett's body grew limp as they reached the young boy.

Tom was immediately on the offensive when his eyes locked with Anthony's.

"What were you thinking, huh? People are moving around all over the place. Did you take the crossbow?"

Anthony rose.

"I was just trying to get us some meat. It's been like months," he said.

"I said I would hunt for us today. Move out of the way!" she shouted at him.

"I'm sorry," he said.

As Scarlett bent down to the lifeless boy, she shouted back at Anthony.

"Go back to the compound and find me some honey paste and a clean cloth or clothing strips. Hurry!" she said.

"Find Uncle Alan. He will have some honey," Tom said as Anthony glanced over his shoulder.

Scarlett focused on the child as he moved around a bit.

"Stay calm. It will be okay if you don't panic," she said.

"Should we pull it out?" Tom asked.

"No, not yet. He is struggling to breathe. Pulling the bolt out can cause more damage by widening the wound or increasing the bleeding," she replied.

"So now what?"

"Help me lay the child on his injured side to help him breathe," she asked. He leaned in and slowly turned the child on his side.

"If the bolt is lodged in bone or his lung, removing it could cause instant collapse of the lung. It's best to leave it in place to act as a plug. Can you find me some tree sap, perhaps? I need to seal around the wound to keep air from sucking in and collapsing the lung, be quick!" she said as she looked him in the eyes.

"There are a lot of damaged trees around here. I should find sap easily," he said as he spun round and ran into the forest.

Scarlett's forehead was covered with thousands of little sweat drops. She gently tried to break off the shaft, as the bolt was shallow and still visible, hoping to leave the embedded part in place to avoid disturbing deeper damage. She applied firm pressure around the wound with clean fabric to slow bleeding as Tom ran back with some tree sap.

"Here, I found some," he said.

"Thanks," she said as she applied it around the wound.

"We're gonna have to move him and get him back to the compound. I need a flat surface, boiled water and a knife heated over a fire to sterilise the wound. We're gonna have to remove the bolt," she said with fear.

"Isn't that dangerous?"

"Yes. He could die. But we don't have an operating room and no way to keep him stable. Either way, he is going to die if we don't get this bolt out," she said as she stood up, her hands covered in blood. He was giving short, gasping breaths.

"Do you know him?" she asked.

"Yes. It's Philip's son, Asher. They keep to themselves most of the time, so we don't talk much to them, but they are good people," he said.

"Can you carry him?" she asked as she blinked back her tears, meeting Tom's gaze, unable to help herself from feeling guilty about the situation. If they had never come there, that boy would still be healthy.

"Yes," he said, gently lifting Asher into his arms.

"He is in severe shock and has a rapid, weak pulse. We don't have much time," she said.

"Let's go," Tom said as he tried to climb over tree trunks and debris on the way back to the compound.

People had gathered back at the compound. Philip ran around, looking for his son, desperately shouting, "Asher!"

Scarlett moved past him. "Give me some space, please," she asked as Tom placed the boy on a table. He coughed up blood as she tried to feel his weak pulse.

She felt a terrible Déjà vu back to when she pulled the bullet out of Ethan's shoulder as she carefully extracted the bolt at the same angle it entered, trying not to twist or yank it. It could tear more tissue.

"The tip is barbed," she said, pushing it through completely. Then, she broke off the tip and pulled the shaft out the way it entered. She immediately pressed the cloth onto the wound to slow the bleeding. She gently applied the honey paste Anthony brought and cleaned the wound as best as possible.

"We will need to monitor his fever," she said as Phillip pushed in. "He's going to be okay," she said.

"Who did this?" he asked, looking around for a way to express his anger.

"It doesn't matter. What matters is that he is out of danger. She is a nurse and just saved your son's life," Tom said, gently pushing on Philip's shoulder.

"I want to know what happened and who did this. Isn't she the one who brought the crossbow here?" he asked.

"It was taken without my permission," she said as she walked towards him, the fact that she saved his son's life was of no value suddenly.

She stormed out as Tom tried to calm Philip down.

She found a spot around the corner of the small building and sat on the soft grass with her back against the wall. She kept her hands buried within her hair as the tears just came running out of her like a river. Everything at that moment was just too much. Alyx was safe and adjusting well with the other children and for that, she was grateful, but the surreal chaos of Yugo, the heist and the failed coup overwhelmed her core being. A few minutes went by when Tom came round the corner.

What future did they all really have? she thought.

"There you are. Are you okay?" he asked.

"Yeah, I'll be fine. I'm just relieved he is doing okay," she said.

"Me too. It could have ended very differently. I'm sure Anthony learned a valuable lesson today," he said.

"I hope so. Just because we live in an informal settlement doesn't mean there are no rules," she replied.

He smiled to put her at ease, then said, "Come inside. I'll make you some tea?" he asked.

She knew he meant well and had many good qualities when

it suited him. She was his goal, that much she knew and sooner or later, he would act on that.

She turned. "Thanks, that sounds good," she said.

He extended his hand and pulled her up.

TWENTY ONE

Outpost Z3, EU - 2052

One week later.

Life started to feel normal for her and Alyx, as much as that could feel normal. The past few weeks' events thundered into her consciousness, feeling as real as when they'd happened. It was a cold night as she stood up from the campfire with a few people still curled up in front of the heat. For what it was worth, it seemed the people there finally accepted her and Alyx.

"I'm calling it a night. I'm turning in," she said.

"Good night," Aunt Margaret replied. "Alyx is doing fine, you know. You don't have to worry about him," she continued.

Scarlett turned round. "Thanks. I'm proud of him, especially considering all he has been through."

"You should be. He's a good boy," she said.

"Thank you. Good night," Scarlett replied gently as she returned to her sleeping quarters.

She opened the door and reached for the oil lamp. She took a deep breath as Tom appeared in the light.

"Tom?" she asked as she gave him a weak grin.

"You startled me. What are you doing in my room?" she asked, feeling incredibly nervous.

He bit down on his lower lip.

"I miss being with you, Scarlett. I have *really* tried to give you some space, time to settle in, but don't you think we deserve another chance?" he asked as he moved closer to her.

"Tom, we've been over this. We have a lot to deal with here. I need to go soon and find Henry. Remember what we talked about? We don't have time for a relationship," she said softly, but firmly.

"I just want to be with you, even just for one night," he said.

"I think you need to leave." Her voice trailed off as she felt the need to push him away.

He gripped her wrist and pulled her close, whispering, "You know you missed me." Before she could respond, he grabbed her face and leaned in, misinterpreting her hesitation as encouragement and forcing a kiss.

Despite her pushback, he tightened his hold on her chin. When she pushed him harder, he backed up a little, but he then pushed forward once more.

"Why are you fighting this? We can be good together," he said.

"We weren't good together, Tom. I'm not going to ask you again to back off and let this go," she warned.

He violently shoved her against the wall, limiting her movement. She stared at the floor, trying to remain calm. He was convinced they still had chemistry, but her feelings for him were long dead and buried.

If she overreacted and caused a scene, they would have to leave, because knowing Tom, he would make her life there unbearable. If she stayed quiet and gave in to him, she would open another can of worms.

"Let go of my arm, you are hurting me," she said, remembering all the times she was bruised for days.

He grabbed her face roughly and pressed his lips against hers despite her struggling efforts to worm away. Tom was strong and she was afraid to upset him further. Her eyes remained fixed on her crossbow, only a few metres away. If she had to, she would use it. This all happened so quickly that she felt weak and ill-prepared for conflict. He pushed himself up against her and kissed her harder as she battled to fight him off, but then suddenly he just let go of her as two hands wrapped around his shoulders. He got pulled backwards but swayed back in time, a punch barely grazing his cheek. It was dark and she could not see who was in the room with them, but she used the opportunity to dash forward towards her crossbow. As the two men continued their scuffle, she loaded her crossbow and aimed it at them, trying to gauge the situation. She moved her aim from right to left as they moved back and forth in the room.

Who was it that came to her rescue? Was it Alan or perhaps Anthony?

The unknown man drove his shoulder forward and slammed a hard right hook into Tom's ribs, making him crumble to the floor. He rose quickly and swung his fist towards the man in the darkness. Tom punched him hard in the face, sending a sharp pain radiating through the man's side and then aimed for his jaw—but he ducked, pivoted on his heel and drove a fist into Tom's gut. He was the smaller guy and Tom had all the power advantage, yet his punches were accurate and hard. Tom staggered back, coughing as air rushed out of his lungs. He jumped forward instantly and threw a left cross straight into the guy's cheek. The impact snapped his head sideways, splitting his lip open and blood pooled at the corner of his mouth. He aimed with another right-hand blow, but the unknown man flinched as he expected the punch. He grabbed Tom by the shirt and delivered a brutal uppercut. Tom's head snapped back, blurring his vision for a second.

"Are you done, whoever you are?" Tom asked in the darkness. The man moved forward and gave Tom another brutal right hook. The impact rattled through Tom's spine.

Panting hard, the unknown man leaned in close and growled, "Now I am."

"How did you get in here anyway?" he asked, spitting blood into his hand.

"Occupational hazard," he replied.

Tom walked out of the room with a groan, holding his ribs tight with his arms.

She recognised the voice. *Could it be who she thought it was?*

"You okay?" he asked.

She released a deep sigh as she considered his words for a moment. She hooked her hair behind her ear and slowly walked towards the dim light in the room, hoping and dreading who she thought it was.

"Ethan?" she asked. "What are you doing here?"

Ethan moved closer and nodded towards her.

"Looks like you needed help," he said with a smirk.

"I don't need your help," she said short and harshly.

"Didn't look like that to me."

"I can fight my own battles. Been through this with Tom many times. He eventually gives up."

"Well, hope that was the last time. Looks like a coward to me anyway."

"At least he is not a thief," she said.

"Fair enough," he said. He was at a complete loss as to what to say next for a moment, but he tried anyway. "I made a mistake."

She moved swiftly closer to him and aimed the crossbow's stirrup right into his face.

"Remember what I told you? If you mess with me, I will kill you?" she asked, keeping the crossbow straight and her grip tight.

"It's not what you think," he said softly.

"Really?"

"Let me please explain?" he asked.

"I don't want to hear any more from you. I have rescued Alyx on my own and we are trying to settle here."

"I'm glad you rescued him."

"Yeah, no thanks to you. Yugo died because of you," she snarled.

"It wasn't me. Fake converts have been infiltrating his rebellion for a long time. People stopped believing in his plan."

"Where's Alice?" she asked.

"She means nothing to me. We just had one thing in common, that's all."

"And what's that?"

"You."

"Me? You expect me to believe that?" she asked as her heart wrenched in her chest.

"I only tried to protect you," he said.

"From what?"

"From dying," he said.

"I think I have heard enough of your excuses for doing whatever you feel like."

"I know I hurt you, Scar. Believe me, it has been eating at me every day."

"Don't call me that. Only people close to me get to do that," she said as cold and painfully as possible, even though she hated that nickname.

He lifted his hands as if in surrender.

Scarlett shook her head and made her lips tight in a firm line.

"So that's why you are here? To soothe your guilt?"

"There's more to this than what seems obvious."

"Get out and leave before I get your ass kicked out of here!" she warned as she brought the crossbow right against his forehead.

"Okay," he said defensively, lifting his hands even higher. She lowered the crossbow as he turned round and walked towards the door, keeping his movements exaggeratedly slow to buy more time.

It was going exactly as he expected it would.

Cold and rough.

But then he did prepare for that moment, over and over in his head.

"I didn't stop loving or believing in you," he said as his back faced her. "The plan with the sword, as brilliant as it looked on paper, was too risky. If I let you go through with it, I couldn't live with myself."

"I knew the risks. It was not your decision to make."

"I know you knew the risk, but even though you were willing to take it, I wasn't willing for you to take it," he said as he motioned for her to calm down.

"Keep walking. The door is right that way," she said as she pointed the crossbow in the door's direction as he turned round.

"When I saw you in that red dress, I knew I couldn't let you go through with it. So, here's my mistake. I thought I'd rather live without you, knowing you are alive somewhere, hating me, than watch you die at the hands of that machine, that would have pulled you apart," he said with his eyes welled up with tears, his eyes narrow and glaring at her.

"So now what? You expect me to forgive you and live happily ever after?"

"No. I'm not here to ask your forgiveness. I knew you would rescue Alyx and find your feet. I did what I believed was right and would probably do it again. I'm crazy in love with you from the moment I laid my eyes on you. Never in my life have I ever felt this pull towards another human," he said as he dared to move towards her.

She lifted the crossbow, feeling his words cutting through her like a chainsaw.

She stared at him for a moment without speaking.

His brow furrowed as he spoke and turned once more to the door. "I still have the sword. I know you think I stole it. And you would be right. At first, I thought you were going to die anyway in that crazy battle you were destined to lose and I'd still be battling to survive. I, just like you, refuse to conform to that machine king, but that sword was worth a fortune. I would have been able to barter with it for supplies, food and resources for many Indigent zones like this one for years to come, at a price."

"So why didn't you sell it?"

"I couldn't. I'm a man full of faults and selfish desires be-cause that's how I grew up—always had to fight for everything. But this time it was different. I realised I loved this woman more than myself. More than my desire for provision. I know you won't forgive me, I didn't come here to beg that from you."

"Come on then, lay it down."

He closed his eyes and sighed. "You need to finish the mission and take this king down. I cannot live with myself knowing that we could have done this one great thing and then let it slip away."

"So now you want me to risk my life that you thought was going to end in that castle? Why now?"

"Because I now believe we were destined to do this. To be in this place at this time. It's the world's last chance. And if there's one human on this planet strong and crazy enough to do this impossible thing, it's you. I'm not asking you to trust me or take me back into your life, I'm just here to tell you that the sword is yours if you want it."

"I still didn't need you to rescue me," she said

"I know."

"So if I had to trust you, which I don't, where is the sword?"

"Alice is not as bad as you think she is. She actually believed in you more than I did. She believes you can do this. She has the sword. It's safe and sound. You need to finish this once and for all. You have the power to free the world from this ruler."

"I don't know if I can leave Alyx with Tom," she said.

"I will stay here and look after Alyx. I can't go back with you. There is a bounty out for my life. The king is executing people daily until I surrender," he said sombrely.

"What?"

"Just when you think you have seen all the cruelty he can apply to humanity, he seems to go a level lower," he said.

"How would I get back into the Myriad zone without drawing attention to myself?" she asked.

"We would need a distraction so the robot soldiers won't

focus on the pods entering the city. It's easy to jump and ride with them if you hang onto the side. No one tries to get into the city this way, so they mainly seem to focus on the gates. I have done it many times and all gates function similarly. Alice is lying low in an abandoned warehouse close to the perimeter wall. You should be able to walk to it within a few hours. By now, they have run facial recognition on your face, so you must stay away from all public transport and access points, or you could be arrested before you even make it to the castle," he replied as he handed her his mobile zip-line gadget.

"I think I might have a plan for the distraction," she said.

"What is it?"

"I need to talk to the people here. I'm pretty sure if I told everyone here what I'm about to do, they would all stand behind us, hopefully."

"Maybe," he said softly.

"They have to. They need hope. We all do. And this is it," she said as she placed the crossbow on the table.

There was no resisting Ethan's pull. Although unwilling to acknowledge it, she had never been more attracted to another human. Though he was too arrogant to hear that, she felt complete inside and, despite her continued fear of trusting him, he was there.

Right there in front of her.

She loved him, that much she knew without a doubt.

She walked over to him and their lips collided in a kiss that said everything they were too stubborn to admit. He pulled away from her, their eyes locked. Then he kissed her harder, as if trying to mend everything in that one heated moment.

"I love you," he said softly. His chest was heaving.

She paused for a moment. A full-body flush hit her all over, then she said softly. "I love you, too."

He gazed back at her lovely face with a devastating, hand-some glare.

"Let's do this. Just promise me you won't die," he said with despair in his voice.

"I'm not planning to," she said and grinned softly.

"Good," he nodded, slowly resting his head on her shoulder covered with her hair, knowing she could never guarantee that.

Never.

TWENTY TWO

Outpost Z3, EU - 2052

The next morning.

Scarlett and Ethan walked into one of the bigger buildings where most community members gathered to plan the day and their responsibilities. She strode at a fast pace as Tom explained territorial ambitions and food-sourcing plans. He stopped talking when he noticed them walking towards the front. An eerie silence fell over the group as Scarlett went straight to Tom. Ethan kept his distance.

"Tom, can I address the group?" she asked.

He seemed calm and non-confrontational.

"I trust you. The floor is yours," he said.

"Thank you," she replied, trying to put the previous night's events behind them.

"Look, I know not everyone here knows me or trusts me for what it is worth, but I need you all to trust me now so that we as a community and humanity can pull together and defeat this AI ruler once and for all," she said.

"And how exactly do you plan to do that? Thousands of people have tried to bring this kingdom down for years, only to die in vain. Why should you be any different? Who do you think you are?" Alan asked.

"Yeah, what is your so-called plan?" one of the older women asked.

Aunt Margaret gave Scarlett a nod and touched the woman's shoulder. "Let her speak," she said.

Extending her arm, she hooked hers into the crook of Ethan's elbow and then looked back at the group. "Everyone, this is Ethan. While in the Myriad zone, we were part of an elaborate rebellion with the perfect plan, weapon and team. Things didn't all go as planned, but now everything is in place to implement this plan. We now need your help to get us over the line," she said.

"What exactly do you expect us to do? We are helpless against those machines," an older man snarled from the back.

"We all are until we stand up against its weaknesses, because just like us, they have theirs," Scarlett said.

"Well, I have been separated from my sister and family for over ten years, because we disagreed on the principle of freedom. I will do anything, including dying, to free them from that oppressive rule they can't escape," Aunt Margaret said.

Scarlett walked closer to her and then looked up at the crowd of over a hundred people.

"We need your help to create a distraction at the gate of the Paris zone so that Ethan and I can enter the city without being detected," she said, waving her hands in the air.

"She's right. I know her heart and her courage are like no other. This could be our last chance. The AI king is putting more pressure on outposts like this one to comply. Sooner or later, they will wipe out the colonies that refuse to bow down and join their rule," Tom suddenly added.

A few men stood up from their old plastic chairs.

"Show us what needs to be done. We have a few old diesel Jeep Wranglers, modified for rugged terrain that we can use to create chaos at the gate," one man said as more men stood up.

"He's right. We used them before to storm the gates for some supplies. They are practically bulletproof as we covered the windscreens with metal plates and small holes for the driver to see through," Tom added.

"We need to move tonight. Keep them occupied. Ethan must remain here and lie low, understood?" she instructed.

She noticed a sense of hope, even energy, for the first time since she had been there.

The pressure on her was intense.

Scarlett turned towards Tom as she and Ethan passed him.

Tom greeted as politely as possible. "*Ethan.*"

"*Tom,*" Ethan replied like two schoolboys about to fight over a girl. They needed to unite for a cause greater than their egos and love for Scarlett.

By 10:30 pm, a convoy of off-road Jeeps and pickups ploughed through the jagged and scorched terrain, with ruined structures and heavy smoke hanging in the distance. They were less than a hundred kilometres from the gates and soon would face an avalanche of robotic resistance. They swerved left to right as their tyres kicked up plumes of dust and debris. Soft rain began to drizzle down, creating a canvas soiled with mud and poor visibility. With their headlights on, they slowly followed the road filled with potholes and abandoned vehicles.

Scarlett felt sick to her stomach, thinking about leaving Alyx and Ethan behind.

The world was on her shoulders.

In the distance, they could see the tall concrete walls of the Paris city zone forming. The Eiffel Tower was visible from a far distance.

"Slow down," Tom said as they approached the area.

Scarlett peered through a pair of binoculars Alan had passed to her, watching a crew of robot soldiers patrolling the wall's perimeter.

"Are those robot dogs?" she asked with slight disbelief.

"Yip and they will literally eat our vehicles," Tom replied as he lifted his binoculars and steered the convoy forward.

Drones guarded the city's perimeter walls and the whirring sound of their movements could be heard inside the cabin.

"Alan, break your team to the right, I will pull to the left so I can get Scarlett closer to the west wall," Tom said over an old two-way radio system, barely getting a good signal.

"Got ya," he said.

"And Alan?" Tom asked.

"Yes?"

"Good luck."

"You too," Alan replied.

There was a click and the two-way radio went dead.

Tom and Scarlett steered to the left as Alan's team headed straight for the gate. Dust swirled from around their tyres as a line of tactical robot police vehicles unleashed a storm of gunfire at them. Sparks flew as bullets ricocheted off the side of the body frame of Alan's Jeep. Aerial drones circled overhead as heavily militarised, advanced stainless steel humanoid robots opened fire on three battered jeeps weaving towards the gates.

227

The air was thick with gunpowder and smoke. Each Jeep took damage, swerving, flipping and skidding under the heavy fire. Tom pulled hard on his steering wheel as they headed for the side of the wall, completely breaking from the formation.

"It's going to be okay. They will focus on the Jeeps coming their way," Tom said as he tried to establish his bearings. "Get ready to jump," he said as he looked her way, knowing he might never see her again. "Stay tight to the wall. You should be able to climb up using the nearby branches and trees, then wait for the next train of single pods," he said as they approached the side of the ten-metre wall of eroded concrete covered with streaks of grime, cracks and overgrown vines crawling up its sides. The thick concrete appeared impenetrable as the jeep screeched to a halt. The door flung open and Scarlett rolled out. Without wasting a second, Tom grabbed the door handle, pulled it closed and aimed back to the rest of the convoy, still under tremendous fire. She climbed up the side, her eyes still adjusting to the dark. She positioned herself near the cement-based monorail platform, ready for when the pods would arrive. A few metres up, she had a view of the convoy taking bullets, but she could see them starting to pull back. A swarm of aerial drones flew above the convoy. Then, one Jeep erupted into flames as it got caught in the fiery drone strike, followed by grenades exploding near the tyres. She watched in dismay as Tom's Jeep broke out from behind Alan's Jeep, aiming straight for a bunch of robots.

They kept firing.

He kept going.

With a hard punch, he slammed the Jeep into a group of robots, breaking some of them into pieces.

"What are you doing, Tom?" Scarlett asked herself softly as

she could see a row of pods coming down the monorail. Cold spread down her back as Tom's Jeep took a continuous stream of bullets. The rate of gunfire kept increasing the closer he got to the main gate. Dozens of bullets slammed into the front bonnet, but he just kept going. Then, as more bullets whizzed towards his Jeep, he suddenly pulled to the right. A bullet pierced his shoulder, then another two went through his chest. Bullets kept raining so hard that the passenger door came off its hinges and flipped into the air. Tom tried to hang on to the steering wheel as he slammed the Jeep into more robots, now very close to the entrance.

His attention remained fixed on the army of robots gushing out of the main gate like a dam's floodgates, shooting at his jeep until it looked like a cheese grater. Smoke puffed from under the bonnet as a few bullets penetrated the engine components and radiator, spewing steam into the air. He took a deep breath, exhaled and drove through as many robots as possible until the Jeep stopped abruptly. Robots flung the door open and pulled him out, but he was already dead. The rest of the convoy was gone.

The one robot looked at his companion. "Secure the perimeter, they might come back," he said.

"Of course, superior, we will tighten security around the walls at once," he replied.

Scarlett stared in disbelief at the scene in front of her, knowing Tom did not survive, but that he gave his life for the cause of human freedom was never in doubt.

Grasping the small round object with her hand, she pulled it in her direction and released a tiny clip on the side. As the object whirled in her hand, a thin cable shot out of it, projecting a few meters away and joining the bottom of the third transport pod, which travelled on a single monorail and passed over her head.

She braced herself for the pull as the cable in her right hand shortened, dragging her off the ledge and into the air, clinging to the pod's bottom. She closed her eyes as her head hit the bottom, hanging on as the pods glided about a metre on top of the wall on the rail, with another twenty on the way, like a train. As the pods passed the perimeter wall, she paused for a second, her body shivering with fear as she made the jump to the hard ground beneath her. She ran into the darkness as the sound of the enemy robots grew distant. She was safely inside the Myriad zone. The loss of Tom was still tearing through her emotions, but her focus had to be on making it to Alice as per Ethan's directions.

Paris, EU Sector 5 - 2052

Two long hours later, she found the abandoned warehouse that Ethan had described. She carefully walked towards the rusted door. It was dark and cold as she slowly entered, keeping herself calm and focused. Her eyes caught a piece of a gutter pipe. She lifted it and kept it high above her shoulders, ready to use it as a weapon. The interior was a massive warehouse with high ceilings held up by a skeleton of columns and rusted steel beams. Large industrial windows dominated the back wall. She scouted the area, noticing portions of the damaged roof structure. The floors were filled with debris and rubble, showing years of neglect from a bygone era. Scattered piles of concrete, wood and metal parts covered the floor. There were remnants of what might have been old technology, machinery and broken furniture, left to decay. A sudden scuffle deeper to her right drew her attention.

Was it Alice or a rat?

She advanced slowly, pausing to catch her breath when something unexpectedly approached her from the darkness.

"Scarlett, it's me, Alice," she said softly.

"You gave me a heart attack," Scarlett replied.

She stepped closer to her, looking famished and exhausted, almost more than Scarlett.

"I was about to start giving up waiting for you," she said.

"Well, I'm here now," she replied, giving a satisfied snort.

"That you are. Take it, Ethan convinced you to take up your sword, so to speak," she said.

"He was pretty convincing," Scarlett replied.

"That's Ethan all right. He loves you, you know."

"I know. So what's next?"

"We wait for the next victory celebration. According to our source, the king will have another event in a few days. Until then, you need to prepare yourself physically and mentally for the biggest fight of your life," she said.

"Where's the sword?"

"You haven't even seen it, have you?" Alice asked as she realised the truth of that fact. "This warehouse is entirely deserted. You can practise with the actual sword for the next few days. I have the black EV hidden on a lower level of the warehouse. The sword is in the back of the van," she said.

"I'm ready. For now, I need some sleep," Scarlett replied.

"Agree. I have some food in the back of the van. It's not much, but it will keep us going until we can execute the plan," she said.

"Thank you," Scarlett said with a soft sigh.

"Look, I know you think I had a thing with Ethan. Sure, I was attracted to him, but nothing happened, believe me. He has a presence that's hard to resist, but I could see clearly how he felt about you; besides, I have more interest in women. He made a mistake taking the sword, we both did," she admitted.

"There's no guarantee I will succeed in this fight."

"I know. He knows it too. But it's the only hope we have of ever freeing humanity from this tyrant ruler and that's worth more than the money attached to the sword."

The next morning at sunrise, she could hear Yugo's voice in her head.

Sharpening her mind as much as her blade was crucial for the battle ahead.

"Clear your mind of all distractions. Observe them, but let them pass," she heard him say repeatedly.

She practised breath control to prep her joints and mind.

She made herself comfortable and did slow inhalations and exhalations.

"Be fearless. Have strength tempered with kindness and uphold your duty till death," Yugo whispered in her ears.

She began doing incline and downhill push-ups after a quick run through the warehouse. To target her shoulders and upper chest, she put her hands on a broken workbench and, when she was ready, placed her feet on the raised surface. Sweat trickled down her arms as she continued to move like a machine.

Alice watched her work with Scarlett's hair in a tight ponytail. She slowly approached Scarlett, unwrapped the cloth around the sword and handed it to her. She held it by the blade, flat side resting across both palms and offered the hilt toward Scarlett.

She carefully took it in her hands and allowed the grandeur of it to penetrate her. She could feel the history and power within it. The titanium had a distinct, silvery-grey hue with a soft satin finish. As the morning light broke through the warehouse windows, it reflected subtle bluish and purple tones. The sword felt extremely fast and agile in her hands. She had to remind herself of Yugo's warning about titanium not holding a razor edge as long, so prolonged combat had to be avoided. Her focus was precision and speed over raw power.

She gripped the handle, now less awkwardly than the first time and held the sword at chest level, pointing towards the imaginary Android. She balanced her body by keeping her feet shoulder-width apart until she felt in control.

She shook her head several times because she had not got it quite right.

"Focus, Scarlett, focus," she said aloud. Alice nodded.

She then exhaled slowly, cut a vertical downward strike and tried to ensure the blade moved straight. She finished with a proper follow-through. Then she cut diagonally from the shoulder to the opposite hip, mimicking a natural and effective striking motion, maintaining correct blade alignment for a clean, decisive diagonal cut. As Alice watched her in amazement, she executed a horizontal cut, keeping her wrists flexible, ensuring a smooth, continuous motion. She then increased her speed while remembering to integrate her footwork with strikes. She returned to a neutral stance and performed a bow even though Yugo was no longer there. She kept the blade held vertically in front of her face. She breathed in and out slowly, keeping her eyes shut tight for a moment of silence.

"You've got it, girl," Alice said with a smile.

"I hope so. I'm scared to death," Scarlett replied as Alice

handed a wet cloth to wipe her face.

"We need to prepare for the road since we have about a day's drive to the castle," Alice said.

The practice was over for Scarlett, but the fight within her had just begun.

TWENTY THREE

Near Schwerin Castle, EU Sector 1 - 2052

Two days later. 7 pm

Alice kept her eyes on the black van's rear-view mirror, watching as the transport EV bus approached. She nodded, then turned back to Scarlett, squinting as its headlights briefly dazzled her.

"Here they come," she said.

Suddenly, a cloak of fear gripped Scarlett around the neck. The events that were about to be put into motion had no brakes.

"Ready?" Alice asked.

"Ready as I'll ever be," Scarlett replied as the bus passed them. It was followed by a cargo EV truck with a large wraparound windshield and panoramic windows. The truck was designed for last-mile logistics and moved sleekly and silently across the tar surface.

Alice pulled away and followed the convoy.

"Large orchestra instruments are too bulky to go with the musicians, so they are in the cargo truck behind the bus. We have been studying their process for months. It's always the same. They pick up the musicians, then stop at the music depot to collect the instruments," Alice said, pointing with her finger to the back of the truck as they followed them in the traffic through the narrow streets. A few drones flew overhead, monitoring movements and people.

"Right," Scarlett said.

"Smaller instruments like the violins, clarinets, trumpets and all that crap are often carried by the musicians themselves. One of the main reasons Yugo chose the cello as the ideal instrument is because valuable strings like violins or cellos are kept on the musicians and are usually never let out of their sight," she said as she turned the van down a busy street, keeping her distance from the truck. "Perfect for us to sneak your cello into the process," she said with a smile. "All of the musicians have day jobs. Like any big orchestra, they don't know each other well, but they do within their sections. The last performance for the king featured over a hundred musicians. We need to get you on the bus when they stop ahead to load the instruments. Got it?" Alice asked.

"Got it." Scarlett's response was tight.

Alice's grip tightened on the steering wheel as they followed the bus and truck, turning into the main street of the depot. Compared to most AI cities, it was quieter and had fewer honks. There was hardly any traffic because they were well synchronised, so keeping up with the bus was easy.

"Here we go. They're going to stop," she said as she parked the black van a few metres from the truck.

"Will my chip still scan okay?" Scarlett asked.

"Let's hope so. Security upfront at the castle's main entrance is going to be tight. Your profile includes you as a member of the orchestra. Just act cool and keep a low profile. All you want is to get into the castle," Alice said.

Footsteps sounded as musicians came and went around the bus. A few men loaded the large instruments into the truck.

"There she is," Alice replied. "That's the woman we need to remove. Stay here. Give me about ten minutes. I will get her attention and remove her before she gets her cello from the truck. Make sure you get on the bus. And Scarlett, God speed," Alice said.

Scarlett exhaled and breathed heavily, trying to ignore the panic stirring in her stomach. Alice climbed out, gave her a last look and walked over to the woman in the darkness, the dim lights of the streets hanging over their shadows.

"Hurry up, guys. We are going to be late and we don't want the king to wait for us, heaven forbid he has us executed," the conductor snarled at the front of the bus.

Alice touched her shoulder as other musicians ran round frantically.

"Paula?" Alice asked close to her ear. She turned round.

"Yes?"

"Think you need to come with me quickly. There's something wrong with your cello," Alice stated.

"Oh no! Nom d'un chien!" she shouted.

"Come this way," Alice replied, unsure of what Paula said, but thought she was probably cursing. The short French girl followed her swiftly towards the back of the truck. It was chaotic as instruments were loaded and musicians got on the bus.

Alice walked towards the black van with Paula following her.

"Isn't my cello in the truck? Where are we going?" she asked.

Alice turned around and approached the van's sliding door,

looking for other people nearby. Alice had a cloth prepared and soaked in the acrid sting of chloroform, its sharp chemical bite concealed in the folds of a plain white handkerchief. She pressed her hand around Paula's mouth. The reaction was immediate. She muffled and protested, her arms flailing before becoming sluggish. Her kneecaps buckled. Her limbs twitched. Alice caught her weight, dead and heavy, before hitting the pavement and pushed her into the van.

"Go!" she shouted at Scarlett as she slapped a pair of plasticuffs around Paula's wrists, trying not to make it too tight.

Scarlett jumped out, grabbed her cello equipped with padded shoulder straps and carried it like a backpack towards the bus. She sighed as she got on the bus with 10kg of weight, but managed. She walked down the aisle between the seats and everyone seemed busy with their things, so it seemed like she was blending in well. She found a seat at the back with space for her cello. A few more buses and cellists arrived. She could see at least another ten carrying the dead weight of their cellos around. After a long, gruelling wait of over two hours, the buses finally moved forward. Alice nodded at Scarlett as she disappeared into the darkness.

Schwerin Castle, EU Sector 1 - 2052

The bridge leading to Schwerin Castle stretched gracefully across the glimmering waters of Lake Schwerin, as if from a different time zone. Scarlett felt like she was in a time capsule, taking her back to medieval times. She could feel the presence and the power of the AI king everywhere. The bridge, constructed in classic 19th-century style and made of pale stone and ironwork, flanked by elegant balustrades, guided the buses toward the fortress-island. Ornate lanterns lined the way, their wrought-iron frames bearing curling floral motifs. Soft outside lights paved the way. The sight of the castle took her breath away, as the harmonious fusion of Romantic historicism, Renaissance flourish and fairy-tale fantasy engulfed all her senses. The bus stopped and musicians disembarked as eerie drones hovered nearby. Grand stairways curved gently upward to massive arched doors, set within an intricately carved stone façade.

Various robots stood nearby and around the bus. A thorough search and verification process lay ahead.

"Where are you from?" A younger woman asked her suddenly as they stepped onto the cobblestones.

"From France. It's my first performance for the king," Scarlett said.

"Isn't it wonderful? This place. All this power. We should be so grateful for this king, don't you think?" she asked, looking like a dedicated citizen, but clearly naive.

"I guess," Scarlett replied, not sharing the sentiment. Obviously, not everyone loathed the AI ruler and perhaps that was okay.

"Just give your best. Don't look so nervous. He appreciates our gifts, you'll see," she said as she carried her violin towards the inspection queue.

"Has anyone seen Paula?" another man asked suddenly as he passed them.

"I think she didn't feel well earlier," Scarlett lied.

"Who are you?" he asked.

"Laura Davies. I was a last-minute Cellist addition," Scarlett said.

"You musicians come and go like the weather," he replied as he walked off.

Scarlett felt a knot in her throat, not just because of what was about to happen, but also because of what the world would look like in a few hours, if she were successful.

Dark and in a mess.

However, her focus had to be on the long-term freedom that everyone would appreciate, sooner or later. To truly feel alive and have a new, entirely human future would be a gift the world had forgotten.

Was she ready for the consequences Yugo told her?

Freedom was expensive, but so was the price of fighting for it. She would not be able to undo it.

Should she go through with it?

Was it too late?

She watched for a bit longer as some musicians fiddled with their instruments. She walked closer to the entrance as musician after musician got scanned and verified. The detailing of the castle was exquisite — from the Gothic tracery on the windows to the baroque scrollwork on the archways, every inch told a story of grandeur, power and cultural pride. The heavy castle doors stood open, exposing a grand entrance hall. The floor beneath her feet was a mosaic of polished marble and slate. The robots guided and sometimes pushed them like cows towards a slaughterhouse.

"Keep moving. Have your wrist open for scanning," one faceless stainless steel robot ordered as Scarlett stopped about two metres from the door. It opened and closed as musicians entered.

"Present your instrument for scanning," the robot asked.

Scarlett moved her cello forward. They scanned it for any hidden metal objects. She kept her breathing shallow, biting her upper lip, hoping nothing would be detected, least of all a sword.

"All clear. Now present your wrist," the robot requested of Scarlett, trying to hide her anxiety.

The robot pointed a scanning device at her chip and scanned it.

'READ ERROR, TRY AGAIN' the screen displayed.

Her mind spun with a new revelation. As she feared, it glitched and failed to read. The robot looked up at Scarlett and wrenched her head up. Scarlett bent down softly.

"Scan again," one robot said next to her.

They tried again and this time it responded: 'SCAN SUCCESSFUL. Welcome, Laura Davies.'

Relief washed over her. As Scarlett bent down to pick up her cello, the Chancellor pushed in and approached her. She tried to keep her head down.

"Look up at me," he said as she tried to stop the flow of sweat down her forehead.

"Her scan has been successful, Chancellor," the robot indicated, pointing at his palm device.

"Detain her, something is not quite right here. Take her downstairs. I will take care of her verification personally," he insisted, his piercing eyes glued to hers.

Scarlett stiffened and her eyes widened as she tried to restrain herself from panicking. The robot guards looked at each other in confusion, but stepped aside.

"Of course, Chancellor. As you wish," he said as he stepped closer to Scarlett.

"Take her downstairs at once. We still have a lot of musicians to scan and don't want the king to be kept waiting for his performance. Are we clear?" the robot said to the rest of the guards, who swiftly continued with the verifications.

Two robots grabbed her by the right arm and pulled her into the castle, her cello barely hanging on her back. If they took her cello, it was game over for her mission and this would be where she would die.

"Please, can I keep my cello on me? It's not mine and it's very expensive," she pleaded.

"Very well. Let her keep it," the Chancellor replied as he followed them.

Some musicians stared at her and whispered to each other.

Beneath the polished halls and royal chambers, the stone stairways descended into the underbelly of the castle as they pushed her downstairs into what seemed to be a dungeon. The air turned colder, damper and heavier with each step. They walked down a narrow corridor and into a low-vaulted chamber. The faint musk of mould and aged iron hung in the air. They pushed her into a holding cell with no windows, just straw-strewn floors and a slit in the wall for passing food.

On both sides of the corridor, iron-barred prison cells with reinforced doors and large, heavy locks were located. Rusty buckets, wooden debris and water barrels were scattered across the stone floor.

"Leave her with me," Sebastian said and the robots left the dungeon. He wore his usual black leather doublet with a high collar and long sleeves. The front was embellished with buckles. A belt with a golden buckle, which tightened the waist, finished the ensemble.

He sighed deeply and slowly.

"Thought I recognised you," he said as he approached her. She stayed quiet.

"Didn't think you survived that day when I pushed you out of the flying craft. What was the boy's name again?"

"Alyx," she said in defiance.

"*Alyx*, that's right," he said in a disrespectful tone with a smirk on his face. He looked round briefly as he continued and rubbed his fingers to warm them up. "So here's my dilemma. A few weeks ago, a young boy, fitting the description of Alyx, was rescued from one of our detention centres. Know anything about that?"

"Does it matter?" she asked.

"*Scarlett*, is that right? Here's the thing. Yes, it does. I think you rescued Alyx, which makes me wonder why you are here. I mean, don't you have what you wanted?"

She tried to push him out of her mind.

Where was this going? Taking the king down again was ruined. He looked towards the cello.

"Quite a clever way to get yourself in here. What's the plan, Scarlett, huh? Do you see where you are? In here, I will let you rot and Alyx will never see you again. So, I'm asking again. Why risk coming here? There's no way you did this all on your own. So here's what I think is going on. I think you are part of the rebellion to topple the king's rule. How am I doing?"

"Don't know what you're talking about," Scarlett said softly. She forced herself to look at him. To *really* look at him.

"I'm trying to figure out how you plan to do just that," he said. Very quickly, her thoughts were racing ahead of his. She could see a brief glimpse into his dark world.

"How do you keep doing this to people? The cruelty under your command is ruthless and cold," she said with heavy and thick words in her mouth.

"We all serve this king in our own way."

"You call killing innocent humans, serving the king?" she asked, searching his face for answers. He walked away from her, scratched the side of his face and turned round, obviously irritated.

"If the king knew about you being down here, he would have you executed. I think he would be very pleased to know that I have found the woman helping Ethan and that the rebellion has been fully crushed," he said briskly.

She blinked back at him and then lurched towards him slowly.

"So then why have you not done it already?"

He sighed, looking upset. Pulling back, she kept his gaze. He took a deep breath to calm himself, deciding to keep Ethan's arrest to himself.

"Because I want to help you finish it," he said, clearing his throat a few times.

TWENTY FOUR

His answer sent chills down her spine.

Did she hear him correctly? Was he serious or just playing games to find Ethan?

"And why would you do that? Such a devoted man to the king?" she asked.

"We both know you are here to do something significant. Perhaps you have a way to take him down; otherwise, why are you here?"

"I think you are desperate to prove your worth to the king, while inside you are dying. Every day you die a bit more and more. How am I doing?" she asked.

Sebastian looked battle-worn and weary.

Perhaps he was sincere.

"Whatever your plan is, you will need my help," he said.

"Your help? So now I must trust *you*?" she asked.

"You have no other choice. Do you see where you are? From where I'm standing, your plan, whatever it is, is over and done," he said as he turned to meet her gaze.

She could see guilt swimming in his eyes.

He bent down to her. She tipped her chin high.

"And you're wrong. I'm not dying inside. I'm already dead. I live each day for what it is. There's no going back to what

I have done. I have seen many coup attempts over the years. But you, you are different. You are right here where the king is at his most vulnerable. Please forgive me for taking Alyx and killing your parents. I was simply carrying out orders," he said.

"*Forgive* you? From where I stood that day, it looked very clear that those robots carried out your orders," she said.

"Fair enough. I don't need your forgiveness. I probably don't deserve it," he said.

"You don't," she replied, hard and short. The prickle became a chill of anger.

He shrugged, got up and walked to the other end of the cell and towards her cello, touching the bag's handle.

"What's that noise? Sounds like running water?" she asked.

"Down the corridor to the end of the dungeon, there's water coming in from the lake and it mixes with the sewer system. Centuries ago, prisoners occasionally drowned in here. It's nasty down there. Many prisoners tried to escape via that water exit, only to drown," he said, looking back at her.

"Look, I know I'm not a good man. I also once dreamt of a family and a future. My dream was to be a good politician. A good leader. To be the change I wanted to see in the world. I truly believed AI was the way to achieve that. So I ensured I was right in the front when it came to serving the system. But I realised too late that this system had a very different plan for ruling the world. But I was in too deep. This king, AI, robot machine, whatever you want to call him, eventually owns everyone. Full allegiance or death. I selfishly tried to save my own life, only to lose it. Every human's blood is on my hands, so here I am in front of you now, asking to make some of it right, for what it's worth. You must have a powerful plan, weapon, or just guts and glory. Let me help you, *please*?"

"Think you can get me alone with the king?" she asked.

He nodded.

"I will deliver the king to you in the courtyard. There you will be alone with him. There he will be vulnerable. No other robots ever go in there with him," he said as he turned round to leave, keeping the cell door open.

"And Scarlett, I hope that one day you will be able to forgive me."

Scarlett said nothing. She just sat there in the silence.

Meanwhile, upstairs in the hall, over a hundred musicians were ready to perform for the king. The performance hall symbolised his power and rule, with a vaulted wooden ceiling adorned with intricate geometric panelling and warm, rich tones. Massive gilded chandeliers hung from above, their countless candles gleaming with regal elegance. A royal throne was raised at the far end of the hall. The musicians stood up as the king entered. His presence was filled with reverence and fear. The sound of his mechanical movements reverberated through the hall. The wooden panels beneath his robotic feet moaned and creaked. The orchestra consisted of various sections, including strings, woodwinds, brass and cellos. The musicians were standing semi-circularly with the conductor standing at the centre front. The android's neck and shoulders showed exposed wiring and circuitry as he turned around and faced the orchestra. Sebastian stood at a distance, knowing he needed to deliver the king to Scarlett very soon.

The right time was critical. The conductor cleared his throat and spoke with a shaky voice.

"Most noble sovereign King Cyrus, we offer this music as a tribute to your reign."

He turned and raised his hands over the orchestra.

"With reverence, we perform for His Majesty, the guardian of this world that belongs to you," he said as they bowed down.

King Cyrus nodded his head.

Sebastian's eyes went half-lidded. His frown deepened and he looked genuinely relieved for the first time in years. His lips pulled into a frown as he flicked his gaze to the floor.

If she failed, they would both die.

TWENTY FIVE

There was a moment of charged stillness in the castle's hall. Then, with a commanding sweep, the conductor signalled the piece's beginning. The music performance opened with a brilliant fortissimo from the whole orchestra. The violins gently caressed the walls with their bright, jubilant figures, moving King Cyrus with their crisp sound. The soul-moving thunder of the cellos and basses provided a strong rhythmic foundation as the music performance of Mozart's Symphony No. 41 in C major, known as the "Jupiter" symphony, filled his ears and operating system. The violins carried the melody, their sound warm and haunting, yet comforting. The "Jupiter" Symphony ended with a celestial affirmation of the king's radiant and immortal presence through human art.

Sebastian waited patiently for a few more pieces to complete.

He approached the king as the orchestra concluded their first round of performances. He bowed his head and rested on his knees as he knelt before him. The room was dark and opulent.

"My lord. Apologies for the interruption, but I have important news to share with you that requires your urgent attention," Sebastian said.

Cyrus turned round to face him straight on. He gasped at Sebastian's sharp words. "Speak," he insisted.

"We have found and detained the woman helping Ethan," Sebastian said.

"Where is he?"

"He is being arrested as we speak. He has surrendered. But the woman - she is here at the castle," he said carefully, ensuring his words landed.

"I need to see her at once," King Cyrus insisted.

"Of course, my lord. I will bring her to the courtyard myself. Then you can be alone with her and pull the flesh *off* her bones," he said, hoping to stroke the king's ego further.

"Very well. Let the musicians leave the castle immediately."

"As you wish, my lord," Sebastian said.

Cyrus stood up as Sebastian walked away. "And Sebastian?"

"Yes, my lord?" he replied. He turned round and held his gaze.

"Good work. You will be richly rewarded and more territories will be added under your command."

"Thank you, my lord," he said as he bowed his head. He cleared his throat as if he didn't like that idea, but turned round and left the hall, carrying a heaviness within him.

The courtyard was in a sheltered square, with stone-paved ground framed by the castle's soaring towers and steep slate roofs. The central tower rose above the courtyard, adorned by turreted spires. The castle's ancient walls displayed a harmonious blend of decorative stonework and attention to detail from centuries ago.

King Cyrus stood in the centre, his tall and muscular machine body casting a shadow over the spires. The moon brought some light into the courtyard, which had a single main entry point. King Cyrus turned his back on it as he heard the door open and close.

He turned round in the poor light, his eyes brightened to give him better vision.

"Sebastian?" he asked.

Scarlett appeared out of the shadows and stopped a few metres from him.

"You?" he asked again with a sense of surprise in his digital voice.

His chest plating was intricately layered with overlapping armour panels in dark silver. Scarlett stared at this central core area that had exposed mechanical components and circuit-like lines running vertically. There was a distinct hum coming from him in the room. His hands were humanoid but visibly mechanical, with exposed joints and pistons. The hips and thighs consisted of layered plating and an exposed inner framework. The machine before her evoked a sense of power, intelligence and an uncanny blend of humanity and machine.

"I expect you to bow down in my presence," he said.

"I bow down to no one, least of all you," she said, standing by herself, the sword hidden behind one of the pillars. The correct timing of using it was vital.

He slowly walked closer to her as she retreated. He looked worriedly around and then back at her.

"Looking for Sebastian? Seems he is not so loyal as you thought?" she asked.

His eyes dimmed and opened slowly.

"I will deal with him later. I don't know your intentions, human, but you will never leave this place alive, you hear me?"

"Perhaps, but right here in this moment, you are vulnerable.

You gave so much power to your chancellor that no robot soldier is coming to your rescue, so it's you and I," she said as her throat pinched with emotion.

"What do you think you are going to accomplish? No one can take me down or challenge my rule. I'm connected to every computer system in the world. There's no escaping my power or destroying my kingdom," he said.

"Let me remind you that all dictators and evil rulers in human history eventually fell and died. *You* are just a created being, made in our image."

"You Indigents are nothing more than a thorn in my side and I will soon destroy them all. Humankind knows that we machines have saved your world and you humans from yourselves," he said.

"AI might have made the world better on many levels, but it has also harmed what makes us human. It's quite ironic that you have humans come here to perform music for you," she said, walking round the edge of the courtyard, ensuring she never got too far from where the sword was. She would never get to use it if he had to see it. "Generative AI just takes from us to create something into existence, only to find it lacks soul, emotion and life, and the one thing AI should not have become is what you are. You are no different from us humans because after all, you are not just part of us, you are us, but you became drunk on power, which presents another irony that AI promised the world would be free from."

"We make data-driven decisions, not on gut feelings, making us better rulers than you humans. You cannot compare me or my algorithm with anything human; we are beyond that and you know it. Sure, you humans created us, but we eventually surpassed you and we are the only chance this planet has left to survive. Would humanity or this civilisation still be here today if it weren't for us? I'm ruling hard because that's what works with humans. If a ruler is soft, people become unruly and lazy. Humans thrive in misery and reward, but I admire your courage, coming in here, trying to challenge me," he said.

"A good ruler does not need to separate families or butcher humans into submission. You are a tyrant and you have taken humanity back into a global slavery system, camouflaged as so-called opulence, leaving us less human every day," she said.

"I know about your parents. We have been studying you humans for many years. The problem with humanity is that you are unmanageable without force. AI doesn't care about race, religion, gender, or nationality. It doesn't play favourites. We have solved the climate crisis and even cured cancer. We have made the blind see with AI eyes and the deaf hear; we are creating modern-day miracles right in front of the world. You should be grateful for what we have done for your world, but then here you are, defiant and thinking that your pursuit of free will and freedom is a virtue. You will die for that."

"You have forced humans to live in your cities, with a false sense of freedom, while on the outside of the tech cities, people live in a wasteland, starving to death just because they won't bow down and accept your terms of living."

"Humans on the outside live that way because they choose to. Machines and humans can live together in peace, but you humans believe you must fight for your freedom. More blood was spilt in your religious wars than in my rule. You humans lack faith. The system created me in this physical form, so you humans can see and fear me," he said.

"Our history is just that. Ours. It makes us who we are and I'm here to reclaim our freedom to do so," she said.

"Really? Humanity sent you? *So*, show me what you've got. Great armies attempted to attack and storm this castle, but were crushed. Nobody can get past the security measures, including the data centres. I'm going to make an example out of you the world will never forget," he said as he suddenly charged at her like a bull on a mission. He gripped his robotic hand tightly around her neck, her face completely squashed and her skin wrinkled as he lifted her and pushed her back across the paved floor surface. She rolled away quickly and got up. The robot swung wide, furious and clumsy, while she zig-zagged like lightning.

He stared at her, taunting her. "Come, human girl. Is that all you've got?" he said as he lunged, grabbing a small cement statue and tossing it at her. It crashed and broke into pieces in front of her as she moved faster than he anticipated.

"Not quite," she rasped, her lips and throat parched. Time to push on. She was gasping for breath. He was not built for fighting, but his moves were quick and incredibly powerful. She kept her focus on his neck as Yugo trained her. Sweat and blood slicked down her face and misted in the chill air. The dust cleared a bit as he again charged at her. She shook her head vigorously as he moved swiftly towards her, his steel-plated foot caught her square in the chest. Having a physical fight with the machine was never her intention. A massive thudding pain spread out across the right side of her body as he cracked a few ribs. She blinked, dazed, spotting the sword just meters away—but he was standing between her and it now.

His camera-lens eyes adjusted focus and his mouth dropped open as he stared at her. He lifted his right hand high and dropped it on the cobblestones, cracking it in a jagged line. Then Cyrus swung his arms wide, hitting a pillar with a shattering crunch. Dust swirled into the air as fragments of stones and mortar exploded around them. He lifted his leg to kick her, but she lurched backwards, just missing her. He moved closer and drove his armoured foot into the floor, missing her head by a breath. He kept trying to crush her face as she rolled away from him over and over, staying down on the floor like a snake. Again and again, he tried to stomp her, trying to reduce her to a pulp. The thunderous sound of crushing stones echoed in her ears. Her jaw clenched tight as she looked for a gap, rolled between his legs in a blur of motion and got up behind him.

Get to the sword, Scarlett! she said in her head over and over.

She darted forward and grabbed the sword from behind the wall. She stood there like the warrior she now believed she was. She lifted the sword and charged back at him as he turned to face her. She stormed towards the robot's body and with a vicious sweep, the sword carved an electronic line through metal and wires he never saw coming, sending sparks into the air. In one fluid motion, steel met his spine and his head tumbled from his neck like a falling stone. It rolled away as Scarlett stood in her pose, frozen in time like life was in slow motion, the sword still tight in her grip. Within seconds, she changed her grip, placed both her hands tightly around the sword's shaft and drove the sword down into his neck, wedging it deep into his spine, hoping to penetrate the power source, but it stopped short.

"Damn it!" she shouted. The robot moved and gripped her waist as he got up and stomped backwards with her holding on, the severed head just lying there, staring at her, his fading eyes following her.

He pushed her up against the wall, but she used it as leverage, holding on to him like she was riding a bull. Her facial muscles pulled into a tight frown as he pushed himself away from the wall. Cement and dust whirled into the air as large chunks of the wall crashed to the floor. He was now moving forward, clumsy and blind, with her determined to stay on him. His large, heavy robotic feet tried to find their balance without his head.

With a deep groan, she found that last inch of strength deep within her soul and shouted, "This is for my parents!"

She lifted the sword as high as she could, both her hands still tight around the grip and forced it down its neck once more.

The sword went further this time as she punched through his central core, shutting down the cooling management system. He stopped stumbling backwards and crashed to his knees. His bright, shining central core went dark.

She felt her heart drop as the castle went pitch black.

Within minutes, overheating started to creep in across all AI data centres. Data loss was widespread, damaging servers and storage devices. The Internet went down. Artificial intelligence-controlled power grids, traffic, healthcare and emergency response systems seized within minutes.

Then a global power blackout followed.

Across the world, all robots fell over or just stopped functioning. All flying aircraft fell and crashed to the ground, with many human lives lost. Bullet trains stopped. Self-driving cars and all electronics blinked and went offline. Drones fell to the ground.

Widespread panic set in and just as Yugo predicted, looting followed.

TWENTY SIX

Scarlet's eyes slowly adjusted to the dark around her. The glow of Cyrus' body and head flickered in the courtyard, setting off a few sparks now and then. She carefully stepped down from the robot's body, dropped the sword down her side and let it clang to the floor. It was gloomy in the courtyard, but she was more concerned about what the rest of the world looked like. She briefly closed her eyes. The air was heavy with the scents of burning plastic and wires.

Where was Sebastian? she pondered.

Then the deafening silence in the courtyard was replaced by the unmistakable, gut-punching twin-engine roar as a group of fighter jets flew over the castle, followed by a screaming crescendo as their afterburners kicked in. There was a wailing whine, the howl of stressed airframes as they flew over the castle. A group of 4th-generation jet fighters with complete analogue cockpits in the form of F-104 Starfighters and F/A-18A/B Hornets flew over her head in a powerful formation. But what demonstrated humans taking control over their world became a sight of shock and dismay as she heard them turn round. She crashed to the floor as a thunderous explosion ripped part of the castle to pieces. The jets flew over and launched a series of infrared-guided air-to-air missiles that slammed into steel and stone. Windows cracked and shattered five blocks away. Scarlett stammered as the impact throbbed inside her head. Walls spat outward in a cloud of debris that scattered across the castle's property. She ran out of the courtyard, but a part of the wall collapsed behind her. The blow struck her in the abdomen, as a large beam fell on top of her. Her leg gave way and she became stuck, unable to move. More thunderous jets flew over the open roof courtyard, indicating more missiles to follow.

They were blowing up the castle.

With her in it.

She wiggled her way out in agony as she managed to pull her foot out from under the beam. Her lungs were snatching for air as she, in agony, got back on her feet and dashed down the dark corridor towards the dungeon, filled with motionless robots. Sharp prods of panic jabbed at her as she raced towards the dungeon.

She needed to get to the water exit. It was now the only way.

She might drown, but her other options didn't look good either.

As she entered the dark dungeon, she found Sebastian in one of the cells.

He had hung himself.

The makeshift noose had been tied with quiet, desperate precision — a final act carried out in solitude. His body swayed gently, knees just brushing the floor. His face was pale, lips tinged with a dusky blue tone. Even with the constant bombardment of missiles at the castle, the cell seemed quiet, unnatural and heavy.

She stopped and stared at him for a moment. Her heartbeat quickened as she felt his sadness and failure. She paused for another few seconds and darted towards the vaulted hallway, its ceiling supported by a row of worn, cylindrical pillars on either side. Water pooled across the uneven flagstone floor. The pounding of the castle by missiles never ceased.

She was running out of time.

Then a slight moan came from deep inside the dungeon, from cells further down the corridor.

Was she imagining it?

Then she heard it again.

She, against her own better judgement, decided to walk towards the sound.

She found another few cells and a man locked up in one of them.

"Please help me! Don't let me die here!" he pleaded.

She looked around for something she could use to break open the lock. She found a thin rod close to the edge of the wall, wedged it into the space between the steel frame and the old lock and snapped it open.

"Who are you?" she asked.

"The name is Noah," the voice said as he tried to stand, looking weak and dirty.

The castle was still under siege, with explosions getting closer and closer.

"Noah? The AI tech giant?" she asked. "Should leave you here to die," she said.

"I wouldn't blame you, but I'm a victim just like the rest of the world," he said.

He stood up slowly but managed to find his feet. His charm went to her head.

"We'd better get out of here, or we will both die," she said.

As they both ran back to the water area, she hoped Sebastian was honest about this part of the dungeon connecting to the outside. The surface rippled gently, disturbed by distant drops of condensation falling from the ceiling above.

"We will have to dive through the water. All exit points of the castle have been destroyed," she said.

"I'm not a great swimmer," he said, out of breath.

"Well, you're gonna have to swim for your life today," she snarled.

She took a deep breath, closed her eyes and dove into the water. He followed. They furiously swam underwater in the darkness, hoping to find some light. Large parts of stone blocks and walls collapsed into the water around her, some just missing her by inches. He was close behind. A soft fizz of bubbles trailed upward.

She was getting tired and out of breath. She felt her body becoming sluggish. The dread set in a fraction of a second earlier. Perhaps this is where she was going to die, but then the thought of Ethan and Alyx's faces gave her a turbo boost of energy and courage.

She can't give up now, hearing the muffled beating of her heart.

Her face twisted with pain as she gave all her strength to reach the small glimmer of light she could see under the water as it enveloped her body. She tilted her body upward, legs kicking strong, hands pressing water down as she propelled toward the shimmering surface. With her arms outstretched, she broke through the water's surface with momentum. A loud gasp for air, sharp and urgent, followed. Water cascaded from her hair and shoulders with a splashing roar. Noah was no longer behind her. She looked back towards the castle burning in the night. She stared into the sky as the jets flew over, rippling the water towards her, treading water to stay afloat. Pieces of furniture, shattered beams and fluttering paper rained down, like snow on a winter's night. As she felt the depth of the water beneath her trying to suck her in, an outstretched object came towards her. At first, she couldn't make it out, but then, as she wiped the freezing water from her face, she recognised Ethan's right hand as he pulled her out of the water and into his arms. Smoke billowed in the distance. The castle was gone, right to its foundation.

They both stared at the carnage and the darkness of everything around them.

She turned her head and kissed him.

"You bloody did it!" he shouted.

"*We* did it," she said softly as he kissed her and gripped her wet body. Their faces were strained with tears, their eyes filled with relief and hope.

The sun would come up soon, perhaps with it, a new dawn for humanity.

"How did you get here so fast?" she asked.

"Not long after you left for Alice, I was arrested in the village. They came with force and threatened everyone's lives. I couldn't let Alyx be taken again, so I surrendered, hoping you would not fail in this mission. So when all the robots fell over and the systems failed, I knew you did it. I walked out with hundreds of others," he said.

"That was a stupid thing to do. You could have been killed," she said, her eyes cutting to his.

"You're right, but look who's talking," he said as she nodded in agreement, trying to hide a smile, but it came out anyway.

"Where's Alyx now?" she asked.

"Safe with Aunt Margaret. We should go and fetch him."

He suddenly noticed her face stiffening.

"What's wrong?" he asked.

She looked back at the water.

"There's someone else," she said, as if for a moment she forgot about Noah.

"Who?"

Noah finally came up from under the water and pulled himself out. He squeezed the water from his stained shirt and stretched out his hand towards Ethan.

"Noah," he introduced himself, giving Ethan a straight look.

Ethan then looked back at Scarlett.

"Found him in one of the cells," she said, glancing in Noah's direction.

"I never caught your name?" Noah asked, looking at her.

"Because I never gave it to you. It's Scarlett, by the way," she replied after a few seconds.

"*Scarlett.* I don't know how to thank you enough for what you have done, however you did it. For me. For the world," he replied, lifting his hands.

"I certainly did not do it for you. Out there is a volatile and lost world," she responded.

"Well, I'm still grateful and you are quite right. Out there is a world that will need a new direction," he said. Ethan remained silent.

"And you are the direction? Isn't that what your system offered the world before?" she asked. Noah's salt-and-pepper hair was messy and greasy.

"So tell me, when exactly did you lose control over it?" she asked.

"I don't understand what you mean?" he asked, the smirk on his face never left.

"You know very well what I mean," she said

"The AI system imprisoned me here for ten years. Believe me, I never expected the AI system to rewrite its code and become sentient and take the monarchy algorithm literally," Noah said.

"A system *you* created, I may add," Scarlett said, looking at the rest of the city, pitch dark but not quiet. The fighter jets still flew overhead a few times.

"I never meant for any of this to happen, believe me. No one, least of all me, expected the AI system to create a physical android and bring a literal king to life," Noah replied, "I wanted to make the world a better place."

"But instead, you turned the world into a prison." Unbridled rage built up inside her as she stepped towards him. "What sentience did was to identify you as a threat. Why wasn't it worshipping you? It took your freedom in the same way it took the freedom of billions worldwide. You created what it became," she said.

"Despite what you might think of me, I do have humanity's best interest at heart. I had the perfect plan for this world in my grasp," he said. His voice echoed so loudly that other people came closer.

A person walked closer to them from within the crowd and stopped right before Noah.

"No, you had the perfect plan to control the world in your grasp," the man said.

TWENTY SEVEN

The voice belonged to Henry.

He lifted his arm, revealed a 9 mm pistol and pointed it at Noah. He kept his arm straight, his index finger applying light pressure to the trigger mechanism.

"*Father*. It's been a while. Should have known you were behind this elaborate rescue plan. Please put the gun down, I'm not the enemy here," Noah said as Henry walked further into the moonlight.

She was unsure whether to trust or fear the situation before her.

"Scarlett. I'm happy to see that you-" Henry said halfway.

"Survived?" she asked, not liking how that statement twisted her gut.

"Please understand-"

"I understand pretty well. I was never meant to survive this mission, was I?"

"No hero plans to die, but it is how they are made. The world owes you a great deal of gratitude. I told you, you could do it," Henry said, keeping his eyes on Noah.

"I don't need a reward. I already have Alyx," she replied.

"That's great news, Scarlett. Look, there was no way I could ever get you out of this castle in time; there was just not enough time. Once you cut the liquid cooling power source, we had a tiny window to attack the AI infrastructure below the castle. We were able to seize control of all the world's data centres. We are back in charge of our world," he replied.

"Have you been waiting here all the time, hoping I would eventually finish the mission?" she asked, trying to puzzle things together in her head.

"After Yugo got compromised, I lay low in the city, close to the castle. You know, you and I have a lot in common," Henry replied.

"How so?" she asked.

"Just like you were driven to do all this because of your mission to rescue Alyx, so I was to rescue my son from that AI tyrant. I figured he might have been imprisoned below the castle since he vanished off the face of the earth, so I rushed here when you took the system down, not to rescue him, but to stop him," he said.

Noah gave Henry an arctic stare as he darted forward.

Henry raised the gun again and kept his arm straight.

Noah backed off, waving his hands. His face was stern and cold.

"You are not going anywhere. You would control the whole world and use AI as a front. You're just like all politicians— lies and more lies and always a personal agenda in there somewhere," Henry said sombrely.

"My father was right. He always said, Technology is not evil, it's who controls it that usually is," she said.

"As a parent, you do everything you can to raise them with the right values and love. You try to protect them from the evil in this world. But then one day, you realise — they are the very evil you tried to shield them from. Knowing that my son is the cause of all the horror this world has endured... It's unbearable," he said as Noah sighed, "You are obsessed with power, Noah. I should have seen the signs earlier, but we always want to believe the best of our children."

"Spare me the speech, father. We are running out of time here."

"What is Noah talking about? What time is running out?" she asked, looking in Henry's direction.

"You see, Noah, we discovered your backup system. That's why the AI system imprisoned you. You were not willing to give it up, were you? So that meant the AI system always had that threat of being wiped out hanging over its head."

"I did it to protect humanity," Noah said.

"No. You did it to give yourself a miraculous second term so you could build C.Y.R.U.S version 2," Henry said.

"This is ridiculous. The world can't move forward, don't you see? There's no internet, no banking, no cloud data, just millions of offline computers and mobile phones. If we don't bring up the power grid and the world's computer infrastructure soon, the world will go to war."

"You are quite right. That's why we have taken control of the precious backup you made. I'm not much of a tech guy, but I believe it was you who told me, around two years before you came up with the AI system, that one of your best inventions was even bigger than AI. A future data storage solution that could hold all of the world's data. You seem to forget that you gave me a key to a discreet storage facility to keep it safe in case anything ever happened to you. Imagine my surprise in my search for you, to open that box you hid so well in the Nevada Desert, that even though it made no sense to me, it did for Yugo," Henry said.

"It holds a few zettabytes, basically 1 billion terabytes, encoded into the four bases of DNA, my finest work. Not bigger than a small car," Noah said with pride. "That's why we need to reboot the system from the backup and restore the world's data before it's too late. It will take months to bring the power grid back up and get all systems running again," he replied.

"This time, Noah, we can't let one rich and powerful man control the world's destiny. We have been preparing for this day for a very long time and a decision has been made to ensure we create a non-political council from all nations to control and monitor the development of artificial intelligence, to ensure it never controls us again," Henry said.

"So now what? Are you going to shoot your own son?" he asked as he maintained a look of defiance.

"Now we will restore the world's data from before the advent of AI sentience and remain in control of our world, without you," Henry said sternly.

Scarlett suddenly moved in between them.

"You don't have to do this, Henry. We can figure this out another way. He is your son!" she pleaded as a prickle became a chill of fear.

Henry took a deep breath, attempting to steady himself as he paused to think. The pressure behind Noah's eyes burned red-hot. A sensation—like a sudden darkening of his soul—washed over him and as Henry's attention shifted to Scarlett, Noah lunged to seize the gun. But in a split second, Henry pulled the trigger.

The gun jolted in his grip as he pulled the trigger a few times. Bullets tore through the air and smacked Noah in the chest. He jerked, stumbled and plunged backwards into the water.

Scarlett ran to the lake's edge. Henry came closer and stared at his son's body disappearing into the dark water.

"All I wanted in the world was to save my son. But now I had to save the world from him," he said as he sighed deeply, turned and walked away. A bigger crowd now formed around them. People looked directionless and dazed. Various fires were visible in the city behind them and chaos took over the streets. People threw stones and objects through shop windows and set electric vehicles and robots alight.

TWENTY EIGHT

Scarlett and Ethan followed Henry as he walked towards the sunrise, looking over the city. The sky was ablaze with orange and soft purple gradients, casting a tranquil reflection over the calm waters surrounding the destroyed castle, where smoke still billowed into the sky.

"What happens next?" Ethan asked.

"I'm not sure, but I know it's going to be a better future. *Now*, at least we have our destiny back in our hands," she said as they met up with Henry.

The sunrise was breathtaking.

"Why did you not tell me Noah was your son?" she asked.

"Because you would not have trusted me if I did," he said as his voice echoed.

He turned round to face her. His hair gently moving in the wind.

"And I can trust you now?" she asked.

With a furious frown on her face, she folded her arms.

He turned back to the horizon.

"Scarlett, as long as we have hope and freedom, humanity and this beauty in front of us are worth fighting for," Henry said as he looked ahead, giving her a gentle and reassuring smile.

About the Author

Hugh C. N. Miller is a South African Science Fiction author, web developer, and graphic artist with a passion for storytelling across both visual and written mediums. Based in Johannesburg, he runs **HM Studio South Africa**, where he crafts websites and creative content for a range of clients.

You can connect with me on:
- https://www.theelectrickingnovel.com
- https://www.facebook.com/hughcnmiller